"GIVE ME THE GOLDEN DRAGON AND I WILL LET YOU LIVE TO SERVE ME . . ."

Baalan's head snaked about as he vainly sought for Dar and Sharlin's hiding place. "Hero! A last chance. You cannot have gone so far as to not hear me. Your petty kingdom lies in ruins, smoldering."

Sharlin made a muffled noise, and bile rose at the back of Dar's throat. *Perhaps,* he told himself, *the dragon lies. Lies come easily to the beast.*

Baalan made a long, slow glide about the valley bowl. Then, bellowing in frustration, he screamed, "No more! I shall squeeze your guts between my talons! The golden one shall fall to me and you will be less than dung."

And Dar knew that Baalan had just declared a private war from which only death could free them. . . .

D0048076

NIGHT OF DRAGONS

R.A.V. Salsitz

A ROC BOOK

DEDICATED TO . . .
our Maureen, the luck of the family, whose
imagination soars beyond dragonwings . . . with
love

ROC
Published by the Penguin Group
Penguin Books USA Inc., 375 Hudson Street,
New York, New York 10014, U.S.A.
Penguin Books Ltd, 27 Wrights Lane,
London W8 5TZ, England
Penguin Books Australia Ltd, Ringwood,
Victoria, Australia
Penguin Books Canada Ltd, 2801 John Street,
Markham, Ontario, Canada L3R 1B4
Penguin Books (N.Z.) Ltd, 182-190 Wairau Road,
Auckland 10, New Zealand

Penguin Books Ltd, Registered Offices:
Harmondsworth, Middlesex, England

First published by ROC, an imprint of New American Library, a division of
Penguin Books USA Inc.

First Printing, July, 1990
10 9 8 7 6 5 4 3 2 1

Copyright © R.A.V. Salsitz, 1990
All rights reserved

ROC IS A TRADEMARK OF PENGUIN BOOKS USA INC.

Printed in the United States of America

BOOKS ARE AVAILABLE AT QUANTITY DISCOUNTS WHEN USED TO
PROMOTE PRODUCTS OR SERVICES. FOR INFORMATION PLEASE WRITE
TO PREMIUM MARKETING DIVISION, PENGUIN BOOKS USA INC., 375
HUDSON STREET, NEW YORK, NEW YORK 10014.

Preface

The life cycle of a dragonet depends upon the hundreds of roe that accompany the laying of dragonet eggs. The roe are eaten either by the hatchling from the eggs or if hatching is delayed, hatch themselves into fireworms, which leave the nests for water and become dragoneels. In eel form, they feed pallan and man and seadrake alike. Those surviving return to land and metamorph into falroth. A crossover in evolution occurs here. Falroth run in packs, are not sexed, and cannot reproduce. They are vicious and rapacious and bear little resemblance to adult dragons despite their common birthing.

A dragonet hatchling feeds not only off the roe, but off the emerging fireworms if it can. Drawn by the migration of the fireworms to the sea, the dragonet will also spend a portion of its time as an amphibian. Only the sea's bounty can fill the bottomless gullet of a dragonet at this stage. A few remain in the ocean—the seadrakes—but their size and bulk cannot match that of the adolescent dragon who returns to the land. The dragon, or strider, in this stage is a massive, bulky, killing machine while its wings begin to form. It has none of the shrewd intelligence it will have as an adult. It is ruled by a rapacious appetite. Lyrith is a soporific when grazed upon in its fresh state and can be used to tame the strider before adulthood. The body then begins to draw upon its muscle and fat reserves as the wings start to grow. The adult emerging is sleek, powerful, and airborne, and uses a native telekinetic power to aid its flight.

Life Cycles of the Rangardian Dragon, *Pallan Histories*, ed. *Pallan Lordess M'reen, Yr of the Disaster, P.T., also known as Year One of Baalan.*

Chapter 1

The wind keened off the plateau, rank with the scent of smoke and fire and carrion. Great shapes kited in its thermal, shapes far too large to be scavengers of the battlefield below. Moans and faint cries were borne upward, of smaller beings wrestling with death amid the carcasses of massive dragons, their bodies bearing deathwounds that could only have been dealt by another of their kind—or by sorcery.

The scene was little different in the cupped valleys below the plateau, though the land here gave way to a more verdant and lush foliage than the thin air off the terraces above allowed. The gliding bat-winged beings dipped low in the sky, circling toward a fire-scorched clearing where an enormous canopy had been set up. Beneath its silken folds their master lay alertly, his tail wrapped about him. Even among dragons, he stood out, his scales of deepest purple, shading to a near black on his head and neck spines . . . except for the gaping neck wound just above his withers. A human worked on his injury bringing hisses from the great and terrible wardragon despite his attempts to be careful.

Baalan looked across the scorched fields, his nostrils flaring. "I am the victor here," he said, sorcery shaping his voice as much as air and throat and tongue did. The pleasure in his tone was evident.

"Yes, my lord," the frail being attending him said,

daubing at the wound without hope he could do much toward the healing of it. "Lord Baalan, it is said that falroth hide . . . it is much like that of your own . . . perhaps . . ."

The beast moved slightly. His neck snaked about and brought the dragon's muzzle low and close to the healer, who suddenly found himself frozen in his tracks, caught in the glowering lamplight of Baalan's eyes.

"What do you suggest?"

"N . . . nothing, great lord. I—I—I—" The healer plowed to a halt, unable to speak further, his fear choking his words within his throat.

"Odd, is it not," the dragon rumbled, "that I, to whom voice is an artifice, should be so much more adept at it than you, flesh of which I'm told babble almost at birth."

The healer made a strangled noise.

"Do you know how that wound was made?"

The healer, having abandoned speech, slowly shook his head. He was a pasty, elderly man, spindly within his homespuns. Char and blood splattered him from the battles that had been fought these last days. The war of the dragons had exploded in the skies above his homeland, a simple country, and had brought cataclysmic change into his life. Of the plateau fortress where a stronghold of the secret people, the pallans, had lived, he knew even less. He reflected now that perhaps his village had not been wise to let the pallans live in peace. Not many villages did. Undoubtedly it was their reviled presence that had called down their disaster.

Wind snapped the canopy above their heads. Baalan wrinkled his muzzle and shook his head, uneasy under the sting of his wound. "A hero," the dragon said, his voice twisted in a sneer, "cut an abomination from my neck. I had been dead in the graveyard, a witch-king's bones across mine, when the Great Resurrection was voiced. My bones were made flesh again, as were his—and our fates inseparable from that moment. He rode my neck as part of me . . . until a hero's sword parted our destiny."

The healer, hearing things he could barely comprehend, began to shake. He knew only that there was no sadness in the beast's voice at the tragedy that had slain the witch-king a second time.

The stink of the fire-scorched grounds hung close in the tent, but could not override the heavy, musky smell of the purple beast crouched between the healer and freedom. Baalan snorted, his breath hot and heavy. The healer licked his lips, knowing then where most of the fire that scourged his land came from. *Dragongods*, he thought. He found his voice suddenly. "L-lord. That is a grievous wound. If I could stitch the edges together, it might heal."

"And you suggest a patch of . . . falroth hide?"

The healer bent his head in abject obedience.

Baalan knew that he would heal, though slowly. Perhaps what this timorous, softfoot of a man suggested had merit. "You are the healer," Baalan said, turning his attention back to the battlefield.

"Yes, great l-lord." The healer scurried from the canopy to order the flaying of a young falroth, taking care to avoid the dragons now winging down onto the field.

Baalan wondered briefly if the little man would return, then stretched and gave his attention to his army. Their claws clutched the rendered remains of most of the enemy and nothing could have been sweeter to the dragon's eye. A dark goblin scrambled down from the neck of his mount and lumbered to the edge of the canopy before going to his knobby knees.

"Master," he said, gravel voice hissing through his tusked jaws. "There is no sign of the golden dragon."

Baalan dug his talons into the char beneath his

pavilion. "There is no victory without her carcass! Look
again. She just did not disappear into thin air—" The
beast blinked languidly. But she had . . . he himself
had seen it and felt the cold chill of the abyss that had
taken them, Turiana and her two riders. Her golden
body ungainly in the way of the female about to lay
eggs, the hero and the girl clutching to riding leathers
—no, Baalan thought. He had not been hallucinating
with pain when he had seen them vanish.

Baalan turned his sinister gaze back onto the goblin
lord who now lay pressed into the ash, eyes hidden
from those of the dragon. Baalan took a long, shuddering breath, and the goblin writhed closer to the
ground. The beast thought of teasing his captain a
moment longer, licking him with flame, but changed
his mind. "What of the youth," he asked. "Tall and
straw-headed."

His captain got to one knee. "We have him."

With that, Baalan was well pleased.

"Tell me where she has gone to ground, wormling,
or there will be nothing left of you to remember you
by . . . not even ash." Baalan traced a claw in the dust
just before the human and watched him pale even as
he hung in his captor's ungentle embrace. The stink of
the boy's fear was perfume to the purple dragon's
nostrils.

It was a far cry from the scene Baalan remembered
as he had winged down across the plateau, ready to
cut down Turiana in her rebellion over his supremacy.
Her wing of dragons had faltered, opened, letting him
through. Arrowing down, filled with venom and sorcery, ready and able to do battle . . . the youth before
him now akimbo, voice cracking with words and power
even as Turiana launched awkwardly into the sky,
riders crouched upon her neck. Then . . . the abyss
where the gold had been. The disappointment and
pain that had finally brought him down. His wing and

army had prevailed, scattering or destroying those who were left behind in sudden confusion.

"Name yourself, boy."

"Ha-Hapwith," the youth stammered. His clothes were torn and singed. The goblins had not been careful with their booty. A flame-reddened welt crawled up the side of his face and into his hair. The welt would heal, but the hair burned there would not return. Baalan made note of it, in case the boy should escape or ever be released.

Baalan rumbled, "Hapwith. Tell me where she has gone. Her laying time is near, very near."

Hapwith shook his head fiercely.

"Don't fool with me. I saw you on the mesa, above, with them. I will not forget you, and a dragon's time is long, long, on this earth. I will torture you daily until you've told me. Tell me now, and save what you can of yourself."

"No."

To himself, the dragon exulted. The voice was low . . . the tone already broken. "Take him," Baalan ordered. "To the stronghold." He paused, seeing the healer at the edge of his glance, flayed skin in his palsied hands. "Approach me," he ordered the village healer.

The falroth skin glittered in the man's fingers, tiny scales taking up the sunlight and reflecting it in a hundred glittering points. *So like, unto me,* Baalan thought vainly. His nostrils flared and he turned his head about, to better watch the chirurgery.

He sensed the aroma, rather than smelled it, veiled as it was by smoke and carrion and the ichor of the newly slain animal. Hapwith's limp form had become suddenly tense, and, curved away though he was, Baalan caught a glance between the thatch-haired youth and the old village healer.

"I—I have the skin, lord," the old man said. "And thread and needle. Perhaps something to numb the pain?" A clay jug hung from his belt and bounced upon one thigh.

"I think not." Baalan peered at the healer. "Let me see the patch."

It quivered before him as the healer hung it for inspection. Mottled black, not spectacular particularly, but pretty enough. Baalan sniffed and edged closer.

"M-my lord," the old man said. "The grafting must be down while the skin is fresh, to work at all. I must trim the edges of your wound and stitch the patch in as quickly as I can."

Hapwith and the elder were avoiding each other's eyes. Treachery rumbled inside Baalan, but he was unsure of what kind or how . . . his nostrils cupped. The flayed skin danced in the wind.

"I see, Healer," Baalan said. He tilted his head, jaw agape slightly. "Let me see the underside, where the blood and flesh was cut away."

"My lord—" the healer began.

The purple dragon exhaled, flame gouting, pouring out, yellow-white in intensity, and where there had been a paling old man, now staggered a burning char. It wheeled and then collapsed. The skin, untouched, drifted to the ground. The side up was bloody and yellow-green, painted elaborately with ointment.

Baalan pricked a talon tip through it and held it in the air. "Poison," the dragon commented dryly. He tossed the hide in the air and let go another burst, and watched the glowing ash drift groundward. "Take him," Baalan ordered. "Out of my sight now. When we meet next, he will be ready to talk."

The goblins dragged the boy from the tent, heels digging ruts into the ground. Baalan sighed and put his chin down upon the ground. He would have to suffer pain and healing another day or two, it appeared.

*   *   *

It was two years later before a goblin captain approached the dreaded Lord Baalan in his stronghold and said only, "The captive has talked."

Baalan paused in his reception of tribute and tithes, and turned his muzzle to the furred-and-tusked beast kneeling to his scarred side. "Has he?"

"Yes." The goblin licked his lips and tusks carefully. "Turiana was not sent where—but when."

"What? What have you said?"

"Your nemesis is lost in time, O mighty one. But she will return, according to the prisoner. The spell is a circular one and yet incomplete."

Baalan raised his eyes to the sky above. The fortress courtyard, crowded with tribute, had become hushed. Time was not on Baalan's side. With every year of life and magic, he faced the return of the disease the magic carried along with its power. The cursed pallans and their cursed sorcery.

"Let him go," Baalan said.

"Master?" The goblin captain was not easily surprised, but he stood now, mouth open.

"He is a witchling of small power. I have already put a leash upon him. It will amuse me to tug it now and then. I will find him if ever I need him. No man will take him in. He is known as the sorcerer who destroyed Turiana the golden and the heroes who rode her." The dragon stretched his lips in a parody of a smile. "The years have not been kind to the truth. Meanwhile, set a watch. We will not rest until the golden dragon lies rent within these claws," and Baalan looked into the deadly cup he made of his talons. He shook his head, spines rattling. "Dismiss the audience for today."

The captain hurried to do his bidding, and caravans of human and goblin and pallan alike scurried to leave the courtyard and return to the campgrounds beyond, to present their tribute on a day when the dragonlord might be in a better humor.

Only a single, slight figure stayed behind. Baalan ignored it for long moments, then said, "What is it, little fly? Are you brave or foolish to defy me?"

The young woman stepped out of the shadows of the fortress walls. Bells on her wrists and ankles chimed with her motion. Her skin was cream and her hair dark as the raven's wing. Her eyes smiled as she did, but Baalan immediately sensed the stink of power about her—a power as vast as any he had ever sensed among the human kind. She dropped upon the flagstone, prone, before him.

"My name, O lord, is Wendeen." Her voice, though low and pleasant, was accented with the tone of the mysterious East. Even Baalan did not trespass the East. The lands were veiled from his foresight and ruled by a crimson dragon that he feared.

"Your tribute?"

"Nothing, O lord."

"Nothing? Nothing?" Baalan crept nearer. Her dusky scent filled his thoughts. "You risk much."

"Not as much as you do, O lord. I know of the curse your magic carries with it—" the girl's confident voice halted abruptly as Baalan hissed, and spittle struck near her. Acid smoked its way into the stone.

Baalan growled, and said, "You carry your own death sentence in your words."

"O lord! Any scholar could tell you as much!"

"Then," the dragon said coldly, "I must remember to burn more libraries."

"But I can help you!"

"The last healer who offered to help me died a horrible death."

She lifted her face and, unflinchingly, met his terrible stare. "I *can* help you. Even now you weaken— you fly fewer and fewer raids, and the lieutenants who fought next to you seek Glymarach in growing numbers. Even the dragongods are not immortal. In my lands, we have found that blood cleanses many wounds. I would bring that cleansing to you."

"What is it you want?"

"Only to tell you what it is I have found, and to stand by yourself, reflecting in your glory. I can beat the curse—and if I can, you *will* live forever."

Baalan curved a talon and lifted the girl to her feet. He bent his head down. "I have a moment," he said. "I will listen."

Chapter 2

Golden wingspan fused into sunrise, pink and gold of its own. An early morning thermal, rising as the land below warmed, took them higher. Aarondar shoved his boots a little deeper into the riding harness and wrapped his left hand a little firmer with the leathers. Packs snugged the backs of his thighs and buttocks. They held the nine precious eggs of the dragonqueen they rode, and she used her power to keep her flanks ember warm against the thin, bitter air. To his fore, the girl riding kept the wind from cutting at him, her body wrapped like a cocoon in a royal woolen cloak.

Sharlin slept in his one-armed embrace, her head tucked into the hollow of his neck. She wore a net of blue jewels, but finer hairs strayed, tickling about his face like the strands of a spider's web except these were exquisite gold rather than silver.

He frowned into the edge of daybreak finding it too bright. Only a fool stared into the sun. "Turiana," he said lowly, but the dragonqueen had already begun to bank.

"Yes, fair son," she rumbled back. The wind could not catch her words for her voice was not the same as his, made by sorcery as much by tongue and throat.

He took advantage of her attention. "When do we cross?"

"Soon. I can feel the edge of the charming now.

When its calling becomes something I can no longer ignore, when I surge after it even as it catches me up—then the abyss will open and we will soar into our own times again."

The girl stirred in his arms. She shrugged from under the dusky blue cloak that matched her riding skirt, blouse, and handtooled leather vest. As blue as she was dressed, it was a pallid echo of the intensity of her eyes. She smiled at him now. "Dar?" she whispered, and he felt the vibration of her question rather than heard it as the wind snatched away the sound. He leaned his lips to her ear.

"Awake?"

"Yes. How far have we flown?"

"All night. Turiana says she's found Hapwith's spell and will be answering it soon."

She shuddered, turning away her shell-like ear away from his whisper, with a laugh. "I think you need to find some more hairroot. You're beginning to tickle."

In answer he scraped his rough chin across her cheek and smiled as she shrieked.

Turiana protested even as her favorite, the Princess Sharlin, did. "Children!"

"That," he said, "was for keeping secrets from me . . . both of you." He tightened his embrace about her thickening waist. "What if I don't want to name my son Balforth?"

"Fort," Sharlin answered promptly, pouting lips to his ear. She nipped him lightly. "I'm calling him Fort."

He dared not cross her on that, but he did not want to. She had told her father she would follow Dar wherever he went. They had let her go, for she had brought them a dragon and dragonmagic to save their kingdom—and fathers everywhere were used to letting their daughters go. He wondered briefly if she had told him just how far they must travel—two oceans and three or so centuries—but that was between them. She had come with him, and that was all that mattered.

An unnameable flame seemed lit in him, not a love or lust for her, but a warmth born of the knowledge they had created something and it would carry on when they had gone. *A son*. He wondered what it meant to Sharlin to know that, centuries after her family's history had become dusty lines in pallan history books and graven temple panels that her son would carry her father's name. Her lifeline, thanks to dragonmagic, would span that gap.

He was grateful to be an ordinary man, son of a soldier turned dairy farmer. He would not have been an ordinary man if he hadn't met Sharlin, for his own destiny had been to carry the soul of another, the witch-king Valorek. If he had not succumbed to the lure of a treasure map and the love of a lost princess, his own soul would be utterly forfeit.

Now he was master of himself, aloft on dragonwing, seeing a view of Rangard that only mapmakers had ever seen before. He realized a kind of power that came from, at last, knowing exactly where he was coming from, if not where he was going to. As if in answer to his thoughts, the sword sheathed upon his back began to warm. If he put a hand upon the hilt, it would speak to him just as it had the first time he had ever touched it, in a sacred place the dragons called the Gates. A dragon must pass the Gates to gain its sex and its power. Dar had gone past those Gates as well, gaining a weapon with power of its own. Had it been meant for him—or had it just simply dropped into the first convenient mortal hands?

Dar shifted, undecided if he wished to listen to the blade forged in far away and long ago Thrassia. Sharlin wrapped her hand in the riding leathers so he could take his arm away as if she'd heard his unspoken thought. The banking movement of the gold dragon straightened, and she dropped a little underneath the leading edge of a cloud bank. He felt the increased moisture upon his face as the dragon took them lower. He thought of what they might meet upon their return.

"Will we face Baalan?"

Sharlin shook her head. A tendril escaped from her net and bannered in the wind. "Hapwith said he hadn't learned that much control. Probably a month or two after the battle. Pray that we'll be in time, whenever we get there."

Her words added to his foreboding. The brand across his back grew warmer. Upreaching across his shoulder, he wrapped his fingers about the hilt despite the heat which scored him. The flare-up cooled as quickly as it had heated.

Draw me.

It spoke in his thoughts, an alien voice among his inner one, but one that had never frightened him before. What could possibly threaten them here, so high above the lands of Rangard that only another dragon could reach them?

Sharlin shifted in the riding harness as he began to pull the sword forth. "What is it?"

"I don't know. But something . . ." The Thrassian sword came free of its scabbard.

Clouds boiled below them. Turiana's sides heaved liked a bellows and Dar could feel her heat between his calves. She worked to keep her eggs warm as well as stay aloft.

Sharlin twisted suddenly, neck craned so that she could see downward. The dizzying heights did not bother her as they did Aarondar. She grasped his bracered forearm. "Look!" even as Turiana crooned, "I have it! The thread which will pull us homeward!"

Dar looked and swayed in the riding harness as vertigo caught him—but he could not avoid seeing the thundercloud that rose toward them—a great, dark dragon boiling upward, his jaws stretched to bellow forth a trumpeting challenge.

He shouted. Turiana veered suddenly. A wingtip as sharp as any blade whipped through the air. It missed Dar's helm, but the defense he put up struck—and the Thrassian sword bit deeply into the beast's sail. The dragon seemed to jump in midair. He had a split second look into malevolent yellow eyes. The beast snapped at them, missed, and began to tumble downward as his wing crumpled.

The turbulence of his fall buffeted them even as Turiana beat her wings, surging her body into an abyss only she could open. With a scream of defiance of her own, she bore them forward.

It was worse than Dar remembered. The sky went pitch black and icy cold. The wind pummeled at them until he thought sure he would lose his half-helm and his ears with it. Sharlin hunched miserably into her cloak. She had her hands and arms bundled tightly into its folds, as much to anchor it as to keep warm. They bucked along the air currents, every jolt a reminder to Dar's stomach about how much he hated dragon flying. Clouds spun about them as they tunneled their way through. He found himself holding his breath—and could not remember if he'd been able to breathe the first time they'd done this.

Turiana panted. They bucked again and Sharlin let out a tiny squeak. "Hold tight, fair children," the dragon gasped. "I am not . . . in control."

The sword's voice had gone silent and Dar decided he wanted two hands to be able to handle the situation. He sheathed it carefully, not wanting to drop it in the abyss. The gods alone knew where it would land. This would be Hapwith's fault again. How Sharlin could ever have believed that baby-faced charlatan could have had the talent they needed—

He could feel something too hot and warm breathing down the back of his neck. He risked a look behind . . . to see the lantern-eyed black dragon winging after them, pulled into the abyss by the draft of the golden beast. Was it her old nemesis Nightwing, the only black dragon he'd every known—or another, different beast, one as malicious and canny as old Baalan? Even as he watched, a gout of flame lashed toward him. The force of the abyss ripped the flame to nothingness, but he felt its warmth across his face.

With a scream of defiance, the dragon lashed out, and talons raked across Turiana, scraping over the packs. They rocked under the force of the blow.

Turiana said, "I can't hold it! We're nearly there, but I can't hold it!"

She began to drop, so alarmingly quickly, he lost his stomach. His eyes began to water. Sharlin screamed for his hearing, "We're going down!"

The tunnel of cloud and wind tore at them. They dropped in its midst, caught in a maelstrom of time and magic. Beneath his hand the riding leather suddenly began to part, adding its own voice to theirs. The harness went lopsided. He grabbed for Sharlin and began to pray as she had requested earlier.

With a roar the attacking dragon overtook them. For precious seconds, they were entwined, wings entangled, each beast screeching its hatred at the other. Dar's ears rang with the noise they made. He kicked out at the sail he'd slashed earlier. Leather skin parted under this blow. With a keening like a sharp whistle, the second dragon ripped free and skewed off. A bucket of air and the black dragon spun away, growing small before his very eyes.

The riding harness made another ripping noise and they began to move sideways. Sharlin clutched at Turiana's spined neck for purchase. Turiana swooped through another pocket of turbulence. Dar felt some-

thing wet splatter his check. He wiped it off and saw
ichor on his glove. The golden dragon had been
wounded. Every wing movement was laborious.

With a last rent the leather harness gave way com-
pletely, bearing Sharlin and Dar with it. They tumbled
into thin air. He kicked free of the riding leathers and
packs. He had a sudden, dizzying look at the underside of the golden dragon who'd been bearing them,
and then the maelstrom of magic and time swallowed
them up. His last glimpse showed the packs being
sucked backward into the maelstrom, and Turiana dart-
ing after them, in desperate pursuit of her dragonet
eggs.

Sharlin stayed in his embrace, as they cartwheeled
through air. Then, an abrupt slowing. A saffron bubble encased them. Sharlin drew a low, sobbing breath.
They gained their feet as the bubble floated landward.

"A sending," she managed to get out, as she turned
and reached for him. "From Turiana, with the last of
her strength."

They were going down . . . and it was the will of the
gods where and when they would land.

Chapter 3

In all her long years, in her first and second lifetimes, Turiana had never heard of a dragon laying two clutches. Chary with one another because of their magic, dragons did not feel the mating urge until death was nigh—and then flew one another only when instinct made it impossible to do otherwise. After spawning, as it were, death was usually close to both mates. The female might linger long enough to cozen her eggs. Turiana had, the first time. She was determined to do so now. Where her death awaited her, she no longer knew . . . the weakening that accompanied laying did not bother her now. And the silver! She had lain a silver egg, as rare a dragon as she had ever heard of in either of her lifetimes.

And so she pursued the packs now, though they led her back into the abyss, severing her from Sharlin and Dar. She beat her wings frantically, felt her heart pump sorcery as well as blood through her veins, fueling her flight after the leather bags tumbling through the air.

Her lips peeled back from her mighty fangs. The leather straps and packs danced before her nostrils. Another drive of her mighty wings and a snap—and she had them. The packs bumped to a gentle stop at her chin—and the raggedy scraps of leather held.

The dragon queen took a long, shuddering breath and sculled, bringing their descent to a controlled glide.

The miasma of time and magic that swirled about them began to dissipate.

She looked out on a land she did not recognize. It was late afternoon, and hazy clouds kept the sun from browning the land. Instinctively she turned to the mountains—eggs meant a need for caves or hollows, and privacy. Water and, if she were lucky, wild gunter. Being alone was normal for a dragon, but she was no longer used to it, and as her sleek shadow chased her flight across hill and dale, she called for Sharlin.

There was no answer.

The purple mountains ahead were sharp and thin in air, but below . . . she saw terraced valleys and jeweled lakes. Turiana banked and turned. A thin blue-gray spiral of smoke laced upward. In her turning she winded its scent. *Lyrith*, herbal incense of gods and kings and dragongods. Its perfume drew her lower yet.

From within the cupped peaks, split as though a lightning bolt had sundered them, she saw a valley. From the upper end, lyrith smoke billowed upward from the fire that had been set. As she dropped lower, Turiana could see huts and fields and common pastures. As her shadow sped across the fields, figures bolted ahead of her. Her keen sight identified the graceful and secret people called pallans by the humans.

She remembered the glory days of the pallans. Days of immense walled cities none the less gracious for their size and population. She remembered the decline of the pallans, for her own first lifetime had been plaited with theirs, on the continent Glymarach where all dragons are spawned and laid, if they can help it. But their loss of the city of Lyrith, on the plains below the dragon graveyard she had not seen, for her own bones had been laid to rest by then. Still, unlike many dragons, she did not regard the pallans with guilt. It had been their own choice to put aside their power for magic and sorcery, a basic part of their nature. Just as it had been a basic part of dragonnature to usurp the magic for themselves.

Unfortunately the talents had proved as deadly for dragons as it did for pallans. Dragons were long-lived, yes, but the longer one lived and the more one worked with power, the more insidious the disease was. It had driven both pallans and dragons from greatness. Turiana was endowed with knowledge that could not save any of them from this final downfall. To her sorrow, after the Resurrection brought about by Sharlin, dragons knew little of their heritage, their lifespans shortening by the generation.

But Turiana liked pallans, and that brought her thoughts back to the now. To be burning *lyrith* . . . what better omen could she hope for? And the mountain ridges edging every side of the valley would surely have a cave or two with good prospects. She tilted her head, packs shifting alarmingly in her grip. The eggs needed to be warmed and soon.

A crowd of pallans gathered about the bonfire, drawn by the sight of the golden dragon winging above them. They stood, hushed and tense, their scaled faces hidden behind gauze masks, hands and arms gloved and sleeved, so that no human might ever be more repelled by them than already were by differences already clothed. Turiana banked and came down to the field that they had leveled so that a dragon might land.

The soil crumbled beneath her talons. Rich soil. Good farming land. She swept her tail across it and found the afternoon sun warm enough. She laid the packs down and cupped her nostrils to better wind the burning *lyrith*.

Instead of welcoming her, the crowd drew back. They held their collective breath in silence. A small, lithe figure to the fore swung her arm about, and a slingshot rock careened off her brow plate even as the mother grabbed her child in terror and pulled her back into the anonymous crowd. Turiana looked after, marking his masked-and-hooded figure despite the mother's efforts. The air stank of fear and hostility.

But they had called her here—had they not? She reared up protectively over the packs containing her eggs. "You burn the *lyrith*," she said, and her voice was bell-like in the silence they maintained.

The one with the striped hood stepped forward. Turiana knew, because she knew pallans who had been unafraid to unhood and unmask themselves, that the luxuriant mane concealed would also be colored and striped. The movement was constrained, the pallan being very old and subject to the infirmity that crippled older bones. "You are early, dragonlord." The gauze veil rippled delicately to the breathy words.

Perhaps earlier even than they expected. Turiana looked about. It was difficult to understand these people, but she knew fear when she scented it. She was not the dragon they anticipated. "The flying was good," she answered finally.

There was a ripple of sound through the crowd, and a slight relaxation of tension. It was important to them, then, that she be in a good mood. And when and where was she that none of them remembered a golden dragon? Pallan memory was legendary. The striped one murmured, "Will you partake of some food, great one? We have blooded a gunter for you."

Her stomach clenched in agreement of her hunger almost before she could agree. Four pallans dragged out the carcass and a tureen of the boiled blood. She greedily dipped her muzzle to the tureen and stopped. Saliva dropped to the ground as she pulled back abruptly.

The pallans scattered. Only the stripe-hooded one was left to face her fury, the others huddling behind the bonfire as if ordinary fire could stop an enraged dragon.

"Who poisoned this cup?" she demanded angrily, the mountains echoing her anger.

The pallan got down on his knees and bowed his head. "I did, O great one."

"And the carcass?"

"Likewise."

Turina shoved the offering aside. She then raked her talons through the newly plowed field, amid grass roots and dirt clods to clean them. "What have I done to offend you?"

"You, great lord, nothing. We have never seen a golden dragon in our lifetime. But you come in the watchdragon's place, do you not, and at the appointed hour, do you not, and we fear the Taking. It is our place and we know it, but we fear it still."

The Taking? Watchdragon? Turiana fine-tuned her senses and picked out threads of thought, always difficult among the silent and wary pallans. It took all of her effort not to rear back in horror. They expected to lose the best of their youth tonight to a dragon, to be borne away and never seen again—to be slain on a cold stone altar that they could all sense but none had ever lived to see and tell the tale themselves.

She drew her packs bearing her own young under her more fully. "On your feet, elder," she said to the striped hood.

The pallan got up stiffly.

"Do you know your histories?"

Like a slap in the face to a pallan, that, but she pursued it relentlessly. "Do you know your place, and your father's and mother's place and your grandsires' places?

"All pallans know their catechisms and their history," the elder answered, no less stiff in voice than in movement. She had struck deeply.

Turiana smiled inwardly. "Have you heard of the golden dragon Turiana?"

A catch of breath. The bold youngster of the sling-shot bolted forward out of the crowd. "Oh, yes," she said wildly. "She was great and good and she died when the sorcerer Hapwith slew her for Baalan's sake."

"Died?" repeated Turiana, turning her eyes upon the child. The hood was gold shot with red, and so the burgeoning mane hidden beneath it must be. Gold for wisdom and red for . . . impetuosity.

"Destroyed," the youngster blurted further. "Destroyed into less than ashes, she was—and the heroes who rode her. Fifty-five years ago this season."

An icy feeling speared her. So many years . . . gone. And Hapwith branded as their killer. Had he lived to know that or died under Baalan's un-tender mercies?

"A lie," hissed Turiana lowly, and she dipped her muzzle low so that she might look directly into the youngster's eyes. "I am Turiana. I was lost, but you have found me—and so long as there is breath in my body, none of Baalan's will ever touch any under my care. Do you believe me?"

"Oh, yes," the youngster breathed. "Oh, my yes." She flung back her hood and ran to Turiana's clawed feet where she flung herself facedown upon the ground in worship.

Turiana looked up. "Can any of you say any less than this child in her innocence?"

The elder approached, the hem of his robe brushing across the body of the prostate child. "It is not unlike a dragon to toy with the Taken. What do you want from us?"

"A high cave, and secrecy, and an occasional gunter—undoctored, if you would. For that, I will keep the watchdragons from your skies and your children safe within your valley."

The pallans murmured. They moaned and keened and cried helplessly among themselves. Turiana watched them beyond the flames of the bonfire.

"And what proof do we have you will keep your pledge?"

"This," Turiana said, as she hooked a talon tip into the pack and opened it for all to see. "The life of my young in trade for the lives of yours."

The silence was complete for a heartbeat, then two. Then the youngster got to her knees and crawled forward. She lifted out a dragonet egg, one of the emerald hued. She held it out, saying, "Look!"

There was no immediate response. It was as if Turiana had frozen her audience. The dragon shifted impatiently. "Will you fight?" she demanded. "Will you be the first of the pallans to throw off Baalan's yoke? I cannot use magic to accomplish my needs, but I can and will use my strength and cunning—and a gold dragon is not easily overcome by any. I have defeated Nightwing, and Baalan won from me only because I was forced to leave the field of battle. Now I am returned. Let it start here, with us. There will be no more Takings!"

The young one stroked the egg before handing it, once more, toward her senior.

The elder took it a moment, reverently, then handed it back. He doffed his hood and tore the mask from his face. "O great one. If you intend to protect this valley and your clutch, you must first rest and eat. The watchdragon normally comes with the tide of the evening."

Turiana dipped her head. "I will be ready."

Chapter 4

Ganth was a poor, humble man. He sold charcoal to bakers and rich widows and other people whose hearths were not as mean as his and wore his charcoal baskets on his back, as if he carried the weight of the world. The high mountain air and rigors of charcoal gathering had made him tough and wiry and bowed. It had not made him cautious. Bandits would never bother with a man of such engrained and obvious poverty as himself—never mind the silver half crowns he carried in his shoes or the rather opulent if out of the way hut he had built near the charcoal fields. Never mind that the lingering cold streaks of the last ten years had made charcoal a very popular item or that he was seriously considering digging up another silver half crown or two buried behind his hut to buy a horse and cart for his business. His poverty was abject and obvious to all who knew him.

Save, perhaps, to the five who jumped him as he trudged through a high mountain cut, bathed in dark purple shadows as day gave way to dusk and his weariness bled into sharp fear. They surrounded him with loud yells of intimidation, which worked admirably. Ganth plowed to a quivering halt, half kneeling under his charcoal baskets—more out of habit than heaviness, as they were empty—took a look at the bandits and went all the way to his knees. His trousers were well padded there, to aid in the sorting of charcoal lumps, so it was not as much of a hardship on him as it must surely look to the bandits.

From under the brim of his floppy hat, he could see two had bows while three brandished very sharp swords, which caught the first moonlight from the Shield coming up over the peak. Ah, if only the Shield could dip downward and cover *him* . . . Too much of a miracle to ask for a poor man. Ganth sighed. "Mercy, I beg of you!"

"Mercy!" cried the largest bandit, the one to the fore with eyes as hard as flint, a long mustache, which wiggled fiercely with every word, and the sharpest sword. "You'll find mercy in us when you find mercy in the dragongods!"

An icy stab of twilight speared through the vendor's heart. The dragongods had no mercy—and neither did the bandits. Ganth sobbed. "I have no hope!"

"But money, we think," jibed the second bandit. He wore his fiercely red hair in thick braids under his cap. He placed the dull, flat side of his blade to Ganth's throat.

"I am a poor man selling charcoal! Take my baskets—whatever crumbs are left, you may have. At least your fires will be warm!"

"We intend to do that anyway," said the first. His mustache danced. "Convince him, Jesta!"

A bowman lifted his weapon and let fly. Ganth found his sweat covered brow suddenly shorn of his hat. The mountain seemed colder than ever before. Winter's very edge was in the twilight. He groveled discreetly, keenly aware of the sword blade to his throat. "Ah, masters, masters! Take whatever you would have of me! My jacket, my clothes—even my shoes!"

"Especially your shoes," said the ringleader. "And whatever you might have buried up on the mountain.

Ganth is not a rich man, but he's not as poor as he pretends, either!"

The cut rang with their laughter as they looked down on him. Perhaps it was because Ganth was miserably being forced to look up that he alone saw it—and knew that even worse luck faced him. Ganth had three daughters awaiting him in his hut: three daughters who had so far survived the Taking. But now a shadow passed before his eyes. He saw the spine-crowned head and far-flung wings cross the sky between the Shield and himself. Sword or not to his throat, Ganth let out an anguished cry and threw himself face first into the stoney ground.

The bandits whirled and shouted as well. Ganth looked up and saw a miracle—two silhouettes jump from the dragon's back and float downward as light as a feather. The dragon disappeared as though it had never been. But it had—he had seen it, and Ganth might be a lot of things, but he was *not* short of sight.

An aura surrounded the two figures, tiny as straw dolls, growing larger by the second as they floated to the mountain's peak. Ganth had seen a lot of things in his fifty-some years, including a few Takings—but he had never seen a dragongod bestowing gifts upon Rangard.

"A miracle!" he cried. "The dragongod gives back what it has taken!"

Jesta put another arrow to his bow and half drew it. They all stared with wide eyes as the two descended . . . and the man was a fighting man, young and fit, in chain-mail coat and bracers and shin guards, with a noble hilt riding his right shoulder. The woman was beautiful, too, all gold and blue, dressed as befitted a queen.

The bandits began to group in confusion. The two alit and the bubble dissipated. Drawing his blade, the fighter stepped out.

"What have we here?" he said, and his words were oddly accented, rich in sound and texture. He kept the woman to his back protectively.

"Bandits!" howled Ganth. "Help, O noble master!"

The two bowmen pulled but before they could draw, one sprouted a dagger in his shoulder and the other went down before the length of that masterful blade. Sharper than a thousand razors it was, such that Jesta's head wore a surprised look as if not knowing it had left his shoulders. And the woman was not a bad thrower, herself.

Ganth scrambled away as blades rang out and the three launched themselves at the swordsman at once. In a blur he met them, parried and answered, and the third man fell away, bloodied and silent. Then, it was just the redhead and the dark mustache. They rocked back a moment, eyes narrowed, swords held defensively, as if wondering just what kind of man this was they faced.

To their foolishness they attacked again. Ganth watched in wonder at a kind of swordplay he had never seen before. The swordsman was undoubtedly a master, fluid and graceful, holding back two men without breathing hard. The blade was a silver blur, meeting and defending here and cutting there, doing its work with a fierce joy.

And then the two began to try and back up, ducking blows instead of meeting them. They panted in unison and cursed in duets as the swordsman pressed them further.

"Dar." The woman spoke softly as the bandits found their backs to the cold stone wall of the pass.

He pulled back slightly as if in answer. He lifted his blade. "Mercy," he said, "because milady asks it. Run, and never let me see you on this mountain again!"

The two ran, their clothes in streamers, bearing

wounds so sharp the bearers did not yet know they'd been touched.

Ganth retrieved his hat with shaking hands and pulled the arrow from it. The third bandit had sneaked away, leaving behind a blood-streaked dagger. He cleansed it and crept close to the royal two, and offered it on a trembling palm.

The woman—no, girl, she was no older than his middle child—took it with a smile. "Thank you," she said, and her voice was no less strange than the swordsman's.

Ganth went to his knees again. "Thank you, O lord and lady, gifts of the dragongods!"

She turned to her lord, who was cleaning his blade. "He saw."

"I'm not surprised. The Shield is full and bright tonight," her lord answered wryly. "Now what do we do with him?"

Ganth went once more to his face in the dust. "I saw nothing," he declared, voice muffled, "if that is what you wish, masters." He cursed his luck, knowing that he had indeed been damned, for there was nothing good about dragons and he would die for thinking there could have been.

"Oh, get up," ordered Sharlin. "We saved you from all that." She looked about. "Do you live up here?"

Ganth lifted his face, nothing more. "Indeed," he answered cautiously. "My whole village. I live higher, to comb the charcoal fields."

"Ah. A vendor? Is that what you carry in your baskets?"

"Yes." He wondered a bit at her boldness. Perhaps she was not afraid of being chosen by dragons. And perhaps the swordsman did not mind her forwardness, though Ganth did not think him the henpecked type. Not after the work he'd done with that blade! Nag twice, and the girl could find herself with a forked tongue before she'd even blinked.

The swordsman sheathed his weapon. He put a hand down, at which Ganth stared stupidly before realizing the man wanted to help him to his feet. Afoot, the old man was even more awed. The fighter towered above him, head and shoulders and more. What a reach he must have!

To his consternation Dar began dusting him off. "Where in Rangard are we, old man?"

"Know you not? Oh, we're in a bedighted land, noble master, for sure. Even the dragongods rarely remember us—" a miracle in itself, but Ganth was not sure if these two could appreciate it—"far from trading roads, with little to offer any civilized man."

The two passed a look, one which he could not quite read. "But where," the man repeated, an edge to his voice, "Are we?"

"The Shalad Mountains, sir."

"Ah."

The lady shivered, even within her cloak. Her full mouth parted as if to speak, but the man responded without her words. He put an arm about her shoulders.

"My wife is with child, old man, and tired. We are not gifts of the dragons, but fleeing them. You, I think," and the deep brown eyes of the fighter assessed him, "can appreciate that."

Ganth found himself nodding vigorously. There was a power of truth in the swordsman that he could not resist! "My hut lies just up the pass," he also found himself offering. "A humble but warm cot and freshly brewed tea . . . my daughters will assist your lady."

"Good," said Aarondar. "Then we will discuss your Shalad Mountains and the dragongods. I am an ordinary man, friend, and if the dragongods do not notice you now, I wouldn't want to change that."

"No," Ganth agreed, falling into step with him. "But we have bandits—something fierce—and goblins."

Dar smiled. "I think we can deal with those . . . quietly. You see, friend . . ."

"—Ganth," the vendor named himself.

"Ganth—there are dragons of good intentions in the world."

"There are?"

"Oh, yes," the girl put in.

"Indeed. Such as the one which brought us here for safekeeping. But those are secrets, and secrets which must be kept."

Ganth knew well of secrets. Had he not kept three daughters and a small fortune to himself?

The swordsman seemed to sense his agreement. "In these uncertain days, some of us must find quiet places, places in which to gather our strength and raise our families."

"Shalad," the old man blurted out proudly, "is an excellent place for that sort of thing."

"Good. But it is better you speak to no one of how we met, or what you saw. Not even a hint, for it might set tongues to wagging and even the wind and stone have ears."

Ganth's head bobbed again.

The girl spoke softly again. "Why would dragongods want to remember you?"

A brush of deathlike cold reminded him how close to winter it was. He turned his eyes to her. "Do you not know?"

She shook her head, and as incredulous as it was, he believed her. "Why the Takings, milady. The Takings by the dragongods of our children, for their sacrifices. Oh, the dragons repay us, or say they do. Lift taxes for a year and some such—as if any amount of money could be worth the soul of a sweet child. But some villages have hard times and they really don't mind losing an extra mouth to feed, I'm told."

"Abomination," she said, and her face went pale.

Ganth stopped in his tracks. He put a callused hand upon her sleeve. "Don't be distressed, milady. Shalad rarely sees a dragongod. In the seventy-two years of Baalan's reign, I have only see a Taking twice in my lifetime."

Her mouth shaped a surprised sound, and her eyelids fluttered, and then suddenly, before he could think of catching her, the noblewoman dropped. The swordsman caught her up with a cry and balanced her in his arms. "We've been through a lot," he said. "Is your hut far?"

"No," Ganth said, and hurried to the fore. "Follow me!"

And thus it was the village of Shalad gained a protector, bold if somewhat circumspect about showing his face. They were known as hermits, the man and woman, and only Ganth had the slightest inkling of how they'd come to appear on the mountaintop.

Chapter 5

From the outpost watchtowers of Rilth, the mountains of Shalad could not be seen. Nor could the vast forests of the Keug nor the mighty river Vandala running through the southern continent. It did not matter, for the watchtower of Rilth looked upon a ridge of mountains that was always tipped with snow, and where the winds always challenged the dragons who approached. It was the honor post, the fortress of Baalan, the hold closest to the mountain that held the Gates of Power. The watchtowers themselves were footed on a mesa that must have once been the foundation of a mighty peak akin to that which held the Gates. What had leveled it, the dragons could not guess . . . or even much care.

Without inner fires like those the dragons had to warm them, humans, pallans, and goblins were always cold in Rilth. The pallans did not complain: their time in Rilth was transient and they seemed to know it. The goblins complained about everything, incessantly, and in their deep-toned guttural words that sounded like cursing even if it was not. The dragonpriests alone wished to complain and did not. Quietly, vehemently, they wrapped their cloaks of crimson about themselves and tried to ignore the iciness creeping into their bones. The hold of Rilth was an honor post—one to which they had aspired all of the time they spent in service. What was a little cold this close to the altar at which they all hoped to be allowed to worship?

On a dreary night the priest acolyte, known only as Third, swung off his cot and set his bare feet to the flagstone. A chill as mortal as a death blow rang through the bones of his feet and thrilled up his legs until it finally dissipated somewhere around his gut. Quickly, to avoid a second such touch, he shoved his feet into battered boots half a size too big. Better too big than too small, he thought, before grabbing up a clay lamp and wrapping his cloak about him tightly. It was his turn to check the dungeons and their holdings.

Scroll tucked under his elbow, Third made his way from his small room behind the kitchens to the even colder hallways and stairs leading to the dungeons. As he descended, he looked out of habit at the upper landings, where Wendeen had lived. Baalan had not yet chosen a successor to the high priestess's position as if denying that the woman had finally given in to her years and left him. Third had only been at Rilth long enough to have seen her briefly before her final illness. Brief though the view had been, it was long enough to confirm all said of her. She had looked barely half of her one hundred and several years.

There were rewards to serving the dragongods in this icy palace. Third smiled grimly at his fleeting remembrance, ducked his chin down, and resumed his trek to the dungeons. He took the steps with dignity as he wished to give the impression this duty was a privilege and not an interruption of his sleep as so many others seemed to regard it.

Third bolted out of the dungeons with a great deal more haste and less dignity. His cloak streamed from his shoulders as if he, too, were dragonwinged, as he sought the immense cavernous room that sheltered Baalan. Goblins came to attention at the door and dropped their swords to bar him from it.

"Dungeon watch," said Third carefully, trying not

to gasp for breath. "I must see and inform Lord Baalan immediately."

The goblins looked at each other, their hairy beetle-brows furrowing in brutish understanding. A problem, their expression seemed to say. They raised their swords. "It's on your head," the bigger one grunted, as Third brushed past him.

The acolyte slowed inside, in the dim expanse of the room, hesitant about waking the dragonlord. His boots suddenly seemed as loud as drums and he stood on one foot and then the other to remove them, despite the cold stone floor. But as he set his bared feet down, he found the stones warm beneath him. Heated, perhaps, as they lay upon it by the inner fires of the creatures that slept here.

He crept forward, his eyes adjusting to the twilight of the hall. There were other bulks lying curled, but he knew his lord's by the sheer size and grandeur of it. There had never been a dragon like Baalan and never would be.

"You creep like a softfoot."

Third jumped and dropped his boots in startlement. He recovered himself. Of course the dragonlord would be awake. How could he think Baalan would not? The purple majesty must have heard Third's steps even as he pounded up the stairs from the dungeon.

Baalan stirred, lifting his head a little, and opening his hooded eyes so that the glowing orbs shone like lanterns in the hall. "Your consideration of my sleep does not go unnoticed, priest, nor does what must be the necessity of your disturbing me at all. What do you wish?"

Third got close enough to drop to his knees and bow in accordance with law. He pulled the scroll from his sash. "My lord, I am Third, and this night was dungeon watch for me. I—I am sorry to report, lord, that there has been an escape."

"An escape? Really." Baalan drew himself upward onto his haunches. "This is a first for Rilth. Perhaps we should look into it, Third. Are we getting lax?"

A herd of possibilities stampeded through the acolyte's mind. Heading an investigation could very well thrust him into the forefront of those competing to replace Wendeen. But he stifled his ambitions. He dealt with magic here, as well as bestial cunning. "It will be difficult to say, my lord, without knowing more of what occurred," he said finally, as truthfully and without guile as he could muster.

"Hmmm." The dragon's rumble vibrated on the man's eardrums. "Be that as it may—how many are gone, and have you identified them?"

"Just one. The human known as Telemark." Third unrolled his scroll and double-checked it even as he spoke. He nodded in confirmation. "I have a patrol readying—"

"Not necessary. Let that miserable scrap go. If he crosses these desolate plains, he will find that there is no place he can go where I cannot find him. Like his mother and grandfather before him, I have a very long leash on him." Baalan stretched his muscular neck and shook himself, spines rattling. "He will soon find he has gone from the jaws to the altar, as they like to say."

Third misunderstood. "But if he was to have been a sacrifice . . . it will be no trouble, lord, for me to bring him back.

"No, priest. I do not want him sacrificed, nor do I want him back, just yet." A singular eye fixed on the acolyte. "But knowing what I do of Telemark, it was assuredly bribery and not cleverness which got him loose. Do find who was stupid enough to collude with the prisoner and bring him or her to me."

Third dropped back to his knees and pressed his forehead to the floor. "I understand, mighty one." He got up and hurried to the door before Baalan's voice spoke out again.

"And, Third."

The acolyte stopped, hair prickling at the back of his neck. He turned slowly. "Yes, my lord?"

"See yourself fitted for a decent pair of boots. You needn't be clumping about."

A very slight smile creased the young man's face. "Yes, lord!" He bolted through the doors before the dragon's temper changed.

He had been born accursed. Cursed and galled and destined to live a life not worth having. He had known it all his days, long before the dragonpriests had sought him out and taken him to Rilth. His witch-mother's milk had been sour from her very teats when he was a babe. His grandfather had been a raving, drunken old man—one whom Telemark was pleased to smother in his sleep as soon as his arms had been strong enough to hold the blanket down. Had he been a little older, he might have hesitated at that. Not because of any conscience, oh, no, but the old man had had a little talent—mostly for pinching food, and Telemark could remember horrible, hungry days after Hapwith's death.

His mother abandoned him soon afterward on the streets of Murch's Flats, a dirty hazer town filled with scroundrels and other bastards just like himself. She'd taken to whoring and he'd been inconvenient. He hated her. The only goal he had in life was to outlive his hated mother and he had a few more years to go before he accomplished it.

He grit his teeth and stumbled across the woolie path along the ankle of a range of hills. Fall and winter and most of spring had passed since fleeing the watchtower of Rilth. His boots were shreds about his feet, held together with strips cut painstakingly from the hem of his cloak. Telemark was torn about which he needed most to live—his boots or his cloak.

As he stopped to gather his bearings, there was a tickle . . . an itch . . . that crawled through the back of his mind. It crawled and crawled until he screamed and thrust both hands into his matted hair and scratched and gouged at his scalp. It did not help. Nothing helped when the dragongod reminded him that he was still within reach. No matter where he ran, Baalan could touch him.

Gasping and bleeding from his scalp, Telemark leaned against a dusty boulder. He hugged himself close and waited until the moment passed, shuddering in the horror of it.

He was not free. He would never be free. He had been canny enough to escape, but not canny enough to understand that Baalan had willingly let him go. He was like a gunter or a woolie on a horn tether. He might bleat or bawl and jump, but one tug on that tether, and he was brought to the slaughter. As a cold sweat beaded on his face and ran dirty rivulets down it, he damned his grandfather anew.

Damn him for destroying Turiana and the heroes who had ridden her. Damn him for living and siring a daughter who in turn he damned for carrying him. They were traitors against mankind, all of them, and none of them should have been allowed to live. He had known most of his miserable life that they were outcasts, shunned by the towns they'd lived in. He had thought it because of his grandfather's irreverent attitude toward the dragongods. It was man's lot to live and serve the dragons, no one could deny it. No one who wished to live and prosper. But despite his grandfather's drunken ravings, the dragonpriests had turned their attention away. Telemark had thought it because the old man had used his meager talent to charm their thoughts away.

And after he had murdered his grandfather, his mother had said little or nothing to him. They lived on

the streets for four more years, then one night she had
just disappeared, gone, as if she never existed. He was
twelve, then he remembered. He had always been able
to find her before, no matter how she hid or what
hexes she'd used to cover her tracks. She hadn't minded
then, either.

But she was really gone this time and he had to
sharpen his wits to stay clear of the bully boys running
the streets, and he was always hungry, desperately
hungry and then, one day, after three months—she
was back. Back, with a haunted expression in her pale
brown eyes, and she never told him where she'd gone.

Soon after, she turned from her living at witchcraft
to whoring, and not long after, she abandoned him
again. He could have followed that time, but knew if
he did, she would not smile at him and rumple his
hair. She would spit in his face, and he hated her for
that.

The crawling in his mind stopped. Telemark stayed
hunched over, cursing, a moment or two longer. It
crossed his thoughts briefly that this is what could
have happened to his mother, and he shoved it away.
To believe that would be to find mercy for the slut and
he had no room in his guts for anyone else but him.

Telemark's eyes focused on the woolie path. The
slot was fresh and he thought he could hear their
bleating above him. Fresh meat for dinner sounded
good, and his stomach clenched with agreement. He
had some small talent himself—sleight of hand mostly,
good for games of chance until the townspeople eyed
his lucky streaks with suspicion—and he could also
charm the unwary close. He was tired of softfoot.

He was short of breath, too, and realized that he
had been climbing steadily. The woolie path and foothills led into a mountainous region and a backward
look confirmed that the desolate plains he'd left were
far below him. Baalan had been scratching at his mind

longer than he'd thought, to have trudged so high without noticing it.

A bell tinkled. Pebbles rolled down from the hillside. The woolies were belled then, and that meant herded and guarded and that meant no free dinner. With a sigh, Telemark straightened his shirt and cloak and ran his fingers through his hair. He had a hat stuck inside his shirt and would put it on before he reached what passed for human. The hat would cover the disarray of hair that needed trimming and whatever bloody scars he had given himself. Thus girded, he took a deep breath and made to overtake the woolies and their shepherd. With a pleasant smile and perhaps a bit of shadow puppetry, he might spend a night inside a hut, with mutton stew and wild onions for dinner. There were curses and there were curses, he thought, and walked onward.

"Evening, Ganth," the pub man called as the coal seller entered the common house for a bit of refreshment and diversion.

Ganth doffed his hat and smiled. He no longer had to bow and scrape to every man in the village. His wealth and investments were known—and protected— thanks to a shrewd moment or two upon the higher mountains. His daughters had married well and left him a comfortable home in blessed silence. And they had brought with them strong backs and hands, husbands eager to learn the coal business and do the digging and carrying for him.

And Shalad, too, had prospered. Word had spread that bandits avoided the mountains like the very plague, driven out, and the dragongods seemed to have overlooked the village. Even caravans nudged their way into town periodically and the woolie herds were growing famous for the soft white cheese their owners produced. All this in three short years. Yes, Ganth was blessed, three-fold, and feeling quite benevolent about it.

The click of dice in the pit alerted him. He flicked a glance at the pub man before heading to the gambling room. "Early for a game?"

Abel, a stick-and-bones sort of man despite his wife and sister's good cooking, shrugged. "For some perhaps. We've a visitor. He's got the dragon's own luck."

Ganth smiled wider. "Send a pot and a plate of whatever smells so good after me, will you? I feel lucky, too." He rubbed his hard-worn hands together and followed the clicking of dice.

By the fall of night, Abel's dinner sat in his stomach like greasy cold lumps of the coal he mined. The stranger rocked back on his haunches and looked over the room's audience. "Quintains? Any bet I can't throw them?" He eyed Ganth with blue eyes as hard as ice. "Bet, master Ganth?"

The coalman shook his head, feebly at first and then more vigorously. The head herdsman slapped a coin onto the betting table. The stranger looked about rapaciously. "Any more? Shall I sweeten the pot a little?"

Ganth squatted, out of the betting and the man's stare, and did a little staring of his own. He could not help but see the man's battered boots and worn cloak . . . and his thatch-colored hair matted as if it, too, were part of a roof. It was obvious the man had walked in, and probably over the plains, too, a lonely, desolate trip. But a man of luck ought not to be walking, as Ganth well knew.

The stranger rubbed the dice in his palms, their clicking music to the coalman's ears. Ganth watched him closely. The throw . . . he had a nice twist of the wrist and a good follow-through as well. He watched the dice bounce in the gaming pit and before they were done, quintains faced up.

The old man blinked and rubbed his eyes with the heel of his hand. He'd seen them twist! He was sure of it. Witchery, and punishable by death when it came to games of chance. Quietly, quietly, Ganth backed off the throw-line and left the gambling room. Shalad might still be small for a village, but they had their law and an enforcer.

He bowed his shoulder against the breeze of an early evening and went uphill, by a path only he knew, in search of the hermit swordsman.

Caught up in the thrill of winning and the chance, Telemark took a moment to realize the gaming room had fallen silent. He glanced up and saw a dark shadow towering over him. His heart took a plummeting fall in his chest. Isolated and quaint these folk might be, they were not the easy fleecing he had thought. Bile rose in his throat. He should have known, he should have known! When would life ever be as easy as this for him?

He stood up and faced the swordsman who was dressed like any herdsman except for the chain-mail coat and bracers and damnable sword upon his back. He wore a woven hat of bark that shaded his face, but Telemark saw the set to his jaw and knew he was dead where he stood.

"Witchery," the man said, and his voice was an orchestra of richness compared to the thin twangy accent of the villagers, "is punishable by death."

"Witchery?" Telemark repeated, his eyebrows questioning the swordsman. He rolled his eyes up, gauging the height of the room. The swordsman would have no problem with an over the shoulder draw. All Telemark had going for him now was the speed of his hands. He palmed the hilt of his dagger in his belt, thinking that he could gut the man before he finished pulling his sword. "I had a bit of luck, is all."

"You do not look like a lucky man."

Telemark sighted the distance to the door. "Perhaps
. . . I'm not!" He threw the dagger.

The sword came out and struck it down midair. The
breath stuck in Telemark's throat, strangling him. He
had never seen such a draw! Never! He staggered back
on his heels, totally unprepared to flee.

The sword blade licked about him. Sleeves, gone,
fluttering to the ground. His hat, in shreds. His hair,
barbered short for him, falling in clumps to the wooden
floor.

The swordsman paused, blade at rest, but cautiously
held. "You are divested of your winnings. And before
you lose anything else, I suggest you leave."

"Some of that money was mine—"

The swordsman's brown eyes glittered. "Take two
crowns, and go. My mercy is borrowed and short."

"You will leave that pot for the pallans?" His voice
reflected his shock.

The pallan traders who had been gambling at the
very last and were standing in the corner came forward. With them was the illusion that they brought the
shadows with them, both were dressed in dark and
somber colors. Telemark cared less about offending
them—he ranked pallans even below goblins and knew
many humans felt the same. It was they who had
brought the full wrath of the dragongods on all of
them.

But the swordsman stiffened, and Telemark was
surprised.

"We are all children of Rangard," the stern-jawed
man said. He did not seem to hear the whispers at his
back, nor take note that the pallans were watching
him closely. He gripped his sword hilt anew, and the
blade tipped glittering lamplight into Telemark's eyes.
"Take your two crowns before I change my mind."

Telemark recognized the coalman, Ganth, in the

swordsman's wake. The old man was grinning at some huge joke. He felt a surge of revenge. It sickened him. He shook it off. He was accursed, that was all, and if not the old man, someone would have seen him cheat sooner or later. It did not occur to him that he might not have risked cheating at all.

He stooped and palmed an extra coin. That left him at least a crown to the good.

"I am a stranger to this region," he said. "I came across the plains, and find no desire to return that way."

"Cross the mountains," the swordsman answered. "You'll find the passes free of bandits."

Indeed, thought Telemark. I bet I will. He shrugged into his cloak, left untouched by that razor-sharp blade. His scalp felt naked. He looked to the pallans and felt his lip curl as he spoke. "May your children be Taken," he spat, and left.

Ganth tugged on the swordsman's sleeve. "Do not leave yet, milord. He had a vile look upon his face."

"I'll stay awhile," the other agreed. "To be sure our unpleasant company is gone."

The night was late, and the smaller moon in its crest, trailing the large moon down the curve of the sky, when Sharlin heard the grass bend and gravel crackle outside the hut's door. Sleepy toddler on her hip, she ran to the door and pulled it open. "Dar? Is everything all right?"

"Yes," he answered, shrugging off his hat, and sitting down on the porch to pull off his boots. "Put him down."

Sharlin paused in the doorway and then let Fort down and watched the pudgy boy toddle his way to his father.

"Your charm worked well enough. He did not seem to be a dragonpriest in disguise or anything else. He was a cheat, though, and I saw him throw at least one pass he magicked."

"Ah." She leaned against a porch post. "What do you think?"

"I think I'm getting slow. He could have gutted me—I'm going to wear the sheath on my left hip from now on. I don't have time to draw from the back." Dar hugged his son close. "I keep thinking I can take the practice dummy down and stop working the drills, but I can't. And I'm not as good as I was."

"And that bothers you? To lose your edge as a fighter? I thought you wanted to perch up here and raise woolies forever."

"No, my girl. You misheard me. I wished to raise children forever. And hoist other things preparatory to that."

"Dar!"

Even in the midnight light, he could see her blush. Fort made a gurgling sound and ran back to her. She swung him up and said, "You've got to go back to bed."

The boy looked back over her shoulder. "G'night, Daddy."

Dar smiled. He waited on the porch till she came back and sat down next to him. He put an arm about her. "Have I attracted attention?" he asked finally.

"Do you think you did?"

"He was a strange one. Reminded me of Hapwith once I sheared him. Sooner or later, someone is going to bring tales of this mountain haven to a dragon or one of those damnable blood-sucking priests. Sooner or later, we're going to have to move on."

She did not ask him what he meant. She was familiar with Dar's habit of shaving the sides of his victims' heads, to mark them of their shame to others and also to remind them of the sharpness of the blade he carried. But to have shorn a stranger and found a familiar face looking back . . . She caught at her thoughts. "But do we have anyplace to go?"

"It makes no difference at this point." He paused. "There were pallan traders at the inn tonight."

"Really? Did you get a chance to talk to them?"

"No. But we've never had word of Turiana before. I have to think—I have to think when she lost us, and went back, that something happened. If she'd survived, we'd know of it."

"And if she didn't, I'd know. We shared her magic. Part of it still burns in me like . . . like the way I feel for you and Fort."

"Then I'll keep on looking. I'll glean travelers' tales the way you do the fields." He smiled. "All the same, milady, you'd better have some baskets woven. We may have to leave in a hurry. I've no wish to face Baalan without an army at my back!"

She had her head on his shoulder, listening to the vibrations of his words in his chest. She turned her face so that she might kiss him. "We do what we have to," she murmured. And then vigorously pulled him down on her. "And sometimes, what we really want to!"

Chapter 6

The hair had fully grown back on Telemark's head and his body wasted almost to gauntness in his travels before he set eye on the wastes of Keldonna. He parted the branches of a smoke tree, its leaves shaking like soundless coins above him, and leaned downhill. His lips were chapped and the insides of his nostrils raw with the dryness. A bad trade two villages back had left him with a poorly tanned water bag that went slimy and foul-tasting on him and now he had nothing to carry water on him except for an inadequate gourd he'd dried. Even it swung half-empty on his belt.

Keldonna stretched before him. It was desert, but not all sand. He recognized the many life-forms that a desert held, seemingly barren but teeming with life if one knew where to look. He sighed. The crossing was no less than he expected, cursed as he was. He would not go straight across if either north or south he could see the shape and shade of foothills, but he couldn't. The only foothills beckoning were dim and faint across the stretches of Keldonna.

A few dried leaves drifted down on him. He shook them off. He palmed his gourd, lifted it, took a sip that scarcely wet the inside of his mouth. A familiar tingle crawled across the back of his head. He paused a moment to focus on it. It fled. Either mighty Baalan had grown weak or he had come far indeed. Or per-

haps it was just a drop of sweat trickling through his
dirty yellow hair.

A treefrog croaked from a branch above his head.
Telemark looked up and blinked. Already it felt as
though he had grit under his eyelids. He looked back
to the wastes. There was no water here, and he had
been assured at the hazer outpost two days ago that
there were no less than three oases scattered across
the Keldonna. He had gambled (and won) directions
to one of them. He let go the branch he held. As it
moved back into place, a curtain of leaves obscured
the vision of distance hills.

As he stepped onto the sand, the crust broke under
his feet, and fiery red biters boiled up from their
underground nest. Telemark smiled. He wet a finger,
leaned down, and scooped up what he could and licked
them from his hand before they could sting him. They
crunched sweetly between his teeth. Where they found
nectar to gather in this barrenness, he could not guess.
If he were not suddenly in a hurry, he would stay and
eat the nest empty, but it took too much effort and he
found himself eager to begin crossing the Keldonna.

Baalan scratched his chin with a talon he had used
more than once to gut rivals. He did so carefully.
When he lowered his claw, he found Third's attention
fixed devotedly upon him. Caught in the moment, Baalan
found himself slightly embarrassed. Before he could
say a word to put the dragonpriest in his place, Third
bowed lowly.

"If it would please you, my lord, I will have several
acolytes come this evening before prayer and oil you.
The air has been dry. We received several wagon
loads of the lyrith-scented oil you prefer this morning."

Baalan lowered his eyelids in thought. The itch was
likely to be caused by a sand mite—those damnable
parasites occasionally got under the edges of a scale—

but an oiling sounded refreshing. "It would please me," the great purple beast rumbled.

Third wrapped his scarlet cloak about him and bowed. "Consider it done." He made a note upon the scroll he kept attached to his wrist by a cord of gold. Baalan appreciated his efficiency of administration—and it was the scroll that made it possible. There was too much business in the day to remember on one's own. Recording the oiling also made it possible for Third to hide his expression from the scrutiny of his master. By anyone's reckoning, Baalan was old. Even for a dragon, he had to be past his prime. The acolytes Third intended to send had more than oiling in purpose. When they returned, they would report to the dragonpriest just how much of Baalan's bulk was muscle, and how much flab. Third revered dragons and his lord—but the dragonpriesthood and the rule of Rangard went only to the fit. There were other dragons being spawned who might one day challenge Baalan and win. Third did not intend to be on the losing side.

He capped his pen and scroll tube. "My lord, if you are ready, Mayor Nicommen of Geldart has come to beg audience."

"Ahh." Baalan came alert. His eyes glowed. "I have been expecting him. Let him in and, Third, stay as well. You will have to make preparations according to the news he brings." As he watched Third leave, he hooded his eyes carefully. With a trumpet he summoned Atra from across the hall.

The sleek black dragon came, throat bared in subjugation. His posture did not fool Baalan. The vivid silver-white eyes glowing in his broad ebony forehead glared at the purple dragon with intelligence and hope. "My lord," Atra said. His twin Pevan watched alertly from across the hall.

"I have a tether I want pulled in."

The dark beast lowered his head and cocked an ear.

"You will have to fly a distance," Baalan cautioned. "My prey has gone very far indeed. You may take your brother if you wish . . ."

"No need," said Atra reedily. He wasted little sorcery on his speech. "Tell me what you search for and where it is."

Across the hall Pevan stretched and bated his wings in jealousy, and hiss boiled like steam. Baalan ignored it. The longer he kept these two at odds, the more secure he was in his reign. Atra was the keener of the two and if Pevan's spitefulness could keep his brother from challenging Baalan a little longer, so much the better.

Baalan stretched jaws wide in a growling smile. He sent an image into the air. "It is this man, and this is where he is to be found."

Atra folded a wingtip over his muzzle coyly before bowing back upon his haunches. "I was hatched," he said, "upon the sands of Keldonna. I know it well."

"A proper dragon," Baalan warned, "is only hatched in Glymarach, the cradle. You would do well to remember it upon your spawning time."

Atra's eyes narrowed to a silvery glint. A dragon only spawned when near death. Baalan's warning carried double meaning and he would do well to heed it. He bowed. "Yes, my lord. I will return as soon as I can." He hobbled toward the immense doors, built for the entrance and egress of a dragon. His trailing tail tip nearly knocked the mayor of Geldart off his feet. The mayor was a young, hale and hearty man, businesslike, well-dressed but not opulent unless one knew the price of the dye of his garb. His dark hair was thinning, but cut confidently, as a man does who moves into his prime and is not afraid of it.

Nicommen recovered admirably, his arms filled with scrolls and an urn. He strode in Third's wake was if it were the only safe path to take into a den of dragons —as, indeed, it might be.

He stopped at Baalan's signal and said, "Hail, O mighty dragongod. Geldart, jewel of the river Vandala and gateway to the mysterious East, sends greetings. Your reign has prospered us and in turn, we honor you." He dropped to his knees and spread out a massive scroll, more map than book. "The temple is nearly finished. It is even more beautiful than the architects have painted it for you."

The dragon tilted his head in curiosity. "Indeed? How grand? How beautiful?"

Nicommen set his hand upon the urn. "I have brought with me samples of the building and decorating materials. The quality is even greater than I hoped for. By the time I return, the temple should be finished and ready for consecration." He bowed his head reverently. Third took the urn from under his hand and shook its contents upon the map.

The paint and gilded ink provided an intricate background for the marble, quartz, ivory and jetstone that tumbled out. Third put his hand inside the urn and drew out lengths of cloth, fabric so thin he could see through its shimmery weave and let it waft from his fingers to the scroll below.

Baalan cared little for what humans and pallans cared for, other than the grandeur. He let his nostrils widen, as if what he saw impressed him. "What," he said to Nicommen, "about the cavern and mud baths, and the altar hall?"

"The mountain was as you said, O lord. We built the temple against it, and, for all the magnificence of the building, it is nothing more than the door to the worship hall and the caverns you desired. The holding facilities and the baths and, above all, the golden altar, have all been completed. We awaited only the interior furnishings for the apartments of your servants, and a trifle here or there."

Baalan reared up. His pectorals rippled. "Good.

You have done well, Nicommen. All roads lead to Geldart, and may they so continue." He made a mental note to tell Atra and Pevan to continue the harassing of other trade routes to ensure both the piety and continued prosperity of the city. "Third."

"Yes, master."

"Next year's Night of Dragons will be held in Geldart. Prepare accordingly. In the meantime, inform the local priests to consecrate the altar when the temple is finished, and hold the local rites as is usual. I myself will be in attendance when the Night falls in Geldart."

Third sucked in his breath. Beside him he felt the tension and joy in Nicommen's stocky form. Baalan had not attended a Night since Wendeen's death. No wonder the old worm was getting lax in his powers . . . he, too, needed the rites and cleansing.

Nicommen got to his feet. "Thank you, lord, for this bountiful honor. My city will rejoice."

"You have done well." Baalan looked deeply into the human's eyes. It occurred to him that Nicommen might be of further use, later. He hummed a tune beyond what he knew to be the range of human hearing, trying to suggest the man return to him alone, privately. If Geldart did not already have spies in the East, it might be good to do so. The crimson dragon who ruled there bothered Baalan. It would not hurt to make use of whatever resources he might have.

Baalan made a few more polite words and watched the humans leave. His attention turned to Atra and the far flung tether he wished pulled in.

Telemark was dying when he stumbled across the oasis. He did not see the sparse smoke trees at its fringe. Sand and gum glued his eyes nearly shut. His tongue had begun to swell in his mouth, choking off what air he dared to breathe into his heat-blasted throat and lungs. His feet shuffled through the dirt,

moving of some volition other than the will to live. His
thoughts were gone, tumbling in the severe wind, never
to be pulled back, never to be realized . . .

With a thump and a woof, he hit the ground belly
first. He tried to blink and scrubbed at his eyes to do
so. Then the visage under his chin became clear.

Prairie grass, wiry as metal, had tripped him up.
Gray-green it was and as he looked ahead, it grew
greener still. Water! Water trapped in this benighted
place. Telemark began to crawl upon his stomach,
followed the prairie grass until it stood tall and lush
upon the grounded edge of the spring. He cupped his
hands in the cool blue water and splashed its life-
saving goodness upon his face.

As it trickled down, he splashed again, ignoring the
sting of his eyes and the myriad cracks of his sun-
burned skin. When he had done washing, he cupped
his hands and drank, deeply. At first his tongue absorbed it all, and his throat cried out, and then the
cotton of his mouth was gone, and he could swallow,
and the first cold drips went down his throat. He lay
elbow-deep in the pool and drank all that he could
swallow.

The first violent stomach cramps hit suddenly. He
arched his back in pain, and then doubled over. Fool!
He'd foundered himself like a lathered beast! When
the cramps stopped, he took a shivery breath. Telemark took a deep breath or two, feeling the pain in his
chest from breathing the too hot, too dry air, and then
the cramps began again. He stood up and staggered a
length away from the pool. When he fell again, he
crashed into a skeleton, its brittle bones shattering
under his weight, and the prairie grass bowed over
them both.

Telemark stared into a skull. Its eye sockets were
deep and dark. The man cried nameless oaths, his
vision blackening. His throat began to close. He could

feel it swelling shut, cutting off his life. The oasis had been befouled, poisoned.

Mark, his grandfather said, and stood from his perch on a nearby rock. *There is a difference between being cursed and being stupid. Cursed we are. Stupid, I had thought not.*

Telemark tried to claw the vision from his eyes. He chased it to the corner of his sight, where the ghost barely held sway over the horizon of the Keldonna framed by the arms of smoke trees.

"Go away, old man! I am dying!"

Not quite. But soon. The old man tottered about, his opaqueness pierced by the reality of the oasis. Telemark found the pain in his stomach again and shut his eyes.

You have some talent, old Hapwith said. *You need not die.*

Telemark levered his eyelids open. He looked for the ghost. "Why did you come here?"

To help you.

"I murdered you, old man!"

You but put me out of my misery. Do you think an eight-year-old child could murder a sorcerer unless he wished it?

Telemark considered that, but rational thought was shoved aside by another racking of pain. His bladder voided vinegary urine and his bowels turned to black water. Soon he would lie in the prairie grass, another stinking corpse until the sun and wind and scavengers make a skeleton of him.

Are you listening?

"Go away!"

Are you listening?

"I am dying!"

Are you listening?

His blood rushed in his veins like a spring-swollen river, and his heart made a drum-like tattoo. His breath rattled like seeds in a dried gourd. "I'm listening!"

You use ghost fingers to turn the dice when you roll them, do you not?

Telemark could only set his head to nodding and could not stop the spastic movement.

Now you must use the ghost fingers. Reach down your gullet and clear out the swelling. And when you've reached your heart, you must grasp it and squeeze it, one, two, one, two before it stops beating. You must squeeze it until you know you're going to live without it.

"I . . . can't . . ."

Then, said Hapwith without mercy, *I'm here to escort you to hell with me.*

Telemark jammed his shoulder against his head and managed to stop his convulsive nodding. Before the cramps could begin again, he thought of his talent for gambling and his ghost fingers. He began to follow his grandfather's instructions. He opened his throat and followed his hand inside of him until he reached the heart, took it in his hand, and began to steady the convulsing pounding with a rhythmic squeeze.

The waters of the oasis coursed inside of him, bringing both life and death. With his ghost eyes, he could see the difference and began to peel them apart. He could hear his blood calm and feel his crackled skin heal and slough off, exposing delicate new skin beneath. He could heal himself . . . he could throw off the poison and take the good water into himself . . . he was going to live.

And then his sight met a spiral of darkness growing within him. He nudged it. Like a thundercloud heavy with noise and fire as well as rain, it moved ponderously aside. Not flesh then, but something else. Telemark made a ghost mouth and swallowed it.

Light flashed before his eyes. Thunderclaps deafened him, told him secrets, and then deafened him again. Rain washed away his voice so that he could never reveal those secrets. Levin light illuminated them, then blinded him again. But one thing he would never forget was that the darkness had been dragonseed within him—the spark Baalan had planted in him, plaited into his own power, and now he was fused with it.

His death had transformed him.

Telemark opened his eyes. The enamel bowl of a clear blue sky met his stare. A smoke tree sighed nearby. He could hear the wash of water at his feet. He stood, toppled to one knee, regathered himself, and stood again. The vision of his grandfather was nowhere to be seen.

But everything else was. How clear his sight! How vast his understanding of the oasis he stood in . . . even to how the prairie grass and the smoke trees and the treefrogs filtered the water from the poison and used the good of it. Telemark smiled to himself. He would filter the poison from the water and find a use for *that*. No longer would he be shunned or cursed on the face of Rangard.

He stepped into the pool and bathed in it, cleansing himself of all that had passed. He emerged and let his clothes dry on him in the intense, arid wind off the Keldonna.

Shadows swept over him, cooling the desert. Telemark looked up again and saw the immense wingspread of a vast, dark beast. He smiled hugely then.

He stepped out of the oasis, shouting. "Here I am! Come and get me!"

Chapter 7

Baalan appraised the man before him. The moment Atra had entered the hall, he had sensed Telemark's conversion. Into what, he was not sure, and it was that uncertainty that had sent him bellowing after the other dragons in the hall. He wanted it clear, absolutely clear, before he spoke to the man.

Telemark did not seem to notice the late fall chill. He stood at ease, meeting Baalan's eyes without hesitation. His face was thin, almost a death's head, but his skin glowed with health.

"It appears your latest travels have treated you well."

Telemark sketched a bow. "Better even than the hospitalities of dragongods."

Baalan hooded his eyes and quenched the flame that flared at the man's insolence. First, he had information he wanted; then, he had to determine the difference in Telemark's manner. And then, he could rend him limb from limb, if he wished. "Perhaps," the beast answered, "we have been remiss."

"And then," said Telemark, as he seated himself cross-legged on the flagstone flooring without regard to Baalan, "perhaps you have not." He looked up, and his eyes burned intensely from his face. "But we both know I am not the same callow youth who occupied a cell below. I might feign before another, but not to one such as you."

"Indeed." Baalan settled upon the stone, warming

it gently with his own interior fires. "And what has happened?"

Telemark scratched his chin, then smiled. "Shall we just say I have discovered myself? That my talent for making dice jump and picking pockets has flowered into something much greater. That I can now hear the whispering in my head which you planted there."

"Tell me what you hear."

Telemark closed his eyes briefly. For a second Baalan was glad to have that blazing gaze shuttered away. He steeled himself to meet it again when Telemark looked out once more.

"It tells me I am outcast, a wanderer, that the only welcome I will ever receive from Rangard is when my feet are upon yet another road. *And it asks me to look and listen for the whereabouts of a golden dragon.*" The man shifted about. "And when I am done listening to the whisper, I think to myself—is it possible I am not shunned or cursed as I have always thought? Is it possible that the great and munificent dragongods have set my grandfather, and my mother, and then me to wandering on a mission so important that even we were never told the truth of it? What have we to do with a golden dragon?" His gaze seared at Baalan. "What have we to do with a golden dragon," he repeated. "My grandfather destroyed one for you, once."

"Once," echoed the beast. "Only once."

"Yet you search for news of one. No." Telemark tilted his head as though listening to an inner voice. "No, not just any news. *Her.* You look for Turiana. Then my father did not destroy her for you."

Talons clicked upon the floor. "You presume too much."

The man smiled briefly. "I'm already a dead man by coming here, Baalan. I might as well die knowing the truth—or live using it. My grandfather was not a pow-

erful man and I don't think it was because you put a
claw in his brains and stirred them up as you tried to
do mine. I don't believe he was capable of doing such
a feat for you. You must have come close to ruining
this golden one, or else you would not have the power
you have today. But she's in hiding, she must be, or
else you wouldn't be searching for her."

"You are too clever."

"Never too clever." Telemark surged to his feet.
"Come out of the shadows, Baalan. I can do far more
for you knowing what it is you truly want than being
nudged. I have no news of Turiana, but make me a
priest where I can walk the roads in honor, and I *will*
find her for you. There are havens all over Rangard
which do not live in fear of the Night of Dragons.
We'll bring that to an end. I walked through one such
a few months ago—a swordsman drove me off, a country bumpkin still smelling of his woolie herd, but with
mail and a sword the like of which I have never
seen—and he used it well. You should fear him, Baalan,
because you don't rule him."

Baalan rumbled, "What of you? Do I rule you?"

The man's face shone. "For now." He made a pass
through the air and conjured up an image of the
Shalad swordsman, face shadowed by the woven hat
and dim lights of the gambling room, jaw set as he
looked down and pronounced judgment on Telemark.
"No one will ever drive me away again. Cloaked in
the red of a dragonpriest, I'll walk wherever I want,
and take whatever I desire. In turn, whatever power I
have, I put in your service."

The resonance of his talent thrilled through Baalan.
Under his scales, skin became gooseflesh. The dragon
had not felt power through a human like that since the
death of the witch-king Valorek and his own beloved
Wendeen. The dragon reared to his haunches and
roared in joy.

Chapter 8

She was a jealous mother. Turiana found a cave not far from a fresh water stream, deep and clear, that would one day carry her young to sea. The trip would be a perilous one, and her cave was not the wind-carven, natural caves of Glymarach, but she could not return there. Baalan would be watching for any rival emerging from the ancient birthyard and deathgrave of the dragons. She had done a difficult thing during the laying of her eggs and withheld a great deal of the roe. Uncomfortable and full unto bursting, she began to release the additional roe as soon as she had the eggs settled. The gelatinous mass filled the cave.

She had not chosen the cave at random, but made a careful selection of it. The sharp, cloven mountains that protected it also allowed her to oversee the most logical points of approach. And, within a day's flight of the cave, lay an azul eye that looked at the sky, a tarn fed by local streams and cut out of sandstone rock. She fed in it once and found the tarn bountiful with fish and frog and fowl. A secret began in her, one she carried to her cave when she prepared it for her eggs.

In a whispery voice made faint by her trials, she also laid down a ward, on each and every egg, and started a thing no dragonqueen had ever before attempted.

The golden dragon took up residence nearby and turned back each and every one of the pallans who trudged up the ridge to see her. Some, she knew, were simply curious. Others were distrustful of any dragon. They would be even more distrustful if they had any inkling of her true intentions.

She met the watchdragon with her own brute force rather than magic. Theirs was a battle that rained crimson ichor down from the skies and deafened the valley dwellers for days with their warring trumpets. When it was done, she crawled back to her cave and lay as near death as the beast she had vanquished. The pallans sang of her prowess and her skill with magic and she listened to the muted song drifting up to her cave as she nursed her wounds.

She allowed the elder, Zachiyah, and the bold female, Anya, his granddaughter, to visit. They brought a fresh gunter. Her nostrils quivered with the pleasurable smell.

She crawled out to eat the delicacy on the wide fronds of a valley tree. The frond, soaked with blood and sweet oils, smelled so good she devoured that as well, much to Anya's surprise. The child's eyes grew large in her face, her gold-shot, flame-colored mane alert as antennae, and Turiana snorted in amusement. "Am I so strange?"

"But—" Anya began and stopped. Then, "You ate a tree!"

"I eat many trees. An adult dragon, unlike the young, is an omnivore. Once bulked up, we maintain our weight, and our appetite for meat alone begins to slow. Otherwise," and Turiana put her muzzle quite close to the little pallan, "you would not have much left for dragons to eat!"

Zachiyah put his gloved hand upon his granddaughter's shoulder. "I have also brought oil for your wounds. It would be a shame to mar a skin as lovely as yours."

It was true. She could not deny it. Scar-and-puckered skin made flying and flexibility difficult. Turiana looked to Anya, who had not worn her traditional pallan garb. "And who might," she said, "volunteer to oil me?"

"I do!"

"Really?" Turiana looked to Zachiyah. "Will you consent to leaving her in my care, elder?"

The pallan nodded somberly. "Till nightfall, then, Anya, or when the queen bids you leave . . . understand?"

Anya was busy stripping down to a loincloth, the sun gloriously dancing upon her patterned skin, so like a dragon's scales, but much softer and gentler. "I will! I'll remember."

The dragon and headman exchanged a look before Zachiyah turned away and headed downhill where there was no trail, but soon would be, if Anya had her way.

The question came later than Turiana expected. She lay in the sun, the little pallan being kind with her sore and wounded parts, when Anya said, "Can I see the eggs?"

"I think not," Turiana answered. She felt like rolling over, belly up, but to do so would squish Anya who lay flat upon her back, vigorously oiling every patch of skin she could reach. "It is not wise to disturb them. They will not hatch otherwise, you see."

"Oh." The young one lay close. "I'm sorry. But I liked the green one you gave me. It was very pretty."

"Ummmm. Over there a little—further—yes, that's it. Pretty is not a word I would have chosen."

"When they hatch then, can I see your babies?"

Turiana fought against the lethargy a gunter meal, warm sun, and oiling was forcing upon her. "No," she answered finally. "Dragonets are not what you expect. They're a vicious lot. I will need to teach them manners."

"Well, then, maybe I can see them."

"No," said the golden queen lowly. "A dragon does not mother her young. They are cast to the water, to be what they will."

Anya slithered down her shoulder, landing under her chin. "Really? You can't keep them?"

"No."

"How will I ever see them? Can't I be here when you hatch them?"

"I think not."

The pallan child persisted. "But you'll protect me. When are they hatching?"

"They will hatch, each and every one of them . . . when they are ready."

Anya stopped in her tracks, skin of oil dangling near empty in one hand. She considered that for a long time. "What do you mean?" she asked finally.

Turiana looked about at her cave, where to her sorcerous eyes, she could see the faint sheen of the spell and warding she had placed on the eggs. "I wish I knew," the dragonqueen answered finally.

Of the ten dragonet eggs, one died. Turiana rejoiced for the viability of the other nine, knowing that the journey they had taken with her could easily have killed more. The abyss of time was cold and chill, death to any young. She was left with two green and two bronze and one each of black, purple, silver, and gold, as well as the strange, murky egg unlike any she'd ever seen. Of the others, a green and bronze hatched first. She looked over them, spiky, spiteful worms devouring the roe that surrounded them as quickly as they could eat. They had a go at each other, gumlessly opening their jaws as wide as they could, unable to swallow the other. The green would be a female, small and supple. The bronze a male, though not as large as she could have hoped. She let them graze as much as she dared, and then she snatched them up.

They should have gone to the river. Her thoughts warred inside her, but instead of uncurling her talons and letting the deep flowing water take them, she beat her wings instead and gained the sky. When she reached the tarn, she circled it lowly, studying it and the canyon that held it. Game abounded on the land surrounding the bottomless pool. Turiana loosened her claws and let her mindless young fall to the water below.

A dragon does not mother its young . . . because a dragon does not usually live to see its hatchlings. That was the way of things naturally. But she, Turiana, was no longer a natural creature. She had not been impregnated by her choice, or in her season, or in her death throes. Perhaps this was a thing that might change all other things as well.

The other dragonet eggs stayed quiet, awaiting their time. In the meantime, Turiana had her time filled as guardian of the pallan valley. She helped them through harsh winters and dry summers, through bandits and baffled traders who tried again and again to broach invisible barriers that gated the valley. When she was not busy, she returned to the stone canyon, with its tarn that was like a bowl of the sky, deep and mysterious, and the creatures that thrived within its depths.

The green died when she became a strider, years later. She broke her neck chasing a woolie up a rock wall, and the shale gave way under her weight. The bronze thrived, however, and when at last his wing buds began to form, Turiana became a common fixture perched on the walls above.

Turiana listened to his dragon speech, his spits and hisses and wails and trumpets, and sang back to him. She watched sadly as the bronze grew to adulthood. Without a trip to the Gates the bronze would never mature in either his sex or his power. And she knew that Baalan would have the sacred mountain guarded close.

The bronze took the name Turan. He coaxed her

down from the canyon walls, and she taught him speech of the pallans and of the humans, and he practiced the use of his wings by plunging off the sheer face of the canyon walls, gliding to the ground. Then came the day when they climbed together to the highest precipice.

Turan turned his face to the wind. "I must go, Mother," he said, "to the Gates. All that you have taught me, all that you have been and I have been is nothing if we let Baalan bar me from the Gates."

Her heart leaped in her chest, for those were words she had both hoped and feared to hear. She stayed so quiet that he said, "Am I not right?"

She draped a windsail over his shoulder. "Both good and right. I have done something no queen has ever done before, and now I will do yet another thing." And she gave him the location of the sacred mountain and burned it into his thoughts so he might never forget it so long as he lived. Then she watched him fly, and she felt a piercing in her heart and thought it very strange.

So she felt with every hatchling when it came their time. The black was a vicious beast . . . a true son of the dragon Nightwing, who had raped her, and she slew his offspring on the spot, keening for forgiveness as she did so.

The stone canyon could hold three dragonets at the most—two in the lake and a strider upon the land's game. When their time came, she sent off the purple Carana and a second bronze, Arel, and watched her silver grow. Carana was slain trying to breach the Gates. Turiana felt it, a spear of ice through her very being, and as she lifted her head for wailing, the silver dragonet huddled against her. It had never been as the others . . . mute and strange as its upbringing . . . and she knew it had no hope at all without reaching the Gates.

Turan flew in once. He brought fresh gunter with

him and news of the outside world. She realized with a shock that some fifteen years had passed and, although she had reckoned time by the growth of young Anya and her own dragonets, she had not really noticed their passage. Her own brief foresight showed her a glimmering presence that was her beloved Sharlin and Aarondar . . . as well as the darkness that threatened them. But her power could not show her if she would live to meet them. How far ahead had they gone?

She told her bronze son then of the man and woman, in hopes that he would carry the legacy if she could not. In turn, Turan told her that Baalan had lost Wendeen and the dragonpriesthood faltered, if only briefly. "I do not know yet what the Taking is, other than ceremony, but it has saved him from the wasting sickness that comes with the power from beyond the Gates. I promise you, I won't rest until I know what it is."

Turiana's eyes glowed with pride. "Perhaps," she said, "there is still hope for us."

The silver huddled against her and turned his dark blue eyes upon her. She gathered the strider in and noticed his wing buds. She left him the best of the gunter. As unnatural as her life had been since the Resurrection, she, too, faced the wasting sickness. It was the great fear that drove all dragons to side with Baalan's evil. Live under Baalan's rule . . . or die. She would rather die and knew now that she could, as long as her brood lived after her. This was her strength rather than the fickle power of her magic.

She said to Turan, "Now I know what the humans and the pallans mean when they say there is hope in their children." They hunkered down in the stone canyon and watched storm clouds sweep by.

Chapter 9

Sharlin stood in the doorway. Her face was in the shadows, but Dar knew without illuminating it what her expression was. It mirrored his own. Abel's gangly son stood on first one foot and then the other in his agitation.

"Hurry! Hurry!"

Dar bent over to strap on his shin bracers. He did so with a mild grunt and grimaced at himself. Fort did not grunt when bending over. Neither did Sharlin. Weathering winters on the mountain had added inches to his waist he did not like. Neither it seemed, did the sword, when he picked it up and warmed the hilt momentarily before he fastened the belt and sheath into place.

You must be quicker, swordsman.

With no one but straw dummies and even stupider woolies to strike at, how could he hone his skills? But he did not answer the sword. For all he knew, it was deaf if not mute. But mainly he did not answer it because to do so would worry Sharlin further.

He straightened. "All in place?"

"Yes." She moved half out of shadow. It made a striking diagonal down her face. The eyes, still startling blue, intensely alive. "Even that ridiculous hat. Take it off, Dar. You'll lose it one day anyway."

"It hides my . . . head."

Sharlin shook hers. "They see the sword. They

might as well see the helm." She stepped close and swept off his hat of straw and reed.

Abel's boy let out a gasp. The Thrassian half-helm rested comfortably, a shining silver accompaniment to the elegant sword. "Your head, milord!"

"Is it still there?"

The boy did not notice Aarondar's wry tone. "It's— it's crowned, with a silver hat, shining like anything!"

"Just one of Sharlin's cooking bowls, turned upside down. Doesn't your mom have metal bowls?"

"None that shines like that." Young Calper stepped closer. "It does have a few dents in it."

"Better the bowl than my head. Now—we're in a hurry, are we not?"

"Yes! Oh, yes!" Calper bolted for the door. "I've got horses out front."

Dar followed after. He paused long enough to brush his lips across Sharlin's cheekbone, but she grasped his wrist. He could feel the strength of her fingers even through his wrist guards. "There was bound to be a Taking sooner or later," she said. "Just don't . . . don't let them take you."

"I have to stop it. We're talking about blood sacrifice."

"You will stop it. Maybe just not tonight, here, in this place."

Calper yelled, "Hurry, sir, hurry!" from horseback.

Dar nodded. She tucked his chin strap into place and let him go.

There was no dragon in the village of Shalad. Instead, as Dar rode in, his horse lathered and tired and at a walk, he saw the two immense griffens pegged down by the inn. He motioned for Calper to drop back and circle the outskirts.

One of the griffens turned his head and spied them immediately. His orange eye caught a glint of moonlight. Dar swallowed. He had never seen a tame griffen in his lifetime, though Sharlin talked often of the aerie her family had had. The eagle head of the griffen was immense and colored like molten bronze, and his body the soft dun of a desert lion, and his wings were flecked with turquoise like those of a butterfly. He lashed his tail as if sensing an enemy.

The horse under Aarondar began to quiver in fear. Bird of prey or beast of prey, whatever they approached was too much for him. Dar curbed him out of his sidling maneuver and then reined him up altogether. Abel had been true to his word and hosted the dragonpriests with food and drink to "honor" (read delay) them long enough for Dar to be fetched. But another moment or two and he would have been too late. The inn doors opened before he had a chance to maneuver his slat-sided chestnut into position, and the vermilion men came out. Their breath was white on the night air as they bid Abel and another who looked like Ganth farewell, pressing scrolls into Abel's hand. Behind them, chained in pairs were two girls and two pallans.

Dar calculated that would be about all the weight, two prisoners apiece plus the rider, the griffens could hold even as massive as they were. Biting his lip, he waited a precious moment longer to ensure that no more dragonpriests came out of the inn.

It lost him one of the riders to his mount before he could pull his sword and charge. With a bay that echoed off the Shalad Mountains, Dar kicked his flagging mount into a surprised lunge. But the griffen bearing his rider let out an answering *screee* and Dar knew he was in trouble.

The griffen still pegged leapt to the extent of his tether and cried alike. His rider circled and danced but could not board the agitated beast.

The mounted priest threw back his crimson cloak

and drew a long, thin sword. Dar saw Abel and Ganth pulling the girls and pallans into the safety of the inn's porch before he came within range.

Fool, the swordsman said, as he swung at the griffen's talons. The dragonpriest's sword made an ugly whoosh as he ducked. He heeled the horse aside, *hard*, for they wouldn't have a second chance to avoid the griffen if they didn't move. Pink foam stained the chestnut's lips. He was no war mount, nor did he have a mouth of iron to be reined about so.

But he could *move* and did so, right in under the griffen's unfurled wing. Dar slashed, deeply, and kicked the gelding out of the way as the griffen lashed out again with an ugly noise. It reared above them, taking the dragonpriest and his sword out of striking range. The man looked down in rage.

Dar looked up. Sweat plastered his hair under the Thrassian half-helm. He had a split second to wonder if he was better off facing griffen talons or keen-bladed priests.

Then the griffen struck. His eagle head darted at them with rock adder swiftness. The bronze beak clacked as it met his sword, but the wondrous blade cut. And it cut deep. The griffen pulled his head back suddenly with a wail, nearly wrenching the sword from his hand. The gelding backed up, reading Dar's mind. He got the sword loose and tightened his grip on it. The dragonpriest cursed him with a loud and fluent tongue.

Dar laughed at him. The man's clean-shaven face turned as red as his cloak. Dar pivoted the chestnut before the fighter-priest could gather his wits. He charged the second griffen, who was still eluding his rider and keening his own battle lust. The swordsman bent down as he thundered past and sliced the tether apart.

The riderless griffen rose dragon-quick. Dar saw

instantly that he had miscalculated. Badly. The freed griffen would not fly but came after him as well.

He found himself before the two of them as they lunged together. Their hot, metallic breath stank of the forge and of the carrion they ate. The horse threw up his head and screamed in terror. Wine foam spit from his lips. Dar cocked his sword. He'd get at least one of the beasts.

The riderless griffen let out a soundless vomit and fell back as pallan arrows feathered his exposed breast. Dar whirled in the saddle, cutting the second on instinct. Blood splattered his face as the sword bit deeply, and the second griffen lolled back onto his feline hindquarters. He collapsed to the ground, wings flapping slowly.

His rider jumped free and came at Dar. Hock-deep in blood, the gelding slipped as the man let out an insane yell of fury, sword ready. Dar found himself unhorsed. He flung the blade up to shield himself as he hit ground.

The swords hit and belled as one voice, their ringing both high and true. They might have been blades from the same master smith or they might have been halves of the same whole. Dar felt the shock of their clash into the roots of his teeth. His elbow vibrated with it. With an effort, he drew back so that he could roll and get to his feet.

The dragonpriest kicked him in the ribs. Breath whooshing out and sight gone black, Dar doubled over. He listened, since he could not see, and moved when he heard the man set his feet. It took power to cleave a man's head from his shoulders and the priest had to gather himself first. He threw himself to his right and heard the blade sing past him. He thrust out, entangling the blades long enough for him to get up. His sight cleared as he did so.

The priest rocked back on his heels and brought his

sword back into position. He smiled, a gash in a pale face framed by coal black hair. "Not bad for a country boy."

His sword was strangely dumb in his hand. Dar shook his head, but the Thrassian helm still rode his pate. He did not answer the priest's taunt. Instead he watched the eyes.

He tried a taunt of his own. "You're afoot now. Do you think the two of you will walk out of these mountains alive?"

The priest dropped his shoulder and Dar answered the move with his blade. They rang again, quick and sharp. The man smiled wider. "But there are two of us."

Dar sensed the man at his flank. He jumped back and whirled, blade flashing. The second priest went down with a cry and a puff of his crimson cloak, as though it had suddenly deflated. Dar leaped over the body, putting it between them. "You were saying?"

"Perhaps," the fighter-priest said, "you are not the bumpkin I thought you were."

If Dar had thought to scare him and let him go, the thought died. "And perhaps you aren't the swordsman you think you are." He pressed the attack with the leadenness in the wrist that comes with prolonged fencing with blades not meant for it. The priest gave before the onslaught until Dar had him with his back to the inn.

The man gasped. "By the dragongods, man," he panted. "Let me go. I will forget we were ever here. Keep the girls. I will take the pallans—"

"You will take nothing from us—but a grave!" Dar wrenched his sword free and cut, quickly. Air bubbled in protest from the man's gaping throat.

He blinked in surprise, then toppled.

Dar rocked back on his heel and took a harsh breath. He pointed at Ganth. "Get a cart and the butcher and

anyone else who'll keep his mouth shut. Drag these
bodies to the middens and build a pyre. Burn them, and
scatter the ashes in the midden ditch. Do it well, or we'll
have every dragonpriest in the area on our necks!"

He approached the chained pallans. They were supple and dainty— female, he supposed, behind their
gauze masks and delicate clothes. They shrank back.
He struck, and their chain shattered. "Run," he said.
He did not watch after them. He knew that somewhere in the village, in the shadows or in a tree or
bush, the pallan archers who'd come to his aid were
waiting for them.

One of the girls was Ganth's youngest. She was
pretty still, though she had two little ones at home. He
smoothed her hair as she clung sobbing to him. The
coal seller did not meet his eye as he approached.

Dar knew the reaction. As deadly as the villagers
knew he was, no one had guessed him to be a mur-
derer. Even for their sake.

He said to Abel, who was trying to shush the other
girl, "I'll take the chestnut back up the mountain.
Send Calper for him tomorrow."

"Yes, milord," the innkeeper returned, but he, too,
would not meet Dar's eyes.

Dar mounted the gelding and walked him slowly out
of town. He did not sheathe his sword until he'd
cleaned it as well as he could on a scrap of his village-
woven shirt. After tonight, nothing would be the same.

Zachiyah approached the cave with many bows and
scrapes. He carried a small, wiggling gunter in each
hand, cleaned until the bristles shone. Turiana bade
her Silver to stay well back in the cave. His curious
sapphire eyes reproached her silently, but he did as
told. She came out to greet the pallan elder. She
sniffed the evening air. The first black frost was not
too far away.

Zachiyah said, "We've had word from one of our brethren. I thought you might like to know right away. There has been a hero who stopped a Taking."

Her crown of spines came up. "Really? Who would have been so bold?"

"We don't have a name. Our brethren were there tracking a pair of renegade dragonpriests . . . but he was a young man, with a blade of greatness and a helm from old Thrassia. It is said he lives a hermit's life in the mountains, and his wife is a lost princess."

Thank the winds for humans hungry for superstition and folktales! Turiana's heart surged inside of her, and her fires flared. At last. At last. She had lived long enough to meet with her own Sharlin and Aarondar again. They could be none other. "Where?" she said eagerly, greedily. "Where can this hero be found?"

Zachiyah went to the ground, touching his forehead. The two gunters squealed in terror to be thrust so close to her maw. "I do not know. The tale has traveled for several weeks . . ."

"Zachiyah. I have no wrath for you. Find out as quickly as you can. And—" She eyed the gunters. "Take your weanlings with you. They are a magnificent gift, but I have already fed."

The headman shuffled backward in the dirt until he felt confident enough to get to his feet, then bolted from her sight.

Turiana watched him go. Silver came out of the cave and hunched in her shadow. She nudged him. "There is your hope," she said. Sharlin had carried dragonpowers once, and still had the spark of them buried in her. Perhaps that spark, meager as it was, might fire Silver. Or perhaps the inherited spark in the youngster Sharlin was bearing. It was risky to even think of such a thing. What she considered was unnatural. But these were desperate times.

Turiana looked up at the full moon. The cloud-ridden sky would soon be dark, and the moon higher. She knew without forecasting it that the Shield would wear a bloody veil. Tonight was a Night of Dragons, and hundreds would die all over Rangard.

She looked toward the pallan valley. "Hurry, Zachiyah," she whispered. "Hurry."

Telemark hugged his cape close. Baalan shifted beside him and the beast's musky, fiery odor drifted over him. They both espied the rising moon. The second, smaller moon tipped the mountain range far behind it.

"Soon," said Telemark, "the Geldart temple will be consecrated. Then, at winter's end, your turn, my great one."

"Then you can feel it."

The man turned in surprise and met the dragon's hot, glowing eye. "Why, of course. How can I not?"

Baalan made a contented noise deep in his throat. "Then you've come far in the last few weeks. I want you to search for a particular resonance. Listen."

Telemark felt as well as heard the echo from the dragonlord. He put a hand up to show he had the tune. "It's her, isn't it?"

"Turiana? Yes. Always her."

"Surely, without the ceremonies, she must have the wasting sickness. Even if she lives, she can't be a match for you."

Baalan had been looking off the fortress's rim toward the great mountain peak that held the Gates. He turned back. "I slaughtered a bronze yesterday trying to breach the Gates."

"It's happened before."

"Indeed. But she carried *her* resonance. A dragonet of Turiana's clutch, don't ask me how or where she still lives, she *does* against all law and all dragonnature. If I had not been so quick . . . I could have crippled the beast and then tortured the truth out of her. Arel,"

Baalan said, and his hiss was like a smutty caress. "She died prettily."

"Turiana hides well." Telemark wrapped his cloak tighter about him, but there was a high flush on his cheekbones.

"I know. But I have faith in you." The dragonlord turned his attention back to the blood-stained moon hanging not far from them. "I have a strong, strong faith."

They returned to the easy silence of peers and companionship, to watch the rising moon. Behind them in the bitter cold shadows of the landing, Third withdrew as silently as he had been spying.

Chapter 10

The wind spoke of black frost and early winter. Dar stopped splitting wood and stood up. The back of his neck ached. Sweat trickled down and dried in a chill crust. Sharlin came to the porch, Fort holding onto her skirt. He held a dried greenfruit in his hand and was eating it with great relish.

"Save some for Dad, huh," Dar called out."

Sharlin smiled fondly at their son. "A small piece doesn't hurt. You're just cranky."

"As a falroth in spring," Dar agreed. He balanced the maul and wedge to one side. "I hate the idea of another winter up here." He did a few stretching exercises.

His princess tucked a strand of honey-colored hair behind her ear. "You can take the man out of the adventure, but not the adventure out of the man."

He appraised her. "It's not adventuring I want, but—"

Her eyebrows raised.

"We won't be safe here after the thaw hits."

"You'll leave Shalad on its own?"

He did a few waist twists and did not see the fleeting amusement that passed over her face. When he turned back, he said, "No. I've arranged with Ganth and Abel to use the common hall for practice grounds. We're building a volunteer militia."

She sat down on the stoop then, frowning. Fort

plopped down next to her. "Dar, that's serious. They can never face down a dragon."

"No. But they can keep the bandits out of the passes and maybe handle a war griffen or two. The dragons are another matter." He paused as if thinking of something else he wished to say, but in the end, he did not.

Fort leaned over his mother and rubbed a sticky fist in the furrowed lines of her brow. "Go 'way," he said.

Sharlin laughed and took him in her lap. She kissed the boy's hand. "Tell your daddy not to make me frown."

Aarondar came to the porch's edge. "Don't turn him on me," he said, only half kiddingly. They looked at each other, suddenly silent. "We may have to leave here very quickly. We talked about this before."

"I know." Sharlin ducked her head, then looked up. "I'm only happy that there's no doubt we'll be going with you."

"Until I find another haven. And then . . ."

"Dar!"

He shrugged. "Something's got to be done. I can't stand around and do nothing. Just like Shalad, there have to be pockets of resistance that can be found and brought together. Dragons who won't bow to Baalan. Somebody has to be the kernel."

"It doesn't have to be you!"

He reached down and ran his fingers through her hair, pulling back the wayward strands covering one blue eye. "You wouldn't have said that before Fort."

"I know." She hugged their child close. "I'm sorry he's made a coward of me."

"That's the way it's supposed to be. But I can't let him make one of me. The sword won't let me. Something inside of me won't let me."

"I know."

They paused for a long moment, touching, a quiet

trio, in a loose embrace of their thoughts and love for one another before Fort became restless and twisted loose. He ran off the porch on sturdy two-year-old legs and began to pile the wood up his dad had been preparing. Sharlin sighed. "He'll be all splinters."

"I'll help you pinch them out." Dar lowered himself to the porch. "I feel twitchy today."

"Twitchy?"

He gave a lopsided smile. "I haven't the powers you have, or even that Fort has, but there's something in the wind."

Sharlin looked across the high stoney peaks that ridged their sanctuary. "You're worried about today. Not midwinter or even spring thaw, but today."

"Or soon."

"Those two dragonpriests have been missed?"

"Maybe. Or they could have been free-lancers, gathering up Takings wherever they could, to bolster their ranking. It could be because we've had a lot of pallans through here lately. I think they're taking a look at us," he answered quietly.

"Who could have sent them?"

"Don't know. I couldn't even begin to guess. Did old Baalan ever know what happened to us? Could he be looking for us? I don't know, I only—"

Fort's excited shout broke off his words. The boy jumped up and down, pointing.

"Dragon! Dragon!"

"Oh, god," Sharlin gasped and got to her feet, racing across the open yard, arms open to catch up her boy, even as purple shadow cut off the sun. Dar hesitated, torn between following Sharlin and going in the house to get his sword. The sword won. He turned heel and took the porch in one bound, bolting through the open door.

Sharlin grabbed up Fort and bent over him. Huddled next to the woodpile, she made a shield of her body. The sounds of wings and the smell of musk and heat rolled over her. She dared not look. Fort's heart beat next to hers like that of a wild thing caught in a trap.

She heard Dar's bellowed cry of challenge. She knew he would be standing in the open, sword in hand, decoying the dragon. Sharlin pressed her face into the back of her son's shoulder. She could not, would not, watch the roar of flame that would take her love away from her.

"Fair children," the dragon's voice drifted down. "Has it been so long you have forgotten me?"

Tears sprang into Sharlin's eyes. She unfolded, letting go of Fort, and got to her feet. A golden sun of a dragon descended into their suddenly cramped yard, sculling to a stop with wings that overshadowed even the house. The woolies in their pasture bleated and stampeded away. She heard Dar curse faintly as he put the sword up. Sharlin laughed, a shaky, uncertain laugh, and ran toward them.

"And so, twenty-some years I've been waiting."

Sharlin rubbed the great queen's jaw. "It's only been three years for us. We tried to catch news of you, but no one talks. The Takings frighten everyone."

Turiana eyed Dar. "I thought," she said, "I'd have no trouble hearing of you. I expected news of a rebel doing great deeds. Instead, I must root for tales of a hermit woolie herder."

If Dar heard the disdain in her voice, he gave no sign of it. "In twenty-some years," he said, "your clutch should have matured. You should have an army of your own."

"Honey," said Sharlin, shocked. She touched his arm in warning.

"No, I want to say this. We've had three years . . . she's had decades. I want to know what she's been doing. It takes dragons to fight dragons."

"The abyss of our passage took one of them," Turiana mourned. "And I slew the black hatchling. Too much like Nightwing. One fell to her death and two have been cut down by Baalan trying to gain passage through the Gates of Power."

Sharlin murmured softly, "Your children . . ."

"Yes. Mine. But yours seems well enough. A bright and sturdy boy."

Dar heard the undercurrent in the dragonqueen's voice. He shook off Sharlin's hand. This was the disaster he'd feared. "What do you want with us?" and even to his ears, his voice was hard and fell.

"We suffer, but our suffering is nothing compared to that of Rangard. The whole world cries. Have you no ears for it?"

"I've bled for it before, and I'll bleed for it again," he answered. "What do you want?"

"A reunion," Turiana said. She lay on the ground, her muzzle at Sharlin's knee, like some tame beast, but now Aarondar could read the tension in her form. He watched Fort as he toddled about her, exploring the dragon's immense body. "I came to see my beloved Sharlin and her beloveds."

He believed nothing. "Shall I ask a third time?"

"Dar! Forgive him, Turiana. He's been edgy all day. The wind, I think." She looked at Dar. "Tell her what you were telling me."

"She wouldn't believe me. She prefers to think that we've been hiding up here, shaking in our boots. She wants to think that so that she can ask of us what she intends to ask."

The dragon raised her head. "Have it your way." The beast's gaze rested on Sharlin. "Give me Balforth."

"Fort! He's my son—I don't understand . . ."

"It's not necessary you should understand. For Baalan's reign of blood and death to be ended, sacrifices must be made."

"That way," said Dar lowly, dangerously, "another reign of blood begins. If you want a servant, take me. I was getting ready to leave the mountain anyway."

"No. Only the boy will do."

"Why? For what?" Sharlin's anguish was in every word. "What are you going to do with him?"

Dar answered grimly, "It's a Taking, Sharlin. Only this is the last dragon in the world we expected it from."

"No!" Sharlin got up and took Fort in her arms. He wiggled and protested as she backed away from the dragon and gained the porch of the house.

"Between us, there should be no need for explanation. Nothing is what you fear and yet—yes, I will take him away from you. And, no, I can't promise to ever bring him back."

"He's just a baby! How could he live with you? How can you think to ask me such a thing!"

Dar put himself between the dragon and his family. He drew his sword even as it told him, *Steady. Strike not yet.*

"Everything I am and have is yours. Everything but my son."

Turiana spat. Steam rolled up from the ground. "Everything else is worthless." She gathered herself. "Keep him then a little longer, but I warn you, Sharlin. There will come a day when you have no choice. Next time I return, you will not refuse me."

The air boiled and swirled as the dragonqueen leapt into the sky. The fury of her wing strokes tore shingles off the roof and the woolies circled in bleating fear once again. Then, she was gone, and the day coldly silent.

Chapter 11

Sharlin tied off a last stitch by firelight, looked up and saw the first rays of dawn lacing through the window tapestry. She sighed and put the bunting down, and then flexed her neck. "That should keep him warm," she said, but her heart wasn't in it.

Dar left the hearth where he had been banking the fire. He stood over her and massaged her neck gently. She took his hand and held it to her cheek. "I never thought we'd leave," she added, "even though we talked about it. And with winter coming . . ."

"All the more reason to get out of the pass before the snow. She didn't leave us much choice, Shar."

"I know." She looked over at Fort's sleeping form. "He'll sleep until mid-morning, he was up so late last night. I'm going to lie down while you're buying horses."

"I won't be long."

"I know." She watched him shrug on his mail coat and buckle on the sword. He held the Thrassian helm in his hands a moment, said, "What the hell," and put it on also.

Sharlin watched him from the door as he headed downhill. Even though she could not see his face from this distance, she would recognize him from his long-strided walk with determination and confidence. She watched until the rocks and the twists of the path hid his form.

Fort made a noise in his sleep. She shut and barred

the door before joining him on the cot. She curled her body about his warmth and fell asleep.

He expected to find Abel up, but Ganth was another matter. Now that he was the proprietor of a prosperous business mostly run by his sons-in-law, the old man was generally asleep on a chilly morning. The occasion might explain why both men stood outside the inn's corral, leaning on the rails and cradling mugs of hot mulled wine.

Aarondar joined them. "That looks like a good idea."

"A-course it is. Calper! Fetch Master Dar a mug of his own." The bony innkeeper took a long draft and eyed Dar somewhat warily. "What brings you down so early in the morning?"

Dar wished now he had not worn his helm or coat, but even the fish-eye stare of the innkeeper was not worth the unease he'd have had without his gear. "I'd like to buy some horses and maybe one of your mules as well."

Ganth seemed not to notice the portent of his words. He waved his mug. "Sell him that chestnut. He's not been worth much since he cut his mouth up, anyway."

"The chestnut's a good horse," Dar agreed. "And despite the roughness, shows promise. I'd like that little bay mare, too."

Abel looked more than ever like a fish, his mouth working without sound. Ganth clapped him on the back in aid of some sort and asked, "Going somewhere, master?"

"I'm leaving the Shalad Mountains."

The coalman blinked. "But—" he said and plowed to a halt. "Damn me. You're going."

Dar nodded.

"But why?"

Abel got out, "Let's go inside and talk, gentlemen.

It's cold out here and I'll need to ask my wife if she wants to let her mare go."

Inside, the nip of morning was held back by ovens still hot from baking the day's bread and by the embers of fires from the night before. Dar sat down and rubbed his legs briefly while waiting for Calper to mull his wine. He had never been a foot soldier.

"This means you're leaving."

"I think it's best."

"What about our militia?"

Dar took the mug from Calper as he came up and joined them at the table. Beyond Calper's gangly height, he saw pallans in the far corner of the inn, by the door to the gaming pit. They withdrew even further into the shadows when they saw his glance. Pallans were becoming regulars in Shalad's out of the way domain. His glance flicked back to Abel, Ganth, and young Calper.

"I've had . . . signs . . . that tell me we should leave, the sooner the better. Before winter shuts us in. If I can, I'll send a veteran or two your way—you'll have your militia then."

Ganth scratched his thinning hair, but Abel nodded. "Signs are not wise to overlook. Calper, go tell your mother I am selling her mare unless she objects otherwise."

Calper made a face, to be dismissed from the men's conversation. Abel turned back. "You'll need supplies."

"Some. We have dried meat and fruit."

"Bread and crackers, then. And what are you doing about your woolies?"

"I thought they might make a payment on the horses."

Abel pulled at his long chin. "Ummm" was all he said to that.

Ganth put a blue-veined hand over Dar's callused one. "I shall miss you, Aarondar."

"And we shall miss you," Dar covered the hand with his other one. Ganth had the coolness that elder people get. "We'll be coming back through this afternoon."

"So soon?"

"It's wisest."

Ganth nodded. His eyes blinked and Dar knew he thought of other times, of dragons and bandits in the past. The coalman said, "Fortune is given, and fortune is taken away."

Dar stood up. "Your fortune, master, is built on hard work and skill. That never fades."

He had hoped to strike the worry from Ganth's face, but it had not worked. The coalman said, "Those pallans brought word into the village yesterday. Next spring will be a Night of Dragons such as we have never seen."

"What?"

"The Takings, master, and the sacrifice which follows."

Invisible, icy fingers touched the back of Dar's neck. "They've rarely touched Shalad."

"No . . . but we've been told that the new temple at Geldart will hold a Night that Rangard has never dreamed before. The dragonpriests have vowed to Baalan that they will walk knee-deep in the blood of the offerants. There will be many, many Takings."

Dar said then, and he held Ganth's eyes steady with his own, "I'm leaving not to run, but to go back into the world. There will be no more Takings someday, if I can help it."

The two men nodded in understanding.

Abel's wife came into the room, wiping her floury hands on her apron. "And to whom might you be giving my sweet-footed mare?" She stopped when she saw Dar. "Oh," she said then, and smiled. "The princess needs a horse. Well, then, the bargain is struck. And mind you, Abel, make sure she takes the tack with her . . . no other leather is good enough for my mare." She disappeared back toward the kitchens. Abel made a bow in her direction.

Calper said, "She treats that horse better than she treats me."

"The horse deserves it," his father said sourly. He clapped Dar's shoulder. "I'll have packs ready when you come back down. Calper, go help his lordship saddle up. Give him that stripe-backed donkey, the one just shod."

Before they had finished saddling, the word had gotten round. Dar led his horses out of the corral, and Calper followed with the donkey on a tether. Dar shook off encouragements to stay. He told them again of omens and portents, and the villagers grew silent.

Abel gave him a tiny scroll for the sale of the beasts. He held the chestnut's bridle to allow Dar to mount. The two men paused a moment as Ganth joined them.

They clasped wrists. There were no more words to say. It shouldn't have been final, but it felt that way. Dar took the donkey's lead from Calper and the mare's reins, put his heel to the gelding, and rode out.

A dark swirl of cloud followed him up the mountain and by the time he reached the woolie pasture and lambing shed and hut, he was ducking hailstones. Sharlin brewed a pot of warm tea for him, saying, "Don't worry. Tomorrow morning is soon enough."

He crouched under a scratchy blanket and pretended to be a monster when Fort crawled in under it to find him. He worried too much, he supposed, and it would be foolish to ride out in the hail.

Sharlin left the cot as quietly as she could. Dar had spent a restless night, and she with him, her dreams half waking, their legs entangled in restless tossing. As she rubbed her eyes gently, she listened for Fort's sighs and yawns. The boy would be up and need to be

changed soon. She wanted to have him fed and comfortable before Dar woke.

The hut was strangely quiet. Sharlin gathered up
the hem of her sleep dress and walked the six steps
to the cot that held their child. He'd burrowed
under the blankets again. She smiled at the sight of
hills and valleys under the covers, knowing what they
were. With a careful hand, so as not to startle him,
she peeled back the top blanket.

Sharlin gasped. "Uh-uh-uh," she struggled and then
found breath. Her scream tore the air. A dead woolie
lambkin lay curled in the hollow made by her son's
sleeping body, and Fort was nowhere to be seen.

Chapter 12

"I'll find her," said Dar grimly. He reached for his sword and sheath. "And when I do, I'll kill her."

"You can't . . ."

He paid no attention to her words, as if he did not even hear her. "What she wants, she takes. A dragon is a powerful beast, but it's still a beast, Sharlin. No different from any other animal. It doesn't look forward to the future, *and it does not love.*"

"That's not true!"

He stopped. The woman he loved looked at him with haggard eyes and tear-swollen face. "Sharlin," he said, and his emotion softened his voice. "I'll bring him back to you."

"Turiana can't have done this to us."

"Can't? We slept through one of the worst nights of our lives, and you don't think she did it? We were charmed, and you know it. Fort didn't walk off on his own."

She passed a hand before her face as though clearing off cobwebs. "I—I could swear we didn't sleep. That we'd have heard anything, *anything*, walk through here. You kicked me once—I felt that." She rubbed her leg ruefully. "I have the bruise this morning."

Dar opened his mouth to answer but a jolt shocked him as he buckled his sword belt. The sword asked, no, demanded that he pull it. His face must have paled because Sharlin immediately said, "Dar, what's wrong?"

He pulled the weapon. Its keen tip scraped the rooftop as he held it up. Like a spear to the sun, it demanded it be saluted. Then, *swordsman, take what you can, and run.*

Sharlin was at his elbow. "What is it?"

"It says to run. Grab the baskets, Sharlin. I don't think I want to argue." He shouldered a basket over his left arm and ran to the yard. He skittered to a halt and looked about.

In the lambing shed, the horses and donkey let out nickers, high and thin. The woolies milled nervously about the pasture. Sharlin stumbled out on his heels, two baskets on her back and one in her arms. He headed to the shed. His chestnut was already saddled. He dropped his gear and tried to saddle the bay mare with sword still in hand. As he gave up and sheathed it, the weapon cautioned him again. *Do not delay, swordsman, and take me up again as soon as you can.*

"Another warning," Dar said, as he slapped the mare as she blew out to avoid a tight girth.

"What's happening?"

"I don't know." He could hear the sounds as Sharlin loaded the baskets, child-size, onto the donkey's frame and strap them into place. "We don't have time to question."

He took the donkey's lead from her and pressed the mare's reins into her hand. "Lead the mare by the nostril to keep her quiet."

Sharlin nodded.

Outside the shed the air was ominously quiet. The woolies ran in aimless circles, bleating. Dar looked toward the path. He shook his head. "We're taking the back cut."

"It's so rocky. What if one of the horses goes lame?"

"We'll walk them. And I like the shelter of the overhangs." He shrugged into his mail coat and led the chestnut across the rear of the tiny farm that had been their haven for the last three years. The horse's nostrils flared. White rimed his eye, but he did not utter a sound. Dar took his free hand from the horse's muzzle and pulled his sword.

It said but one word. *Run.*

Dar yelled, "Run!" at Sharlin and slapped his chestnut into motion.

A whirlwind hit the valley. Air sucked out of his ears, taking his hearing with it. The donkey lagged back on its lead, and Sharlin passed him by, the bay mare practically dragging her into the sharp cut in the rocks that backed up their little hut. It looked like a slice in the strata, the eye of a bone needle, and it was just wide enough to swallow her whole. Beyond, the tunnel would open up and widen into angular walls. The chestnut pulled his arm sharply and Dar let him go, taking the donkey with him.

He entered the cut last, squatting just inside the rocky gate, and saw evil blast into their haven.

Dragonpriests rode the dragons, cloaks billowing at their backs like streamers of blood. A purple led the fore, flanked by two blacks, and Dar's blood froze. Old Baalan! But he did not look old. His jaws gaped wide and his fangs shone as whitely as a newly winged dragon. His trumpet deafened. Pebbles rolled off the rock and rained upon Dar. He ducked deeper into the cut, knowing that there might be no safety from those sharp eyes.

The dragons wheeled over the grasslands. They flamed the woolies in spite. The little beasts ran and squealed in terror, their greasy hides alight until a dragon swooped low and swallowed it whole.

There was a movement at his back as Baalan began to vent his spleen. "My god," whispered Sharlin. "We were just *there.*"

Baalan himself rent the hut to shreds and splinters. The two blacks fired the green forest that edged the pastureland and lay the rest of the woolies out. Their gutted, steaming bodies littered the charred ground. The lambing shed exploded into kindling. Above the roar and destruction, Dar could hear the laughter of the dragonpriests.

Small wonder, he thought, *Turiana had accused him of cowardice.* Then his spine stiffened. How else could Baalan have known they were here if the golden dragon had not betrayed them? Did she think to shock him into action by bringing evil to their very doorstep and laying it down?

Baalan sculled to motionless flight above their hut. "Hero!" he bellowed. "I know you hide from me! I can hear your watery blood pounding in your veins! I can smell the fright in your bowels! Give me the golden dragon and I will let you live to serve me."

Barely audible, Sharlin said, "Don't answer."

He shook his head. He had no intention of doing so. The rocks would withstand a lot, but not the sorcery and firepower of three dragons.

Baalan's head snaked about. He saw the fleeting glint of his yellow eyes, but no gaze caught their hiding place. The dragonpriest shifted on the beast's high withers. Something about the man nagged at Dar. He had no time to catch at the thought.

Hold, the sword told him.

Dar laughed silently, grimly. As if wild horses and griffens could pull him out of the rock.

"Hero! A last chance. You cannot have gone so far as to not hear me! Your petty kingdom lies in ruins, smoldering. The village of Shalad is no more!"

Sharlin made a muffled noise at Aarondar's shoulder. Bile rose at the back of Dar's throat. All he had done to make it safe, come to this. Perhaps, he told himself, the dragon lies. Lies come easily to the beasts.

He wanted to yell it and caught the sounds in his teeth.

Baalan stopped sculling and made a long, slow glide
about the valley bowl. The two blacks had landed and
were picking prime bits of meat off the woolie carcasses. The stink of offal filled the air.

Baalan bellowed in frustration. "No more!" he
screamed. "I shall squeeze your guts between my talons! The golden one shall fall to me and you will be
less than dung." With a screech he took to the wind
above the mountain ridge, the two blacks hastily launch-
ing and following after.

Dar did not move for a long time, then realized his
legs had gone to pins and needles. He stood up. "Let's
go," he said to Sharlin. She was cold at his side.

"Where?"

"To what's left of Shalad."

They could smell the burning long before they
reached the village. It hung chokingly in the air. Hope
and lives had been fired here as well as brick and
mortar and timber. Smoke billowed from still smoldering ruins. Sharlin pressed a trembling hand to her
mouth and nose. There was nothing that could de-
scribe the stench of burned flesh.

A frightened gunter pounded through the broken
street. It was little more than raw flesh and bawled
with every jump. Dar's horse sprang aside to let it
pass. Sharlin's mare stumbled over the rutted ground.
She looked down to see what tripped her. The streets,
still muddy from yesterday's hail and rain, were grooved
as if raked. Then she realized she looked at dragonsign.
Even the very earth had been ripped and fired by the
beasts.

Not a building had been left untouched. A few were
lucky enough to have lost only half a roof, or perhaps
a wall, and their owners dazedly worked at them,
shoring up weaknesses in the frame of nailing blankets
over to keep out the cold. There were bodies in the

street, charred to a crisp, contorted in an awful death. No one paid attention. With winter at their heels, the living came first.

Of the inn the only thing left were the brick ovens, roof-high, where Abel's wife had done her baking. Below the inn the massive root cellar was also intact. Dar reined up at the building and looked down. Abel had a leather apron on and was busy reconstructing what had been a floor and now must be a roof.

Ganth was helping. They looked up.

"May the gods help me," Dar said. "I didn't leave you soon enough."

Ganth swung up. Coal dust and soot blackened his face. There were angry blisters on his hands and the dark hair across his forearms had been singed away. He smelled of fire and death.

"To your credit, milord, this might have happened long ago. We were foolhardy. We forgot that all lands are cursed by Baalan's rule. We thought we'd been blessed by your presence." His voice, grown formal, was flat with his tiredness. "You told me to tunnel underground if I wished to be truly safe. I didn't believe you then. But my daughters did. Two out of three of their homes withstood the attack. For that, I thank you."

Dar kept his restive horse curbed. "I brought this on you."

"We brought this on ourselves! You alone fought back. We waited too late to think of doing the same thing ourselves!" Abel bellowed up from his cellar. "Anyway, you warned us. Hell, the pallans who rode out late last night warned me, but who listens to them?" He kicked saddlebags in the corner. "I've still got your supplies—but they're a mite smoked now."

Dar said, "I would send you up to my place, but the dragons burned me out, too."

Sharlin only half listened. A knot in her was growing tighter and tighter. A sound trespassed on her hearing until finally she turned the bay mare around to pinpoint it.

A woman, weeping, the heel of her hand pressed to her mouth. Sharlin recognized the soap maker. She sat her horse numbly as the woman's cries became clearer.

"The babies, the babies."

She put a heel to her mount. The bay mare approached skittishly, her head held high as if she might shy away. Sharlin swung down and put her hand on the woman's thin shoulder. "Gitta, come away. Come to the inn and help there."

The woman stayed in her squat, rocking, back and forth, forth and back. She pointed at the ruin of her house and soap works. Tiny flames still flared up from the embers. "Nobody hears but me. Nobody!"

"Hears what?"

"Th' babies. They're trapped down there, in the pantry. But nobody hears!"

Sharlin herself could barely hear anything but the woman's sobs. Yet, faintly. She thought she heard a mewl. She dropped her mare's reins. "Where should I dig, Gitta?"

"Dig? With what? The men have all the tools. And they don't hear it. Nobody hears it but me." Stark-faced, the woman grabbed at her.

"I'll use my hands, if we've got nothing else." Sharlin kicked aside a burned timber. Sparks eddied up. The floor creaked ominously under her weight. She could hear the muted sound from below. She got to her knees. "Is this it? Tell me!"

The woman crept along next to her, unmindful of the hot stone and melted residue digging into her knees and hands. "Here."

The two of them dug like frantic dogs after softfeet. The noise grew louder. "Here," sobbed Gitta. "They're down here!"

Sharlin's breath roared in her ears. Anybody's child might be down here. What if it had been Fort? Her nails broke and tore, and smoke made her cough and spit. "Faster!"

Sharlin, what are you doing?" Dar at her shoulders, shaking her.

She brushed him off. "Get away. Help or get away!" The wreckage came up as she clawed at it, then solid board met her nails. She picked up an end and wrenched away at it.

Gitta threw herself on her stomach. She grabbed into the hole in the earth. With a squall a mangy looking cat ripped up her arm and dashed away through the ruins, disappearing into the streets. Close to hysterical, Sharlin leaned back against Aarondar.

"A cat? You did this for a cat?" Dar braced her as she leaned against his knee. The effort for breath racked her.

She rubbed her face against the cloth of his trousers where it bunched above his falroth boots. "I thought . . . I thought I heard a child. If it had been Fort, you'd have—" She stopped as Gitta leaned down, murmuring a prayer and pulled up a small child by her arms. The little girl coughed and could barely breathe. Cat scratches raked her face and arms. Her eyes were red-rimmed and swollen.

"Kitty," she gasped weakly, "was very frightened in the pantry."

Gitta let out a tremendous sob and swept up her daughter.

Abel's wife handed out cracked mugs with weak but hot tea. "Th' good crockery," she mourned, "is destroyed."

Sharlin's hand steadied as she wrapped it about the mug. "Never mind. Tomorrow will be better."

"How many dead?" asked Ganth, of no one. "We can't stop to count."

Dar said nothing. He sat on a charred barrel, pack over his knee. She looked at him reflectively and he did not meet her glance.

"Dar, what's wrong?"

He looked up, then. "You're not going with me."

"What? By the Pit of Hells, I am."

"No."

"I have to! Or else Turiana will tear you apart when you find her."

His brown eyes had caught the smolder of the entire burned-out village. "I'm not going to let you get between us. She has my son."

"No! You don't know that. Anyone could have taken him—even the dragonpriests."

He shook his head. "Think, Sharlin. If Baalan had had him, he would have used him this morning. No. I know where I'm going and you're not to stand in the way."

The mug began to shake in her hand again. "He's my son," she protested. "And I'm going to find him. I won't let your . . . your guilt and your revenge stand in the way."

He stood up slowly. "Do you think I'd turn aside from his trail just to avenge myself? Do you think anything comes between me and my family?"

She sat with her mouth open, so full of rage and sorrow she could not answer.

Ganth plucked at his sleeve. "Don't fight among yourselves. You are not the enemy."

"Old friend, I have a favor to ask of you. Will you take in my lady until my return?"

"Surely. But—" Ganth stumbled to a halt as he read Sharlin's face.

"The boy is Taken," Dar said. "But if I have to ride into the Pit, I'll follow until I can bring him back."

Chapter 13

The knots that Dar had tied were gentle but stubborn. Not a one of the coalman's daughters would yield to Sharlin's pleas to unbind her until the day had passed, and then a night and a new day. She had spat like a trapped cat until too hoarse to curse any longer. She spent the night in astonished sleep that Dar would do such a thing to her.

When Amzel, Ganth's eldest, finally knelt by her and sawed a dagger at the ropes, Sharlin kicked free. She rubbed her chafed wrists and rolled new thoughts in her mind around about her husband. She'd seen him at his fiercest, but he had always been mild when it came to her.

Sharlin half smiled to herself. He had known she would follow him, no matter what. Like a madman, he'd ridden out in the first snow of the season. Now, with a storm blocking the pass, she could not.

Amzel laved her with a rag smelling of sweet salts. Even the bath stank a little of the fire—there was no escaping it—but Sharlin let the coalman's daughter attend her. There was no sense in going after Dar while her arms and legs were still weak. And tomorrow, the early snow would probably have melted, for the season was too new to hold it. She hoped Dar had spent a cold night.

Amzel had helped deliver Fort. There was sympathy in her eyes as she pulled forward a tray with a mug of mulled wine and stew. "Surely your husband knows best," she comforted.

"My husband," retorted Sharlin, "knows less than nothing if he ever sets a hand on me again!"

Amzel shrank back. Sharlin, impatient, grabbed the tray from her hand and began to eat as if starved. It wasn't until the plate was empty and the mug drained that the truth of it hit her.

Now she had neither son nor husband.

She rocked back on a three-legged stool and looked about the root cellar. Their baskets of belongings were there. One had been pulled open. From where she sat, she could see the pouch that lay across the top of the carefully folded clothes. Without thought tears brimmed her eyes, dulling her sight. She leaned past Amzel and pulled out the bag.

Its ties had been waxed shut. The bag showed signs of wear and even a black splash of goblin blood.

"What is that, milady?"

"A pledge of his return." Sharlin could say no more and hugged the pouch to her chest. Within it lay not a fortune in coin or gems but nothing more than ashes and bone fragments—the remains of his mother and father. Dar never went anywhere without his pouch. It was his sign to her that if he could, he would return. As if she could ever doubt him.

She sat at dinner with Ganth and his daughters and sons-in-law and their children. She ignored the stabs of pain as the children jostled one another and rolled about, so like and unlike Fort. But she did not ignore the sidelong glances the coalman's family gave her and one another. There was no doubt she had the hospitality as long as she needed it—nor any doubt that once winter cleared, Dar would be expected back, and if he did not come back, she could expect her status as free and single to be understood.

These were villagers after all—unused to the hardships such as she had faced. It might even be a year or two before she could hope to see her husband and knew she might never see her son again. If Turiana had taken him, she might feel surer, but she felt that the golden dragon would never betray her. A stranger, then, had taken him—who and for what reason escaped her. Dar would look for Turiana and perhaps find her. But she was equally sure Fort would not be found along the same road.

Those thoughts and those glances, convinced her that she must strike off on her own as well. It was only a matter of when.

Thus it was that, three days later when the early snow had ebbed from the ground, a lone pallan left the ruins of the village of Shalad, which had once nestled in the mountains of Shalad. The figure went unnoticed and unremarked in the dawn's first light, for pallans, though rare, could be seen now and again.

As if he knew he might be trailed, Dar left very little spoor. The sign Sharlin found might have been left by anyone—the scattered ashes of a fire, a hoofprint struck in a muddy clump of grass, but she knew it had to be his. Behind her makeshift version of a mask, her lips set. The ground stayed hard and chill after the snow, and though she'd left the mountains, she was riding into winter's face. Whoever it was who had taken Fort had also taken the winter bunting. Gods willing, her child would be warmer and safer than she felt riding alone on a trail she could barely discern.

Something icy crusted on her cheek behind the veil. She wiped it off with leather gloves gone stiff from sleet and rain. The little bay mare stamped. Her hide steamed in the morning air. Sharlin murmured something comforting and patted her neck. She lifted the reins and pointed the mare across the wastelands where the grass had seasonally gone a purple gray, and the horizon of looming storm swept across it, until she could not tell land from sky.

When the sleet hit, she guided the mare toward a copse of trees, urging her into the biting snow and rain. The wasteland was bare of almost any shelter and the thin group of trees was likely to be all they would find. But distance on the flatland tricked her. The mare's steady lope seemed to bring them no closer to shelter.

Her mount squealed in protest. Frost patched both of them. Sharlin hunched into her cloak and thought she would never know warmth again. When she blinked and rubbed stiff eyelashes, the copse was finally within a few lengths. Suddenly the mare pitched forward, sliding on the iced ground. Sharlin went head over heels after a frantic grab for the mare's neck with hands too stiff to catch her. She landed with a brittle shock and lay a second, fighting for breath. Her ears rang.

The mare made a low moan and began to thrash around, trying to get up. Sharlin rolled to her elbow and caught her lip between her teeth. One slender foreleg dangled impossibly wrong. Snapped in two on a bad patch. Sharlin got up and stumbled to the mare. She had to sit on her neck to still the beast's thrashing. She stroked the frightened horse a moment.

Then she pulled her dagger and went straight for the throat where her father had taught her death came quickest and cleanest. She jumped away before the blood could splatter her and the mare's eyes glazed almost immediately.

"Shit!" Sharlin kicked at a clump of the treacherous grass. Sleet exploded away from her boot toe. She looked up. The copse seemed further than before, but it was all she had.

She unpacked the mare. She unbridled and unsad-dled her as well, the strenuous effort bringing warmth back into numbed limbs. With a grunt she began to carry all she had until it was obvious the tack would be too heavy to carry. She left it on the lee side of a hummock of winter grass.

One more step. She took it, heaved her goods to a stronger shoulder, then took another. Her packs felt as though the entire weight of the winter storm rode them. She shifted them again. The wind and hail bit at her face. The pallan veil threatened to tear off and float away. The heat she'd gained bled away. Her feet felt leaden in her boots. Another step. And another.

She fell into a slogging walk. The treacherous ground grabbed at her. She went to one knee and got back up, lips too cold for even cursing. The meager shelter beckoned her. Only five more steps. No, six. No, four. And the Sharlin stumbled into the trees and found a respite in the midst of their grouped trunks.

The ground between them was not iced, though cold and damp. Sharlin threw her packs down and sat on top of them. She tented her cloak about her and she sat, shivering, trying to warm herself.

There was no inner heat to warm herself with. Her teeth chattered. She threw back the cloak and stood up. She was going to die here without a fire. With stiff fingers that felt as if they could snap clean off, she raked up a pile of twigs and old leaves. Deadwood she peeled off the trees and laid across the kindling. Then she brought out her flint and rock and began to try to spark a fire.

The leaves she had combed out were still dry and brown. They flamed immediately, but their life was so fragile that the sticks did not catch. Sharlin frantically began to push more leaves into the tiny flames. Her hands shook so that she could scarcely control her movements. Finally the needle-thin twigs caught on.

Holding her breath as if an exhalation might blow out the fire, Sharlin began to feed it carefully. Just as

black dots began to dance before her eyes, the larger
kindling caught on. She sat back on her heels. Now it
was just a matter of time.

The fire smoked a little, but its warmth reached out
and licked at her, until her nose began to run and her
ears to sting and she knew that she was going to be all
right.

Sharlin held out her gloved hands, then stripped the
gloves off and chafed her bare hands in the glow. The
fire would hold until the storm blew over, but what
then?

Unbidden tears streaked her face. The pallan mask
clung damply to her skin as she realized she'd lost all
hope of catching up with Dar. The mare dead, winter
coming in for real . . . she would never be able to
track him. The realization and the loss balled up in her
throat until she could barely breathe. Her child was
gone. Beyond her reach.

Sharlin slumped back against the packs. She balled
her bare hands. Reddened skin protested and a knuckle
cracked. She sucked at the tiny wound. The fire licked
higher. She wouldn't go back. She'd freeze solid or
starve before she'd turn back. Her husband . . . her
child . . . was in front of her, not behind her.

She peeled back the gauze veil and then the mask
underneath. The sudden rush of warm air brought a
stinging tingle to chilled flesh. She put her hand to her
face. What had happened to the girl who'd stolen a
war griffen from her father's aerie and ridden in pursuit of a golden dragon to save her kingdom? To the girl
who'd disguised herself as a pallan and lived among
scoundrels and thieves and hazers long enough to find
a map to Glymarach, the hidden place of dragons? Or
even to the girl who'd slit that map in two and dared a
swordsman to keep pace with her? Why had mother-
hood made a coward of her?

Not a coward, by all the gods! Any hunter or ranger

could tell you a mother with young was the fiercest creature of Rangard. No, then. What *had* it made of her?

Someone with different hopes and worries, that's all. She'd found Glymarach, and found Turiana, and even found her way home through the abyss of time. And, if it took the end of her strength, she'd find Fort.

Sharlin let out a small laugh. Of course, if she was then too tired to bring him home, a lot of good it would do her.

The sound, though barely audible, cracked through the atmosphere of despair that hung about her and opened it up, like a heavy stick would when cracked over an ice-rimed bucket of water. It allowed the good, clean feelings below to bubble up. She drank deeply of her memories and resolve. Then she opened a pack and found her day's ration of food.

How to find her son now that she could no longer trail Dar remained a paradox. She sat cross-legged, chewing on soggy biscuits and watching her gloves dry by the fireside. The boy was all right. She *knew* it, with more than a mother's instinct. There was that tiny bit of dragonmagic left in her, and it linked her to Fort. Now that link was stretched over unknown distances, but she could still feel it. He was *there* and she was here.

Sharlin put down her meager dinner. She closed her eyes and stood. Her shoulders brushed a layer of chilled air that the fire had forced away. Tree limbs rustled above her, a thin roof badly needing patching but staying the weather as best it could. She could hear the heaviness of the air—sleet had turned to snow and snow muffled the wind and fury of the storm.

The cord that bound them was like a web, a fine and gossamer thread. And like a web, it seemed always to brush against just the side of her face, grazing her temple until she dropped her hood back onto her shoulders. Then she turned until she could see that silvery thread as it bridged a span of nothingness, a lazy coil in her mind. But it stretched that way, and that way she would follow it.

Sharlin opened her eyes and saw that she had turned full face to her left. She marked the direction with a handful of rocks and pebbles so that she could not forget in the morning. It would be a long walk.

By the time she reached mountains again, she had walked out of a land where winter touched it with snow and ice and gone south enough so that winter meant black frost and dead grass, but the storms brought mostly rain. She had walked enough so that the heels of her blue leather hand-tooled riding boots were worn down. Her pack had gone light against her back and she relied now on another trick of dragonmagic to keep her fed—a humming song, a charming taught her once by Turiana. It served to put softfeet and chitterers to sleep, so that she could then kill and skin their furry little bodies and make a meal of what was left. It was not sportsman-like, but it was survival. She had walked enough that she was as sure of the silver thread guiding her to Fort as she was of her own right hand.

She stopped on a befogged morning and looked at the blue-gray ridge facing her. There was a woolie track running up it. She knew the sign from the years she and Dar had spent herding the airy-headed creatures. There was a bigger track running below, but she hesitated to step upon it. She had not seen a village or encampment, trader or farm for days. She did not like the idea of running into anything bigger than a softfoot or chitterer. With a sigh Sharlin acknowledged her decision. Woolie track it would be. She stepped high into the cut and began to climb.

By noon the fog had burned away, but its chill still

clung to wisps of bush and shrub. Sharlin paused to drink and eat the remains of last night's meal. If she had time, she would pick some of the herbal flowers along the path and brew a tea for the evening. Perhaps even heat some water for bathing. She must smell like a gunter.

She heard the hissing first, like a caldron boiling over. Sharlin leapt to her feet, forgetting her pack. She knew the sound and it froze her blood. Falroth and more than one, a pack of the foul beasts, headed her way.

She drew her dagger, kicked her meal back into the pack, shouldered it, and ran. But the curving track took her toward the sound, not away from it. Panic thumped in her chest. Even one falroth was death with the weapon she had. Sheer wall hemmed her in. She could not climb.

The woolie track veered suddenly. Sharlin skid to a halt and found herself on an overhang—a precipice tilted over the canyon floor. The hissing and snarling of the falroth boiled over toward her—but her heart began to slow. The falroth were on the trail below.

Falroth lived for the slaughter. She wondered what their prey was. She lay down on her stomach as other sounds began to reach her—the click of rock and pebble as something raced swiftly toward her.

It burst around the bend into view. It came on two feet, light and graceful as any she'd ever seen—a pallan, in full flight, quick as lightning. And doomed to lose its race. Sharlin wormed to the edge of the overhang. The trail ran below her.

She could hear the rabid voicing of the falroth pack. She could see the first sunlight glints off their dragon-hard backs.

"Jump!" she yelled and swung her pack down to the extent of its leather straps.

The masked and veiled face looked up. Without a

break in its stride, the creature leapt, arms up, reaching for her. Sharlin braced herself, for the weight of the pallan could pull her over and then they would both face the ravening pack.

The pallan caught. The pack made a groaning sound but held. The sudden impact made her gasp as her arms strained. But the pallan scarcely paused, using its forward momentum to swing its heels up. And, with a grunt, the creature was beside her on the ledge, grasping and pulling her back.

Sharlin's voice squeaked a little as she looked back. "Are we high enough?"

"Perhaps," the pallan answered softly. Though its chest moved in and out rapidly, it did not sound any more out of breath than normal. "My thanks."

The pallan could not say more because the pack streamed into the track and the air was filled with their vile hisses and snarling and spitting. They flung themselves in the air over and over, talons scrabbling at the rock face for purchase. A large, diamond-backed and black-spined one licked its chops, then trotted away from the pack. Sharlin froze in the face of such an enemy. The pallan touched her lightly on the shoulder.

"It is not safe to remain. Already one goes to double back and see if it can catch our trail."

She shouldered her pack and stood, well back from the overhang. The woolie track twisted back on itself, and she stepped upon it. The pallan matched her steps.

They loped down the trail quietly, the pallan scouting to ensure it did not bring them downhill and to disaster. The vision of double-rowed jaws snapping and frothing at them over and over filled Sharlin's eyes until they topped the crest.

The pallan tapped its chest and pointed. "My clan is there. Would you honor my hospitality for the night?"

The silver thread tugged her in the direction the pallan pointed. She had been alone for a long time. Sharlin smiled. "All right. But I'm not—" she pulled her veil down. "I'm not a pallan."

She got the distinct impression the creature behind the other mask grinned widely. "Of course not," it answered. "No brethren could be so clumsy. But you are welcome, whoever you are. These are desperate times in Rangard, and friends and allies must be honored wherever they are found."

Dinner, a bath, and now fireside and beer. Sharlin felt herself grow drowsy. The pallans had stripped her of her makeshift pallan costume and adorned her with new clothing: rich, midnight blue shot through with silver. The pallan she'd saved had said proudly, "If you must dress as us, you will not go in rags!"

They repaired her riding boots and gave her walking boots for the journey—crafted of tough falroth hide, and now she knew why they'd camped just outside the mountains. The range she'd crossed was famed for its falroth dens, and the creatures were notoriously lethargic in the winter.

She'd also been given the names of her hosts, but she could not remember their sibilant words except for Silreen, the pallan she'd helped, and the one who'd clothed her, Mahbray. The two flanked her now.

"Where do you travel, dressed as one of the most humble servants of Rangard?"

She closed her eyes a minute. Then, having caught the thread in her mind, she looked up at the sky and watched the course of Big Sister and Little Sister. "South," she answered finally.

The two must have looked at each other. Silreen thumbed his clay bottle of beer. Finally he said, "Then you must come with us. Our home is to the south. You will never cross the Keldonna on your own."

"The Keldonna?"

"It is desert," said Mahbray softly. "Even the oases can be deadly. We use it and the salted sea to shield our home. We live in the canyons southernmost yet. Even dragons do not bother us . . . often."

Sharlin gave a quiver, in spite of herself. "No one," she remarked, "is beyond the reach of dragons. I know."

Her host added quietly, "While you bathed, we talked among ourselves and searched our memories. Princess, we know who you are. We don't know how it is possible that you are the same young woman who sheltered among us almost eighty years ago, nor are we the same brethren who helped you, but you are in our memories. Once, you fought to set all pallans free. Once, you faced Baalan in hopes of saving Rangard the misery which chains all of us now. We do not understand where you came from or why you've been guided to us now. Only we do understand that we must help you however we can. Just as we know who you are, you know who and what we are. Yet you have never hesitated to save us. How can we do any less?" His voice trailed off.

Sharlin sat very still. There were few people on Rangard who could say they had ever seen a pallan without a mask and veil. She had. She knew what lay beneath and why they hid, a folk not human but scaled, a folk scorned and abused even as they turned away from the world.

Sirleen and Mahbray sat without a word and awaited her reply. As long as the thread stretched south, she could see no reason why she shouldn't go with them. Trust might bring her search to a much wanted end. She took a long draft of the beer. It was clean and dry and washed the hesitation from her throat.

"I would be most honored," she answered. "May luck follow us."

The pallans clicked their bottles to hers and drank deeply as well.

Chapter 14

The goblin wore irons. Dar watched the boatmen herd him aboard. They wielded their spears and pikes clumsily and stayed out of reach of the shackled being. The creature had been left his bow and quarrel and a fairly good short sword rode his right hip insolently, but neither were within his reach. The leg irons were attached to a chain that rounded the goblin's waist and then to wrist irons, his hands kept within a thumb's length of his belt buckle. Dar ran his tongue over his teeth reflectively.

He didn't like goblins. Next to dragons, he despised goblins most. His falroth boots were splashed with fading black splashes of goblin blood. If he had to sail with one, it was well the beast was in irons. But at the same time, his mouth quirked in sympathy. The goblin moved with grace and speed, and it was obvious he was three times the fighter of the boatmen who poked and urged him along the gangplank.

"Well, swordsman. A mug of yorth for your thoughts."

Dar spat over the railing. It landed on the gray-green swells and floated away. He hated yorth, a fermented milk drink, almost as much as he hated dragons and goblins. "Where'd you pick him up?"

The captain of this floating tub hooked elbows next to Dar. "He's wanted overseas. I'm getting two crowns for bringing him back."

"And who wants him?"

"Baalan himself."

His eyebrow might have arched. A bad habit that. But Dar was sure the captain didn't see it, for the mangy churl was busy throwing moldy bread to the fins circling the boat and barking for attention. He scratched his forehead in case someone might have seen him twitch. This was dragon territory—trade routes protected or scourged, depending on how devoted you were. But the dragons were gods along these shores and Dar had to keep his true feelings to himself.

He and the gnarled half-dwarf captain bantered a moment or two longer, but Dar's heart wasn't in it any longer. Goblins were across the sea, where he'd once fought wars long ago—and so was Baalan's fortress, and the mountain of the Gates. After weeks trailing, he neared the final leg of his destination. Winter's edge had lifted enough here that he could ship out and his mind was on his eventual destination. There was no doubt that Turiana wanted him at the Gates.

He had been there once before. She knew he could find his way again, dangling Fort as the bait. And once there, he would help her fight her way in so that her young might pass the Gates. It had been a ruthless thing to do and he hated her for it, but all the same he'd spent much of his early years plotting just such power plays and understood it.

Boots clomped and chains rattled on the deck behind him. They came to a stop and Dar's nostrils flared with the odor of the goblin fighter.

"There's a swordsman," the being said. Dar turned to see the goblin thumbing at him. "Let *him* take my weapons from me."

The goblin had had his tusks filed down to make human speech easier. Dar had seen it done once or twice. They appraised each other while the boatmen gabbled in confusion.

The goblin wasn't handsome as such beings go—and

his warty, dark skin was nigh bare of the coarse hair that usually pelted them. He'd either had some sort of mange or fever that balded him or . . . perhaps . . . dragonfire had singed him badly enough that it never grew back. The batlike ears stood proudly on either side of his head. There was a light of intelligence in the wide, dark eyes.

Dar shook his head. "You earned them, you keep them."

The goblin's face split in an ivory-shot smile. He was laughing loudly when the milling boatmen finally mustered enough nerve to put him back into a trot and down into the hold.

They sailed on the evening tide. Dar found the rail again and watched the shore grow distant. He sent a thought to Sharlin. She might even catch it, in her fey way. He was almost there.

The crossing was rough. Heavy winds kept the sea swells high, but it was at their backs, and the sails billowed full and the boat crested the swells as if it rode a demonic tide. If anything, the ship threatened the captain's control of her and her name, *The Angry Witch*, was apt. Dar's stomach settled the second night out. He kept himself busy with the sailors, for he'd shipped out before. As a paying passenger, they could not force him to work if he didn't want to. He worked just enough to pass the day.

The goblin they kept in the lowest holds. His throat poured out each day until he grew hoarse.

Dar poked his head into the hold on the ninth day out. It stank vilely of vomit and urine and dung. Even a goblin did not deserve to be left rotting in that. Plus, the smell was beginning to wind its way into the upper hold and his modestly hammocked corner of it.

"Why don't you let him out," he said to the captain that night.

Captain Barl scratched his gray-haired chest and belched yorth-sour breath into the air. "Can't."

"He's in irons. He isn't going anywhere but overboard and if he tries that, he'll sink quicker than a dragon can light a fart."

The ugly little man squinched up his face in a braying laugh at that. When he'd finished, he said, "Can't help us any. He's in irons."

"He can mend nets. And you can use the bilge water to flush out that stall of his. Pah, it stinks down there." Dar slid the bag of yorth over to Barl. "We could use some fresh fish on the table, but the net's too holed. The fins were chewing at it, I'm told."

"I like th' fins," Barl grunted. "They come begging to me."

"As well they should. You keep 'em fat and happy. But we're out of port now, and the nets should be repaired. With this wind and run, there's no hand free enough to sit and weave except him."

Barl squirted foaming yorth into his mug. He gave Dar a baleful glance, then said, "I'll allow as the beast could be useful. All right. Out he goes—if you'll pledge for him."

"If I what?" Dar's voice rose and took an edge.

"You heard me, swordsman. Pledge his custody and I'll bring him up tomorrow. Otherwise . . ." Barl shrugged and lifted his mug to his curling lip.

Dar went to his hammock in a reel to keep a steady walk as the ship bucked along the swells. He could not see on deck, but envisioned the sails billowed white in the moonlight, under the Shield and the Little Warrior, a boatman on the mast with a knife in his teeth, prepared to open it up if the wind took the sail too full. The sour smell of the lower hold reached him as he tried to sleep.

His own sword belt poked him in the ribs. He'd

hidden his half-helm under a leather cap so battered
no one was likely to touch it. The sword now, was
another matter. The boatmen laughed from time to
time and asked Dar to barber them. He wasn't fooled
by their laughter. The sword was valuable and his skin
wasn't. Consequently he slept with it closer than he
had his wife.

The hilt ground into him now. It said to him, *steel
makes a brotherhood.*

"What the hell does that mean?" he grumbled back.
"Strike or hold was good enough."

The hilt stayed warm in his rib cage. Too warm, in
fact. He was going to have a brand there in a moment
if he didn't get up. Dar sat up quickly and swung his
feet over the sides of the hammock. The sword shifted
away from him. Now that sleep was gone, he could
hear the faint, guttural voice.

"Water. Waaaaterrrr."

Shit. He wasn't going to be able to go back to sleep
over that one. Dar picked a lantern off a timber hook
and lit it. He made his way down to the pitch-black
hold. The stench of it put the last of his stomach's
contents into his throat. He clenched his teeth and
made his way to the stall where the goblin had been
chained.

"Waaaterrrr," the being moaned as he strode closer.

He felt a moment of pity and curiosity. What had
this goblin done to incur Baalan's wrath? Peed on an
altar . . . or perhaps rebelled? A rebel could be of
value to him.

The goblin moaned again. His blue-black tongue
hung from the corner of his wide mouth.

Dar moved forward. "Shut up, wart bag. I know
goblins. You're like a humpback. You can cross a
desert for weeks without water."

The chains rattled as the goblin sat up. "It was
worth a try," it said cheerfully. "I might have gotten

you close enough to throttle and make my escape.
That sword of yours looks like it could cut chain like a
hot knife through butter."

"It's pretty good on goblin necks, too."

"Is it?" The goblin eyed him.

In point of fact, Dar hadn't had the sword with him
during the goblin wars. But he didn't doubt its abili-
ties. "Yes," Dar repeated. "It's very good."

The goblin merely smiled. The faint light from the
lamp caught the ivory of his grin. His ears flicked.
"Midnight watch," the goblin said. A moment later
Dar heard the heavy shuffle overhead of sailors chang-
ing duty. They waited in silence until the hold was
quiet.

"I've an offer for you," Dar said finally. "Can you
mend a net?"

"Is it anything like tying knots in cats' tails?"

"Similar."

"Then I can do it, man."

"And will you pledge not to free yourself?"

The goblin lifted his hands and spread them the
thumbs' width allowed by his chains. "Where would I
go?"

Dar continued as if he'd not heard him. "Not,
mind you, that I think a goblin's word is worth
two spits in a can, but Barl insisted. Yorth soused,
I think. I told him I'd put the offer to you. Fresh
air, on deck, if you mend the nets and whatever
other small jobs they give you. And they'll pump
the bilge water through here and clean the stall
out."

The goblin sneered at him. "Are you a buggerer?"

"Not interested," Dar said. He started to turn
away.

"What then," the goblin shouted at him, "do you
want from me?"

"Nothing," Dar answered.

The shackles rattled furiously. "I don't need your pity, softskin."

"Stone head," Dar returned in a friendly voice. "I'm a passenger and you're a prisoner. But we're both fighters and I figure that puts us up above a deck swabber any day. Let me know if you're interested in the captain's offer."

He nearly got up the hold ladder when the goblin called out hoarsely, "Wait!"

Dar turned, and held the lantern high, so that its light might illuminate the stall. The dark being within got to his feet.

"I'll pledge," the goblin said. "But only to you."

"Go to sleep then. We'll talk about it after morning watch." Dar ascended the ladder and returned to his hammock. The sword stayed cool this time and let him sleep.

As Dar might have expected, the goblin was a tricky creature. When hauled on deck, he swore not to Dar but to Dar's sword. That satisfied crusty old Barl but displeased Dar. He knew goblins. He knew that Mwork, as the being called himself, would not consider himself forsworn if he killed Dar and took the sword. After all, it was the weapon he had pledged himself to. The boatmen gave the goblin a corner of the deck, plunked twine and net in his lap, and left him.

Dar shadowed him a moment. "Stone head, I'll be watching to see the twine you use goes into the net— and not into a noose."

Mwork flashed him a smile. "I'm happy, man." He stank some, his clothes still soaked from the bucket of seawater they'd dumped over him earlier, but his lot had improved. The temper of the boatmen improved, too, for the goblin had been persuaded to set aside his weapons.

The storm wind at their backs slowed. The ship's passage dwindled to a reasonable run rather than the storm-driven pace it had been. Dar stood in the bow and watched over the straits. As if reading his mind, the goblin to his flank grunted, "Seven more days."

"How do you know?"

"The shorebirds are flying within range. And I can hear the wind break off the cliffs. Can you not, softskin?" His thick, broad hands worked the net twine swiftly. Dar looked a moment at him. Like all goblins, his arms hung to his knees. And he was big, bulkier than Dar even though his forehead met the point of Dar's shoulder. His reach would be greater. Mwork laughed as if he read that glance as well as the earlier thought. "I need practice. Care to fight a round or two with me tonight?"

Dar would not mind siphoning off whatever information he could about the watchtower Rilth and the lands spanning the distance between the coast and the mountain he journeyed to. And, despite the natural enmity he felt toward goblins, this being was a fighter, like himself. For the first time in years he did not feel like a fish out of water. As for the practice, he'd bitched at Sharlin often enough about that. He scratched the line of his jaw. "Barl seemed awfully relieved when you disarmed, and I have no weapons to lend you."

"Hand to hand, then."

"I am not a stupid man."

"Well then." The goblin stood up. He raised his coarse, gravelly voice. "Captain! Give me my sword back. I have a wager with this windbag of a softskin that I can beat him two rounds out of three!"

Barl poked his head out of the forecastle "A wager?" said he. "I'll have a piece of that. You'll never beat the long sword."

"Ah, but I will. He stinks of woolies. Our swordsman has been a herder longer than he has a fighter! Do I get my sword back?"

"Mebbe." Barl hitched up his perennially sagging trousers. "What's to keep you in my custody?"

"Leg irons," the goblin answered promptly. "Just peg me down with enough room to circle."

"Done then." Barl burped. "All right with you, sir?"

Dar was shaking his head in disbelief. He put his hands up, saying, "I won't be covering any bets. Your money is your own."

"Understood. Before dinner then," Barl said happily. He ducked back inside.

Mwork shot Dar a look as he reseated himself. "There is," he said, "a way to do just about anything."

The boatmen were busy muttering among themselves, placing bets. Dar squatted in front of the goblin.

"And how about deposing Baalan? Is there a way to do that?"

The mischievous glint in the goblin's eyes went out. Abruptly he gathered up the twine and began knotting it swiftly. "I may be brought back, but I will not be an easy death for Baalan. I won't condemn myself out of my own mouth."

"Then tell me this . . . where do you go once we make port?"

"The dragonpriests will come get me. I'll probably have a nice soft ride in one of their carts back to Rilth. Once in the watchtower . . ." Mwork looked up swiftly. "It's the death of one of us."

"Tell me about the cart ride. What kind of terrain? Wilderness? Only one road?"

The goblin smiled. He touched the tip of his blue-black tongue to one filed down tusk. "An incentive, woolie herder. Beat me two rounds out of three and

I'll tell you what you want to know. *If* you'll tell me why you want to know it."

"Maybe," Dar said as he straightened up. "And perhaps you won't live long enough to tell me." He left the startled goblin with the reminder that, even at practice, swords occasionally slip, and he crossed to the stern of the ship.

Chapter 15

"First round, Mwork. Hold and break when I drop my hands," grated the dwarvish captain. Sweat dripped off his grizzled pate and his eyes were bloodshot with excitement and effort, as if it had been him fighting.

Dar tightened his grip. He had let Mwork get by the first round, hoping the goblin's days in the hold would work to his advantage. But the goblin was tough and he knew it, and the light in the goblin's eyes showed him that the goblin knew he knew it.

He gathered himself as the deck moved under his feet. The captain dropped his hands and Mwork came at him. By an unspoken code, they kept to Mwork's circle of movement and the shackles seemed not to hamper him within that circle, though they had to be heavy.

"You cannot count on me dropping as you can a tired woolie," the goblin jibed at him.

Dar did not answer. The sword felt heavy in his hand as though reluctant to be wielded at all. It had not said any words to him, but he was used to its customary silence. It had said more to him in this past season than in all the years before that he had had it. He parried blows quickly, stepped back into position, and began an offensive that put Mwork to the far extension of his chain and breathing heavily. Dar re-

lented at the last because the goblin could retreat no
further.

"Point there!" the boatmen shouted. "He'd have
had him but for the chain."

"Point," agreed Barl. He was encircled by his
men. The wind was filling the sails with a silken
touch and the crew had taken advantage of easy sailing to watch the bout. They left a respectful area for
Dar and Mwork despite their avid interest.

Mwork did not let him breathe. The goblin was at
him again, short sword more than aided by his long
reach. The blades clashed. For a moment Dar was
taken back to the fight in Shalad and the blade that
might have been a twin of his. *A brotherhood of steel*,
his sword had said. Was there such a brotherhood?
And if there was, what might his own place be in it?

"Point!" yelled Barl. "Break. Aarondar, remember
that Mwork is handicapped."

Dar shook his head. He scarcely remembered his
last movements. Mwork bared his teeth at him in
more grimace than smile. Sweat rolled off his sooty,
warted brow. The large ears moved until they nearly
lay flat against his knobby skull.

"Perhaps," the goblin said. "Not so soft a skin,
after all."

Dar gulped in a deep breath. He felt the pull of
muscles across his back and in his wrist. He mopped
his own brow. He should not be so winded.

They sparred again, and Dar felt Mwork falling
back before him, too easily, and then the final point
was given to him. The goblin took a drink of water,
washed his mouth out, and spat it on the deck. Why
expend energy on a round that was already Dar's? his
expression seemed to say.

Dar had not expected such craftiness from a being
he knew to be mainly brutal. Had goblins changed so
much in the eighty-five years or so since he'd fought

one? Was Baalan culling forth an elite army of goblins with the same skills he found in Mwork? If so, there would be little chance of standing against them. The goblins' biggest weakness was their inability to work smoothly with each other.

"Final round," Barl announced. "Any more bets?" The boatmen grumbled and cheered and jostled each other noisily to that.

Mwork lowered the tip of his sword to the deck. Dar did likewise. A few extra moments of rest would not be unwelcome. The goblin turned his face seaward, where low clouds hid the fallen sun. Soon, the dark expanse of sky would be inseparable from that of the ocean. He heard something, Dar was sure of it. He looked, too, but their view was off the port side.

"What is it?" he began, but Barl overrode his voice with a "Break!"

Mwork lunged at him. The goblin's footwork and handwork became a furious blend of brutish strength and fiendishly clever cuts. Dar met him blow for blow, driven back, until the chain stretched taut. The goblin then drew him back. He was being manipulated, Dar thought.

Sweat blinded one eye. His ears roared with the cries of the excited boatmen. His wrist ached and so did his right knee. One more pivot and cut and he would be down, he knew it.

The creature gave him no choice. The short sword swung at his left temple. Dar spun away out of instinct and prepared to swing back. The knee went with a rip and a tear. Dar fell in agony, and his blow chopped to the deck, far short of Mwork.

But not of the chain. His blade cleaved it neatly in two just as Mwork had supposed it might. The goblin lunged free with a cry. Dar flung his left arm out and caught him in a hard-muscled thigh. Mwork stumbled as Dar leapt to his feet, unheeding of the injured knee.

"Now," Dar said. "Without restraint. Meet me."

The goblin looked seaward as if drawn. Then he shrugged and took position opposite the swordsman. "Just," he said, "to break the tie."

He had fought in pain before. He had fought in mud and with blood streaming down his face and in sleet and dust storms. He had fought with his lady to his back and with no one but enemies at his back. He had fought dragons and goblins and demons and falroth and he had little fear that anyone could defeat him.

He had always known that a man defeated himself. He grew weak or weary or careless or injured or vain. Dar smiled thinly to himself. He ignored the captain who shouted, "Point!" from time to time as if it was still a practice round.

Mwork's flat nostrils were flared wide for breath. His strangely hairless skin shone with his exertion. "I take it," he husked, "I fight a man of honor."

"You do," answered Dar grimly. He watched the other's eyes and shoulders. The slightest drop of a shoulder could signal an attack.

"My mistake," Mwork said. He moved.

The blades rang on each other. High, low, high, side to side, until the short sword slipped and gave way. Mwork disengaged.

"A most unfortunate time," he added. "Captain, you're being boarded."

A loud cry of "Brigands!" was aborted by a scream. The ship rocked suddenly as if rammed.

Dar remembered the goblin's interest in the shore. "Shit," he said and went after the being with vengeance. Around them, the crew broke into action with shouts of fury. Barl yelled, "Brigands! To your posts!"

The sound of the canvas being ripped apart under full sail rent the air. Mwork gave a shrug of apology as they crossed blades and leaned full weight into one another.

"The strait is full of brigands," he said. "Only the most devout pass freely to Baalan's shores."

"You heard them coming."

"And smelled. You're right." Mwork gave a grunt as he forced Dar back and off his blade. "Under his chains or another's, I have no intention of going meekly back to Baalan. Guard your back!"

As suddenly as they had been fighting each other, they whirled and met the pirates accosting them out of the dusk. Back to back they fought until the decks were slick with blood. The ship shuddered and groaned.

"She's taking on water," Dar panted. He watched the pirates skitter and hack just out of his range. His wrist trembled. He could not fight much longer. Mwork faced the railing. He evidently saw what Dar could not as twilight curtained much of the ship.

The ship shuddered again. In her death throes, *The Angry Witch's* mast splintered and fell. It boomed upon the deck, taking the lives of brigands and boatmen alike. They found themselves momentarily without foes.

Mwork took a deep breath. "I believe the captain has cast off lifeboats."

"A live coward is better than a dead hero," Dar said. As one, they turned and leaped for the rail and the bitter dark sea.

"I had that last round," Mwork said. Heat and thirst puffed his blue-black lips and made him hoarse.

Dar lay on his back, watching the endless blue sky overhead. The tiny flap of a sail and mast of the dinghy scarcely marred it. "I had it won," he returned. He took a sip from the water bag and threw it to the goblin. "We'll be drinking urine before another day's out," he said.

The goblin took a carefully measured drink. He

wrinkled his nose in distaste. "Not I. I think I'll try warm blood instead."

Dar sat up in the boat, not liking the edge to the fighter's words. His sword came easily to his hands.

Mwork let out a baying laugh and another. He laughed until tears ran down his face. He slapped his knee. "Softskin, you worry too much." He sighed. Then took a deep draught of the afternoon air. "We'll be ashore tomorrow." The little sail filled with a breeze. "Save your strength for your oar. We might be running a reef."

"Treachery, one way or another." Dar wearily lay back on the floor of the craft. He did not let go of his sword even though he closed his eyes. Rain and wind woke him. Mwork yelled over the din of the storm, "Put your oar out. We need a rudder, or we'll be in the rocks.

Dar could not see where the wave bore them, but he put his sword down and took up the second oar, copying Mwork. The muscles on their shoulders and forearms bulged with their effort as the tiny ship skimmed across the storm-driven tide. He could feel their life in the water. Blue-black waves crested like glass over the oar but he held it steady. He could see little in the rain. Perhaps they had already drowned, for everything was dark and his ears roared. His body began to shake with effort. Dar bit his lip until the blood ran.

Then a tremendous crash jarred him from the boat and he went flying. A darkness baffled him and then went silent.

He awoke in the too bright sunlight, his face stretched and crusted with salt as it dried. His eyes felt as though they had been skinned. His head pounded and his twisted knee, which had almost been free of ache, throbbed with pain. Sand ground under his shoulders as he moved. A shadow fell between him and the sun. Mwork stood over him, cradling both swords in his ink-colored arms.

"Now, softskin, we should talk about why you want to know the way to Baalan's fortress." The goblin smiled nastily.

Chapter 16

The pallan ferries across the salted sea gave Sharlin time to catch her breath. There was a wait at the shoreline encampment until the weather cleared. Here in the south it was mainly a matter of fog and heavy rain. Until the weather calmed, cold drakes to harness and pull the barges could not even be raised to the lake surface. It shocked her that dragon-like animals could be tamed to such an enterprise.

"They're almost as old as we are," Mahbray explained. "They live in these warm waters and never leave. My parents and my parents' parents used them to pull the barges. In return, we do what we can to see the lake is never fished out nor its waters spoiled."

Sharlin rubbed away gooseflesh. The only cold drake she had ever met had been at open sea—the great beast Nightwing—and he had sunk the ship they rode. But then, Nightwing had not been a proper cold drake. He had only been swimming the ocean because he'd been too injured to fly the return to Glymarach.

She swallowed her trepidation and boarded when Mahbray told her their ferry was ready. She had never been on a ferry. The barges slid gently across a sea that held waves only if the wind saw fit to send them. It was rather like being rocked in her mother's arms as she walked a slow and steady ford across a river.

The barges held the wagons and carts; other pallans pitched tents. She and Mahbray shared a wagon and a tent. It felt palatial compared to the shelter she'd endured so far. Best of all, each day's passing brought her farther along the bridge, the slender thread that linked her to Fort. She applied a cream to her care-worn hands and let Mahbray trim her hair a bit more neatly than she had first chopped it so it would fit under pallan mask and veil.

She emerged on the morning of the fourth day. Her hands felt as if she could stroke soft cloth without snagging it again. She felt as if she could bear to ride a saddle again, the awful lesions from riding and then walking until she was chafed healed again. She was tougher, too. The pallans rose customarily early in the morning, faced inward in a circle, and did a slow and stately dance for the sun. Likewise, in the eventide for the moons. She had thought little of the dance until she participated. It required a grace and lim-berness she was not born to have, but Sharlin per-severed until she at last acquired a suppleness moth-erhood had stripped away.

Mahbray offered her a newly brewed tea. Sharlin took it with a smile, saying, "How early do I have to get up to make *you* breakfast?"

"Early enough," the pallan answered, "that you would see me without mask and veil."

The talk was more intimate than the pallans had ever invited. Sharlin blew gently across her mug. Fra-grant steam dewed her face. "I have seen many pallans without mask and veil," she answered quietly.

Mahbray looked up quickly. "This is true, then," she said. "Not the time you were sheltered near Kalmar, but at the Nettings during the liberation . . ."

"This is true. For a brief but wonderful time . . ."

"We must find our memories of it." Mahbray touched her veil hesitantly, poignantly, as if she would like to take it aside. But she did not.

They both sipped their mugs of cooling tea. Finally

Mahbray broached the subject again. "Then, if you saw, do you remember?"

Pallans had the talent to persuade and confuse. Few humans, dwarves, or others who saw the naked countenance of a pallan would be able to recall it. Sharlin smiled. "I remember, and I cherish the memory."

Mahbray's hands trembled. She nearly dropped her mug. "Thank you, " she said finally, breathlessly. "Thank you."

Sharlin put out her hand and barely touched the pallan's sleeve. "It is not a gift I give you. You are you, and I am grateful to have known you. It is you who endows me. Never forget it."

There was an awkward moment of silence. She heard an almost inaudible noise from behind the mask and veil. Did the pallan cry? She wasn't sure. After that moment, Mahbray said, "That makes it easier what I must ask of you. You, who sheltered once in need among us, why do you come to us again?"

"I have a son," Sharlin answered simply. "He's been stolen." Her throat closed. For simple words they seemed to have torn a jagged hole in her. She shut her jaw tightly against the emotion that fountained now and threatened to overwhelm her.

"Dragons?" whispered Mahbray.

"No. No, not a Taking. If it were . . ." she plowed to a halt. Astonishingly the pallan seemed to mirror her emotions. The two leaned forward and embraced lightly, comforting each other.

"Our children are our only hope. Each year, they grow fewer. And then, the Takings . . ."

The ferry rocked gently beneath them. Sharlin drew back. "All that we do is for our children."

The pallan nodded. The gauze veil fluttered a moment, as if Mahbray had difficulty catching her breath. "We will help you, princess," the pallan vowed. "Silreen has given me the right to make this vow to you. We will help you with all our lives."

There was a step upon the ferry. Sharlin started to see the pallan Silreen overlooking them. He stared down. "That is not a vow given lightly. You know more of us than any human has ever known before—but you do not know that our tribes are intertwined. We are one nation, though the dragons have scattered us like ashes to the wind. Yet, we remember, and we communicate and we have our libraries. Mahbray has not given you the word of just a tribe. She has given you the word of every pallan ever to have been born or yet to be born upon the face of Rangard."

"But how—"

"Don't ask what you can't possibly understand. The question we must ask now is, will our aid be enough?"

Sharlin put on what she thought was a hopeful face. "Surely it will be."

The pallan shook his head. "You do not understand. It is with difficulty and shame I must tell you this. An enemy did not take your child. It was one of our own tribes."

"What?" Shock peeled away every defense she had left. "What are you telling me?"

Silreen paced a step away from her, as if her naked emotion was an unsheathed sword in her hand. The lines of his body visibly shook. "I'm telling you of a disgrace we must bear all the days that a pallan lives upon Rangard. We shall never forget the shame, even as we never forget the kindnesses you have done us. You tried once to take us out of slavery. And we have repaid you by taking your child. We won't rest, princess, until we find him."

"Then you must know who has him!"

"No."

"But I—I don't understand."

"We have word of a renegade tribe of our people

who have done a terrible thing. We have word of renegades passing though the village of Shalad and spying upon a reclusive swordsman, a hermit. We have word of a human child among a pallan tribe. We have word of a child stolen from Shalad. Do you understand? Linked, we have a form of the truth. But which tribe, we cannot tell. Where they have gone, we do not yet know. With what purpose, we can only shudder to think. Forgive me for not offering you more."

Sharlin caught her breath. She couldn't think of what to say. Then, as if bursting a dam, "Is he alive?"

"Yes."

"Then," and she bit her lip to quench what seemed to be a bottomless fountain, "that is enough. That is more than enough. Thank you." She put the edge of her sleeve hem to her eyes. Damn. She had cried enough since Fort's being taken two months ago to fill a lake. A bottomless lake.

Silreen left, whisper silent. Mahbray stayed with her, rocking back and forth, in quiet sympathy.

"There," said Mahbray. "Our harbor." She pointed across the flat deck of the barge. "Silreen has promised to send word ahead that you need to talk to our elders and consult our libraries. We'll put out official notice of our vow to help. No pallan who wishes to remain in our memories will refuse to help us."

"How long will it take?"

The pallan shrugged. "I can't tell you how long it will take. About one and a half weeks, overland. Then, you must have patience."

"Humans aren't known for patience."

The mask moved slightly. "I know," answered Mahbray, "I know."

They watched the cold drakes slow as they drew closer to port. The driver sent a signal through the harness.

The great lake-locked beast stopped and turned belly over in the water. As the barge caught up with it, the driver took out an immense gaff and unhooked the harness. The pallans who had been sharing the ferry now went to their posts and took up oars. The barge resumed its slide across the water.

Sharlin watched as the cold drakes righted themselves and undulated through the wakes of the ferries. They were rounded and blubbered against the water's sometime chill. Their wings had blunted into immense fins, their crown of spines also stunted and oftentimes carrying a sprig of lakeweed. Their eyes were large and liquid and seemed to take her measure. What relation had these creatures to the savage lords who instituted a blood rule?

Mahbray began to collapse the tent and fold it. Sharlin helped her, feeling useful. "What do I do when we reach the caverns?"

The pallan raised her head. "It'll be lyrith season," she said. "You can come harvesting with me."

Silreen waited for her on shore. "I have other duties which call me," he said. "I leave you in capable hands."

Sharlin wasn't quite sure what to say. In the end she embraced him lightly, which seemed to affect him. He nodded stiffly and left without another word.

The cliff of caves faced the morning. That way, as Mahbray explained it to her, the sun could warm them and they would retain its heat into the night, if needed. If not needed, then nighttime could cool them better. As the great caravan wound its way to a halt, Sharlin looked up the cliff. The caves were reached by hand and footholds. Young pallans scrambled down them at a breakneck speed that made her catch her breath.

Then Sharlin let it out. "I don't think," she said, "I can get up that way."

Of course you can!" Then Mahbray eyed her. "Well, maybe not. You are a little bottom heavy."

"Thank you," retorted Sharlin. The pallan snickered.

She relented, adding, "I'll have a catch harness woven for you like we do the first walkers."

"I'd be grateful." Baby harness or not, Sharlin did not want to scale the cliff face any other way. All the caves were a considerable height up. Natural protection, she guessed. But it reinforced her understanding that, as human-like the pallans had come to be to her, they were still very unhuman in other ways.

Mahbray signaled one of the pallans who'd come running out to greet them. They paused and spoke in their native tongue, a soft, fluid language. The pallan tossed her head toward Sharlin—at least, Sharlin thought the pallan was also female, from the size. Her hood-mask and clothing shimmered in dun and gray. The pallan raced away.

"What did she say?"

"Our brethren is surprised that I need a baby harness for you—says she will have to do some improvising."

"That can't be all she said."

Mahbray's veil fluttered. "No, but since you're a guest, I will spare you the rest of her remarks."

Sharlin laughed, in spite of herself. They bent to unloading the carts and wagons. A ground level cavern, dusty and gray, acted as a huge livery for the vehicles when not in use. She paused, dusty and sweat-soaked herself, to watch the wagons being rolled in. Mahbray tapped her shoulder and passed along a dipper of cold, sweet water.

The water carried away some of her fatigue with it. The barge trip had rested her, but she seemed tired and worried more often now. Fort and Dar were always at the back of her mind. Without them she would be marooned again. She took a second long gulp, then passed the dipper back to Mahbray. She eyed the livery.

"It's been here a long time."

Mahbray nodded. The gauze veil was still wet from where she drank through it. "We call this 'Old Home' in our tongue. We were here before . . . and we returned after."

"Before what?"

The dark eyes looked at her. Then Mahbray shook her head. "It is not for me to tell you. Ah! Here comes your harness! Good. I want to get you up the cliff before dusk. Don't look at me like that—trust me. You will be scrambling up and down the rocks like a treefrog on a greenstick long before you must go to the elders' meeting."

"And where is that?"

"The topmost spire. And you must get there yourself," Mahbray said. "But we have a week or so to practice."

Sharlin's heart did a most peculiar thump in her chest as she tilted her head back and looked at the rose-and-gray cliffs.

"What is important to you," the elder said, "is not necessarily important to us."

Sharlin sat and listened to the wind howl through spires it had eroded whistle holes and needle eyes into. Her harness she had folded and tucked under one arm. She looked about the solemn circle of pallans. Many of the colors here were muted, whites, silvers, grays, duns—color patterns that must have aged as the pallans themselves did. She looked to the speaker, in white shot through with gold thread, and said, "I know."

"Silreen is young and impetuous. He has overstepped his bounds, but our word is given, and we will not fall back on it. However, what we can and will do, will take time."

Two dusty weeks she had waited for this meeting and still they talked of time and waiting. Sharlin stirred. "The Night of Dragons falls at winter's edge. I'm told that Baalan will do everything in his power to make the streets run with blood and the chill of winter never leave. Do you wish this?"

Mahbray stirred beside her as if to object, but she kept her peace.

The elder she faced put up a gloved hand. "We're well aware that it is mostly our blood which will serve. Always it has been, until our ranks are so thin we do not know if we have a future. It's well that you know, too, for when Baalan is done with us, he will turn on human folk."

"Then what can be done? I must find my son and my husband. I know the way—"

"The trail is false," the elder said. "I'm sorry."

His words fell like stones into her hearing. False? False? Her link to Fort was a lie? "What do you mean?"

"I mean, princess, that pallans are not without some innate power of their own. They have turned you aside. We know this from our last sighting of the renegades. They go not south, but west."

She found it difficult to breathe. "No—"

"Many of our tribes are coming to Old Home for the season. We'll have more word then."

"Then? Then? I thought you had communication with your pallans. Can't you find him *now*?" She fought for the breath to speak with, for the calm to deal with this implacable facade across the circle from her. Mahbray leaned into her lightly as though giving her strength or perhaps warning her.

"We can," said the elder, "if they want us to. Suffice to say, they do not. All we can do is wait for sightings. In the meantime, you have our hospitality."

Her throat swelled with anger. She did not want their hospitality, she wanted her son back! But the words did not spill out. Numbly she let Mahbray get her to her feet and fasten the climbing harness on her. She put her fists to her stomach where her gut clenched. At the lip of the cave she overlooked the valley flooring hundreds of feet below. It had taken her the better part of the morning to climb here. It would take her minutes to rappel down. She turned to Mahbray.

"He lied. Fort was here, wasn't he? And he's embarrassed because the renegades brought him in and took him away."

"Perhaps," Mahbray murmured. "Come picking lyrith with me tomorrow. We're not the only young and impetuous pallans gathering at Old Home. Like you, we know we must face the dragons sooner or later."

Sharlin nodded. She felt nothing as she gathered herself and threw herself into the air and the wind whistled its scorn of her.

Chapter 17

"Let's talk," said Dar. Salt crust crackled aside and slid from his face as his lips moved. It opened up raw streaks and he winced as it did so.

The goblin paced up and back a step. Behind him loomed a view of sandy cliffs and trees twisted by a savage wind. Dar had a fleeting thought of his wife, with the mark of the house of Dhamon on her throat. Dhamon, who supposedly controlled the wind and promised his demonic aid to the kin of those who'd once tamed him. Dhamon only answered a call of blood. Fort had that same mark. Then Mwork crossed his sight again and blocked his view. "A wise decision. What is your interest in Baalan?"

"And what is your interest in my interest?" Dar answered wryly. "We could dance this dance all day. But let me tell you something you'd believe. If I wanted to be a captain in Baalan's magnificent army, I wouldn't ask you for directions to Rilth. I'd crawl to the nearest port and ask the first dragonpriest who stumbled over me." He hiked himself up on one elbow and licked salt-swollen lips. His knee felt as though a fire had lit behind the cap, and his clothes were drying in stiff, scratchy layers. And that warty son of a bitch had his sword!

"Surely you don't think yourself as hero enough to enter Rilth and slay Baalan!"

"No?" Dar narrowed his eyes. "And what would you do?"

Mwork made a coughing noise. "I hold the steel. I ask the questions, softskin." He kicked Dar lightly in the ribs, coming into contact with the chain-mail coat that Dar had concealed under his outer clothes. The goblin felt the contact. "Or perhaps not so soft, at that."

Dar did not regret the discomfort of the mail but as he shifted, he noticed his bare head and realized that the sea had done what pirates and swordplay and days adrift had not. He had lost the Thrassian helm. Before he could answer, the goblin added. "I do not know what to do with you."

The goblin also relaxed his stance, ever so slightly. Dar did not trust in the kindness of strangers. He scissored his legs out, caught the goblin off guard, and then they were sparring in the sand.

Wrestling Mwork was like wrestling a falroth. The goblin bulged with muscles Dar could only guess at— and the creature had no rules against pulling hair or trying to gouge eyes or doing other unpleasant things to his body. Dar responded with some gutter holds of his own. He caught scraps of cloth for his efforts at scratching, but his boots made an impression.

He tasted blood and spat it and grit from swelling lips. The goblin cursed vilely as Dar gave him a half throw. A second later Dar's own feet went over his head in a toss that made his neck give a startling pop as he rolled over his shoulders into a belly flop. Both he and the goblin dropped their holds from each other in astonishment. Dar flexed his neck and shoulders to assure himself no real damage had been done.

Mwork said, "We're doing Baalan's work for him." He sat back on his heels.

Dar crawled past on his hands and knees and retrieved his sword. The hilt warmed comfortably in his hand, but the thing stayed quiet. "We do indeed," he said, "if defeating him is what you have in mind."

Mwork grabbed his own weapon and stood up. He used the ragged edge of his billowy sleeved shirt to clean away the grit as he talked. "The only good dragon is a dead one," he vowed. "In the old days, the wasting sickness took them, good or bad. Now . . . only the good wither away. The weak and the evil take Baalan's way."

"The bloodletting?"

The goblin shook his head as he answered. "I don't know. All I know is, the bitch Wendeen taught him blood sacrifices . . . and it appears to work. But you and I both have walked in the lifestream of our enemies. Tell me—do you feel any cleaner?"

Dar did not let his face reflect his surprise at the creature's philosophy. Had he perhaps met the prince of goblins? Here was a nobility he could not deny, yet thought a goblin would never possess. "No," he said. "But war is sometimes necessary."

"Slaughtering helpless victims is far from war. And tell me who can stand against a dragon's rampage? Baalan has us where he wants us and he'll quit grazing among us when we stop being grass and start being *blades*." Mwork gave him a hand up. "Now why are you here? What do you want from me?"

"That all depends on what you have in mind."

Mwork looked back over the straits. "I did not have going to Rilth in mind, But my captors changed those plans." He looked back at Dar, meeting his eye. "Rilth will never fall to an enemy. Betrayed from inside, perhaps, but never to a siege."

"I don't want inside. I want past, and quietly,"

The goblin's jaw dropped, revealing the blue-black tongue. "Past? What is past Rilth?"

"I want the mountain, and the Gates."

Mwork sucked his breath in quick and sharp. His filed down tusks made a whistle of it. "Ah, swordsman. You *are* daring. But you couldn't hold the mountain against Baalan for long."

"I don't need to hold it for long. Just long enough for a dragon or two to get past, without having to kowtow to Baalan's blood pact."

The sun gleamed in the creature's eyes. "Dragons with power Baalan cannot control—at least for a decade. The wasting sickness can take that long to set in, if the dragon is a young and healthy beast. You have possibilities!" He clapped Dar on the shoulder several times. "This is a sortie that requires some planning. Where will you get the dragons? How will you signal them once we've got the mountain?"

"Don't worry," Dar said as they began to walk along the sands. "The dragons will be waiting for us." As the goblin drew him along, he told him a little of the dragon who stole his son. His sword became a hot brand even through its sheath. Dar stopped talking and put his hand to it.

Search the sand.

He paused, quizzically. The tortured shore of the beach was littered with driftwood and scrub brush, shells and fine pebbles. Then, lodged in a branch of what might be driftwood or the remains of a boat, he saw a battered leather cap. He ran across the sands to grab it up. The leather cap had suffered, but the Thrassian helm it held seemed in good shape, impervious even to saltwater. The goblin joined him and Dar showed him what he'd found.

Mwork eyed the gleam. "Where we go," he said, "you'd best keep that under the cap. Men have lost their head in the Throat for less."

"The Throat?"

"The only legal port here. To enter it is to start the downward slide down the throat of Baalan. You'll like it. Cutthroats, whores, good bars. Lots of excitement. It'll take us a day or two walking. The marsh birds are tasty. We'll eat grass for water. Maybe it'll rain if we're lucky—wash the salt out. You ever drive a chariot?"

"No."

"We'll steal one anyway. I'm a better bowman than a driver, but we won't walk to Rilth. You'll see."

Dar hesitated as Mwork flashed a grin and strode out ahead. The Thrassian helm seemed to reflect his boots, stained with old goblin blood. He wondered if even fey Sharlin could make sense of what was happening to him now. He had a feeling she'd approve of nearly everything except possibly the whores. He started after his newly found comrade in arms.

Harvesting lyrith's first buds was a festive affair. The wagons and carts were hitched up to take the pallans out to the high hills. Sharlin jumped the side of her cart, alive with the excitement of the others. The carts would return for them at the first sign of dusk.

The heady blossoms filled the air with their aroma. She had never scented so many—it made her dizzy at first. Mahbray steadied her, laughing, and pushed a basket into her hands.

"I've heard you humans get drunk on this."

"We can." Sharlin sighed. "But it has more important uses. What do you use it for?"

"Dragons, for one. It makes them tame enough to eat out of your hand. When we lived on Glymarach, we grew it for the purpose. Like a moat, we grew fields of it about the city. Young dragons, striders, are savage with only one purpose: to fill those caverns they call stomachs."

Sharlin imitated the pallans about her and knelt to pinch up the yellow buds. "Who did you bring me out here to meet?"

Mahbray essayed a look around. "They're not here yet. I beg of you, this is not a wise thing I do. I do it because you saved Silreen and because you're the lost-found-and-lost-again princess. I don't have word of your boy, but we can ask. Someone might search their memory and find word."

Sharlin caught up her hand. "Then ask about a golden dragon for me. If she didn't take Fort, she can still help me find him."

Mahbray looked up with a start. "Do legends still live? Do you speak of Turiana the fair?

"Yes."

Mahbray hissed in excitement. "We thought Baalan had destroyed her. You might have swayed the elders if you'd told of her."

"She's still a dragon. These are bad days for dragons, and to tell the truth, I don't know her heart anymore."

"Ah. This is a sad thing for you to say."

Sharlin nodded. She swirled her hand about in the basket, stirring buds. "I knew a pallan named M'reen once. I asked her about dragons, and she told me about the heart of pallans. I know about the mountain called the Gates, and that the magic within used to belong to you, before the dragons stole it."

Mahbray sighed. She hunched back into a squat, her basket resting on the high meadow beside her. "It appears we don't have many secrets from you."

Sharlin kept picking the herbal flower. She said, "But she never told me why you didn't just rise up and slay all the dragons, and take your magic back."

"The wasting sickness."

"But even a few years of power would be enough to put Baalan down—"

"So some of us think. Some of us are even willing to risk it. But the dragons are much less susceptible to the illness than we, and there are those of us who think that our original plan of watching and learning is better."

"Plan?"

"Yes." Mahbray ducked her head as though shamed, even though mask and veil hid it. Sharlin also wore her mask and veil, to avoid offending the other pallans.

Mahbray said, in a very small voice, "it is better, you see, for a dragon to die of wasting sickness than for one of us. He is, after all, little more than an animal until he passes the Gate. Our doctors watch and learn, and perhaps one day will understand why one dragon lives two years and another ten before the illness hits. One day, we'll be able to take up our powers again and know that we won't die from it."

Sharlin shrank back from her friend. "You let them die . . . on purpose?"

"There is little we can do about it. We didn't purposely let them steal our powers, but once done—it was a fitting justice, the elders thought. And useful to the doctors. That is why we built on Glymarach, the cradle. And, the graveyard."

The coldness of it shuddered through Sharlin's body. "You play with lives," she began, but shouts filled the air. The two of them straightened. The high meadow rang with noise, and she could see pallans running in terror. Automatically she looked upward, but saw no wheeling shadows. "What is it?" she grabbed at Mahbray.

The pallan pushed her away. "Run!" she hissed. "Run and never look back. If they catch you, take off your mask and veil. It's your only chance!"

The pounding of hoofbeats and catcalls came up the knolls. "But—" said Sharlin in bewilderment as Mahbray took to her heels. The baskets of lyrith spilled out, unheeded.

The pallan screamed over her shoulder. "Slavers. *Run.*"

Nets and whips filled the horizon, and men in dark leathers slinging them from horseback. A king's ransom in lyrith was trampled by the horses' hooves as they stampeded through the meadow after the fleeing pallans. Sharlin had only a terrified moment before she, too, turned and bolted. The bruised grass slipped under her boots. She lost her climbing harness as it fell from her vest.

No matter. They were far from the cliffs of safety. She was alone—pallans keening in their high-pitched voices as they ran in panic. Bodies thudded to abrupt halts, tangled in nets. She ducked her chin down and kept running. Her boot heels twisted awkwardly on the ground. Not made for running. She could hear the horses after her now. She changed direction. Curses and whistles followed her.

Hooves drummed. She could hear the horse grunt with every jump. A whip popped at her ear. She couldn't help it—she jumped and swerved. With a swoosh the net sailed past her. She threw it off her shoulder and gasping for breath, ran harder.

Sweat plastered the mask to her face. She could barely see through its confines. *Throw off the mask and veil*, Mahbray had said. But she couldn't slow. There was no time to do anything.

A dirt clod skittered under her heel. Sharlin let out a cry of pain and this time, the net did not miss her. With a bruising tumble, she fell to the ground. It dragged her along until the man brought his horse to a stop.

Sharlin clawed at the net. Through its rank and dirty webbing, she looked and saw the slaver laughing at her. "That's it," he said. "Th' master likes 'em with spirit. They last longer."

She bit her tongue until blood filled her teeth. If he thought he had netted a meek and humble pallan, he might just live long enough to regret his thoughts.

Chapter 18

"Food and water and proper middens," Sharlin shouted through the cage door, "will bring you a greater profit!"

The slaver stopped in the aisle of cages. His whip was looped about his shoulder. He looked more like a hazer, one of those who herded gunter on the high ranges, than a trader in flesh. He spat to the side. "Who cares," he said. "You're all dragon fodder anyway."

Sharlin tightened her fingers around the greenstick bars. He disappeared along the row of cages. Most were empty. The ones filled with pallans were quiet. This was a stockyard like ones she and Dar had bought horses from, and they'd been carted in like gunters for slaughter.

The pallans would not fight. She knew how they conducted themselves in human hands and in human cities. They would bow and serve and die, mildly and quietly. Mahbray had come back to the slavers hoping to decoy them away from her—all she had accomplished was getting caught as well.

Sharlin sat down to think. There wasn't a spot of her body not bruised or scraped and she sucked the lip she'd fattened trying to throw off her net.

A lithe figure sat down next to her. "They don't know you're not one of us," Mahbray said.

"No," agreed Sharlin. She stripped off her gloves to

examine torn and broken nails. "Maybe I can chew my way out."

"Chew?" The pallan's slim shoulders moved in quiet laughter. "Even if you escaped, where would you go?"

"After Dar." That pouch of his shifted along her ribs where she kept it secreted inside her clothing. She touched it gingerly as if to reassure herself it was still there.

The pallan gently scratched her mask-hidden temple. "We're to be picked up by a dragonpriest later."

"What do you mean?"

"This is one of the main slave yards outside of Geldart, where the new temple was erected. The dragonpriests take whomever they want. The elder has told me I'll be one chosen."

Sharlin looked about the cage angrily. "Who made that decision?"

"Does it matter? All of us face this sooner or later. The worry is gone for me. I've been chosen."

"He has no right!" Sharlin grasped the pallan's arm. "I won't let you go. When the dragonpriests come, let them do their own choosing. They'll never know to look for you."

"I must step forward," the pallan said in astonishment. "How could I let someone else take what is fated for me?"

"Don't let anyone step forward."

"You don't understand," the pallan protested.

"I understand," said Sharlin bitterly. "I understand that if no one ever does anything, we deserve to be dragon-ridden."

Mahbray hesitated. A low mutter came from the other side of the cage. Sharlin did not understand what the other pallan said, but Mahbray ducked her chin in and looked downward. "I have talked too much."

"To an enemy perhaps, but not to a friend. If we get out of here, can you get us back to Old Home?"

"Of course," said Mahbray. "Why couldn't I?" She shrugged out of Sharlin's hold. "But we are not free."

"We will be," Sharlin answered grimly. "We will be!"

"You'll have to hurry," a tall, bent-shouldered pallan said from across the cage. "The auction is tomorrow."

It took most of the night. The pallans were awake and restive anyway, grooming with the buckets of fresh water brought in for that purpose. Some of them ignored her, but she was able to get most of them to cooperate. She had to do it without telling them who she was, though pallan memory being what it was, she was sure several had guessed. But if they would not stand with her, neither would they betray her. Several others were too timid to help with the breakaway, but they agreed to provide distractions.

But their greatest strength lay in numbers. She had to persuade each one singly of her purpose. If there was skepticism, doubt, anxiety, hidden behind the masks, she had to read it in their low-pitched voices. By morning she had a group of twenty ready to stand with her.

The sound of the slavers rousting the other cages woke her. Whip handles jarred the greenstick cages with a rattle. Hoots and catcalls brought her to her feet. Her pallan conspirators had all slept near her. They came awake as one. "Remember," she said. "We wait until the sale is made. The weakest link is when they're transferring us to an owner."

There were nods of agreement. The air stank with the poignancy of the middens, shallow troughs to the rear of the cages, and Sharlin felt sick to her stomach by the time the driver came to their cage and prepared to open it up.

He had a scroll in one hand, whip in the other—and a stinger on his right hip. Sharlin's spirits sank when she saw it. The dart guns were very effective—and the darts could be tipped with any kind of drug or poison. those black feathered were drugs, red were poison.

"Separate yourselves," he said, reading the scroll. "Step forward when I call your lot numbers."

Sharlin stepped out of the pack. "If you please, sir," she said and bowed low. "There is a group of us here, artisans and technicians of high skill who would benefit any guild hall or administrator, and who would serve you best if sold as one lot."

Her captor looked up. He was swarthy and ill-shaven, and a deep, scarred pock in one cheek showed that he had had intimate familiarity with a stinger dart himself, once. His heavy, black brows frowned. "What the pitted hell are you talking about?"

"Please, sir," and Sharlin bobbed again. She heard a snicker behind her at her lack of grace and prayed the man would not be able to tell the difference. "Dragon fodder we may become—but in the meantime, could we not enhance a holding with our skills? We have among us a skilled weaver, and a lantern maker, a potter, several cooks . . ."

"Hold your tongue," the slaver said. He looked over his scroll. Sharlin held her breath as well. Had she imagined the flicker of interest in his eyes?

He slammed the cage door shut with a booted toe. She watched his departure.

"Why would he listen to you?" Mahbray asked. "He thinks you're one of us."

"He's greedy," Sharlin told her. "All such men listen if they think there's money to be made. We wait."

It seemed a forever wait. Two cages of pallans next to theirs were emptied. Beyond the rows of enclosures, she could hear the snap of the whip and the sharp clink of chain and the singsong whine of the auctioneer. She shuddered. She had never thought of this . . . had never seen it . . . never thought it could still happen. The air in the building was stifling. It weighed down on her until her mind grew drowsy.

Sharlin flung her head back. Lyrith! The slavers were burning lyrith in the smudge pots to the rear of the barn. Lyrith, to ensure the passivity of the slaves. Here, the world was so backward, it did not know the common weedflower on the high meadows was worth a fortune elsewhere. Sometime, somewhere, that was a knowledge she might be able to bargain with. But not now. Now her thoughts swung about and she could scarcely . . .

"All right, you lot. Get to your feet. The auctioneer says we've got several large plantation owners out there. He'll try setting you up—but if it doesn't work, we'll sell you however we want."

Sharlin put out her gloved hands and urged her pallans to their feet. Voice lowered, she said urgently, "They're burning lyrith. Shake it off. We'll be in the fresh air soon." Her head throbbed and her eyes burned behind her mask.

They stayed together behind her as if she were a lifeline and they had to hold on to her. As they approached the outside, fresh air felt cold being sucked in. The pounding in her head began to diminish.

The driver pointed at the rough wood platform. "Up there. Keep close. Do what's told to you."

Mahbray joggled her elbow as they mounted the steps. "We're here," she said, as if Sharlin needed to be reminded. Her breathy, slight pallan voice was a little slurred with the effect of the lyrith-laced smoke, but she had wits enough to be reassuring her, so Sharlin hoped for the best. She stumbled crossing the plat-form. Jeers followed her. She could feel her face flame red behind her pallan mask. She clenched her hands to steady herself and took a deep gulp of clear air.

". . . a tribal group that offers more as one lot rather than singly. We have artisans and household technicians, and a household manager as well. Her skills have already impressed us as she negotiated to keep her clan together. Ladies and gentlemen, the addition of this lot will increase your wealth, your holdings. Word of your weavings and pottery will spread as far as fair Delgart, our neighbor to the north. Any money spent here will return three, no, fourfold to your hands—"

A tall, balding man called out, "Do I have your guarantee on that, Tregev?"

The audience laughed. Sharlin heard the sound like a muffled echo in her head. *Gods*, she thought, *I'll be hallucinating if my head doesn't clear!* She felt herself waver. Someone slipped a steadying arm under her elbow.

"You there. Step forward and state your skills."

A black hood with mottled gray diamonds looked toward Sharlin and then stepped forward. In his reedy pallan voice, he said, "I am a glazier. I mold and grind glass."

A murmur ran through the crowd. Tregev, the auctioneer, shouted jovially, "An excellent skill! Real windows for your household. Even a dragonpriest can use a good glazier."

There was a flash of several crimson cloaks on the outskirt. Sharlin could not quite see the wearers, but she thought of the riders who had burned Shalad and her home to cinders. The pallan who'd spoke stood in abject misery, unhappy to be the subject of scrutiny. Sharlin put out her hand and drew him back into the group.

"Who's the manager?"

Tregev looked over them and as he repeated the

question, she stepped out before he'd finished talking. Another murmur. Too bold, and she'd have them knowing their woolie was a falroth in disguise. She looked at her toes.

"Put your head up! What can you do?"

"I am a mathematician. I do household accounts, and I can write, as well." Was her voice meek enough? Light and breathy enough? Would she pass? The sun beat down on her. It was boiling under her mask and veil. Her thoughts swirled as the lyrith stirred in her lungs and blood. Perhaps she should just cast aside her seeming—

"How much? How much am I bid?" The auctioneer wove his words around them. No one took her sleeve and urged her back with them. She was left alone and wavering at the edge of the platform.

The bidding stumbled at first. No one seemed to quite know what to do with a pallan who could do more than shovel out a stable or wait tables. Tregev halted. "Five crowns for the lot? Is this all?" The sound of his voice grated on her.

They would be broken up. They would lose their strength in numbers, the strength her plan depended upon. Out of the twenty, at least half of them should be able to gain a horse and flee—she could see the ring of mounts and carts and wagons at the crowd's edge. The auctioneer and his staff would never expect such boldness—not from pallans.

"Five crowns for the lot," she blurted out. "You spend more on horses."

"*Princess*," Mahbray hissed behind her.

Laughter again. She bit her tongue, but the audience seemed amused by her outburst. She clenched her hands tightly.

From the rear. A man who stood oddly with one shoulder higher than the other. Leaning on a cane perhaps? Or just a peculiarity? He wore purple, the price of his dye alone proclaiming wealth. His hair was silver, but his brows and eyes as dark as coal. "I'll see fifteen crowns for them," he said.

"I have fifteen, fifteen, fifteen. Is the bidding done?"

"That's a lot of money," a heckler called, "for sacrifices Baalan will pick up sooner or later."

"Ah," Tregev answered, "but that's the beauty of it. While you have them, you can learn their skills for yourself. And then the secret dies with them. Dragon fodder they may be, but that should not keep you from wringing them dry."

"Eighteen, a sharp-faced woman called. She held a scent stick in her hand and kept waving it under her hook nose as if something stank unbearably.

"Twenty crowns," the purple man said. He looked to Sharlin as if he could see behind her mask. "And if I pay as much for you as a horse, you'd better be prepared to work like one."

"Done!" shouted Tregev before someone changed his mind. "Kalander, send your retainer up here to take charge of them."

Sharlin felt a thrill. The crowd had begun to mill around. A vendor hawking cold drinks and hot rolls called out, and they were moving in that direction. The retainer would never reach them in time. "Now," she hissed to Mahbray, and bunched her muscles for a running leap.

"Master!" cried a knife-edged pallan voice. "She lies! The manager lies! We stand here not to serve you but to escape!"

Kalander had forced his way close to pay Tregev's banker. He looked up, and his cold eyes met Sharlin's as she froze on the edge of the platform. Instantly, it seemed, the man and platform were surrounded by drivers with whips and stingers.

She felt the pop as a dart pierced her skin. She lost

her sight, pitching forward into darkness. Oddly she
heard laughter.

"I'll take them anyway, Tregev, and the ringleader,
too. What a manager she must be if she can organize a
pallan rebellion!"

She lost the rest of herself to cold, ringing, laughter.

Chapter 19

Horses stamped and chafed impatiently in the alleyway. Their sides steamed into cold, midnight air. Aarondar shivered in spite of himself and clamped his teeth shut against a chatter. The weather on Baalan's continent was ill-begotten cold! Mwork seemed not to notice it as he eyed the informal picket line behind one of the Throat's most frequented brothels.

"Two hardheads on watch," he whispered in joy. "Thump 'em and we've got it."

Dar sourly eyed the two goblins walking the horse and cart line. A thump would scarcely get their attention. But he knew Mwork knew that—a goblin's hardhead was a source of pride and joy. He wasn't exactly overjoyed about Mwork's choice of transportation, either. A chariot looked unwieldy and overexposed from the rear. But they were equipped—the one Mwork was licking his chops over held a shield, bow and quiver and packs from the looks of it.

A door opened at the rear of the establishment and two men reeled out, one of them a dragonpriest. They flipped a coin at the nearest goblin and made for the chariot Mwork coveted. He made a sound like a low groan. Dar caught his arm. "Let's follow," he said. "We haven't lost this one yet. We can always come back if we have to."

"True," Mwork grunted in return. "There's no dearth

of business here." He joined Dar as they shadowed the chariot through the alleyway.

The horses weren't drunk, but they veered and wavered as if they might have been. Mwork shouldered Dar. "Bad driving," he muttered. "He'll topple the chariot and break the axle or snap the tongue."

"Then we'll take the horses." Dar was liking the idea of a chariot less and less anyway. They'd make better time on horseback, but the goblin seemed to have some objection to it that he would not express to Dar.

Mwork made a growl deep in his throat and made an effort to catch up with their prey.

The stalking took them through the most odious parts of a town that was hock deep in it. The chief coin was not metal, but flesh, and the younger, the better. A suckling babe was worth a great deal of barter—but only because the owner could offer it to the dragonpriests or Baalan and receive beneficent attentions for it. A trader wishing to keep his caravans safe or his chief rival's business hassled found children his best method of persuasion. And all because of the coming Night.

Dar abhorred it. The hackles rose on the back of his neck and stayed up the moment they stepped foot in the Throat. He did not mind that it had been days since he'd eaten or drunk well. The food and drink here stuck in his throat like ashes and stank in his nostrils like carrion. All of it was corrupt.

The chariot came to an abrupt stop at a gutter, hub grinding against it. They pounded at the back door of a shop that eventually creaked open as sleepily as the proprietor. They dodged into a particularly dark niche and watched it.

"Ah," murmured Mwork in his deep voice. "They're buying *silth*."

"Silth?"

"A dream drug that kills pain. Most buy it to be free of pain—some to be chased by the dreams."

Dar thought. Lyrith? "An herbal?"

"No." Mwork turned an amused face to him. All Dar could see was the flash of his ivory fangs. "There are many vices in the world, swordsman."

"Maybe," agreed Dar. Silth was not one he'd heard of.

"They will sample the wares," Mwork continued, "to ensure its potency before making a buy. Follow me. We'll strike when they come out of the shop."

It was simple and quick. The wait was the most difficult part, for Dar was positioned crouched by the wheel hub, and his knee, while nearly healed, complained at the strain. His sword did not speak as they waylaid and dispatched the two. Mwork disdained the dragonpriest cloak, but picked the cleanest and best one out of the gutter and threw it about Dar.

"You may not be a softskin, but you're still thin-skinned," he observed. "And it gets colder still on the road to Rilth." He hopped onto the platform. "I'll drive," he further said, "until we're well on our way. Then you must learn to drive, because we may need my skills with the bow."

Dar wrapped the cloak about and mounted the chariot behind Mwork. The cloak was rent in several places and muddied and bloodstained. He crouched down. He was weary.

"Sleep," the goblin said. "I'll tell them you're drunk. The cloak stinks of it and the silth. They'll believe me if we're stopped."

Dar shut his eyes. Just before he slept, it struck him that they were, finally, on the weary way to the last leg of his journey.

He woke to a morning that glowered and hung damply over the face of the land. The road, if it could

be called such, bounced and jostled over desolation, a
countryside of ash and cinder. The trees were blackened sticks hanging at the edge of his vision. Frost
rimed dirt that was already blackened in despair. He
uncurled and stood up, bracing himself to the rear of
the chariot.

"My god," he breathed, looking out over the waste.
"What is it?"

"Dragons," said Mwork companionably. "They scour
the road every other day or so. It keeps the trespassers
off it."

"And how will they know to miss us?"

"They won't. We didn't buy a pass in Throat. But,
don't worry. We have one chance in two that today is
not the day for a dragonwatch." He clucked encour-
agement to the chariot team.

Dar could not look away from the blistered lands.
"The horses," he said, "won't go much farther without
rest and feed."

"There's mash in the saddlebags. The dragonpriest
we capped last night was evidently going to head out
as well. We stopped for a while last night and slept a
little."

"All right," said Dar defensively. "I just don't want
the horses misused."

"Why?" asked the goblin. "Do you think we'll need
them for a return trip?"

Dar could not answer that. If he made it as far as
the Gates, and if he lived to ransom Fort, then perhaps Turiana would carry them home to the Shalad
Mountains. If not, then he would have no need for
mounts. He ended up shaking his head. The goblin
guffawed and snapped the reins.

For all the creature's heedless ways, he had good
hands with the horses. When they finally found a pool
of rain water and stopped to rest them, Dar examined
their mouths when he took the bits down to let them

eat their mash. The gums and tongues were foamed with tiredness, but not cut or bruised. He would be pleased if he could drive half so well.

So would Mwork, Dar thought later, as he labored to keep the horses in tandem and the chariot upon the road.

"No, no," frothed the goblin. "Wrap the leathers through your fingers like so," and he threaded the reins through again. Instantly the chariot horses slowed and steadied, their hoofbeats in rhythm.

Dar flexed his neck and shoulders. He tightened his fingers a hitch. "*There*," said Mwork, pleased. "You're getting it." He bent to pick up the bow and quiver.

"Good quarrels," he said, pleased. "Tough enough to bring down a falroth."

"How about a dragon?"

"Doubt it. Not unless I get a clean throat or belly shot. The beasts are malicious and shrewd. They know their weak points. We'll be dead before I'm given a target like that."

"Too bad," mourned Dar. "Here comes a dragon now."

The crimson cloak about him wrapped him from the inclement weather, but could not keep the deathly chill that crept about him now, as he saw the winged creature drifting out of storm clouds and sailing its way toward them. His hands were full, but even if they weren't, he had no flanking advantage, no way of attacking the beast unless he went straight down its maw. He was helpless. Gorge rose from his stomach.

Mwork grunted at the back of his throat. Then, "Keep driving," he said. "Chances are it's not scouring the road. It's flying too high. Baalan sends out messengers all the time."

The horses began to toss their heads and fret as the beast grew near and its scent came on the storm wind that bore it. Dar felt their panic being telegraphed to

him. He tried to steady them. At his shoulder he felt
Mwork nock an arrow.

"Just," the goblin said, "in case."

But the dragon showed no interest in them, one way
or the other. It snaked its head due east and banked,
sailing in another direction.

Dar felt his heart stagger a beat or two. "But," he
said, "all it had to do was look us over. He'd have seen
no signature spell."

"Not his job," Mwork answered. "That's the way
they are. Spiteful, lazy beasts." He relaxed his bow-
string and took the arrow away. "Close, eh?"

Dar leaned over the side of the chariot and was ill.
He felt better once the foul taste of the meals he'd had
in the Throat were gone. The horses stayed in tandem
and never seemed to notice his hands gone lax on the
reins.

Mwork thumped him. "Soft stomach, too, eh? Believe me, swordsman, you'll see much worse by the
time we get to Rilth. And then . . . curse this small
cart as you will—beyond, when we cross the ice fields
and mud pots, you'll wish you could be driving it yet."

"I have no choice," Dar answered. "I'd follow this
road if it led up a dragon's ass."

The goblin laughed dryly at that.

"Calling him a dragon's ass," Sharlin spat, "would be
insulting the dragon. Who shot me?"

"The new master did, princess." Mahbray held her
aching head in her lap. Cool, gloved fingers massaged
her mask gently, soothing even through the fabric.
"He seemed to enjoy it. I fear we have gone from the
cooking pot into the fire. Please forgive Nevny. He
panicked. It is difficult to ask a pallan to stand firm in
the face of such an enemy."

"It's all right. Argggh."

Sharlin groaned as she endeavored to sit up. Her

vision whirled and one arm trembled violently, the muscles in a spasm she could not control. Mahbray patiently switched from massaging her temples to kneading her arm. In the center of the twitch was a fiery sore spot where she knew the dart had pierced her. The flatbed wagon jostled her about, and she saw that part of her problem in sitting up was that they were packed in it like eels in a fishing basket. The slavers had given them more room. Already she detested this Kalander.

"The question is, Mahbray, where is this fire?"

"I'm told the master owns a large plantation alongside the Vandala, not far from Geldart. He is spoken of as rich and powerful. And . . ." Mahbray's voice trailed off.

"What?"

"No pallan has ever come back from there."

Sharlin patted her hand. "I'm no pallan," she said. "And I'll get you out of there, somehow." They leaned against one another companionably. The flatbed's jostling settled into a swinging rhythm and they eventually fell asleep to the background of a pallan's thin voice singing a mournful, wordless tune.

Chapter 20

She had not thought to see luxury again in the lifetime she'd spent following Dar about in his quest for whatever he was looking for. The pouch of bone and ashes she carried inside the vest of her pallan costume, she carried for him. When he was settled somewhere, he'd always said, for good, he'd then scatter the bone and ash on his grounds. It was the only thing she'd managed to hold onto in these last few months.

But it was the lot she'd wanted and asked for, and Sharlin knew she'd not have been happy settling for less. Yet, as the plantation wagons pulled into a lane bordered by shrubbery grown for fencing, and she counted the stone pillars that marked the vast acreage of the holding, something stirred inside of her. In her time and place, she'd been a princess. She'd been brought up to the responsibilities and accountings of a fiefdom that was now, according to pallan history, non-existent. But it had been.

As she looked out now over the vast fields and pastures and even timberland, she tallied wealth close to that of the house of Dhamon. Another hedge lumbered past, followed by a stone column. She could smell the sticky sweet odor of the flowering crop of the field it bordered.

"What is that?" she whispered to Mahbray.

The pallan answered wearily, "Silth. And the fields beyond are sugarstick."

The day had warmed some. Pallans were out in both fields. Weeding in the sugarstick and harvesting in the silth. A winter flower, then. Must be an herb of some kind. Sharlin twisted in her narrow space in the wagon to watch as they were driven past. Two men on horseback watched the workers, but there was an awful lot of land between them and their charges.

"We have a chance." She pitched her voice for Mahbray's ears alone, yet a restlessness stirred through the wagon. Sharlin sat back and decided to keep her counsel to herself for the moment. She counted the stone pillars marking acreage as the wagons turned into the lane heading for the manor and major outbuildings, none of which could be seen from the road.

Her upper arm ached dully from the dart wound as the wagon finally bumped to a halt. Her hips felt pounded into mush as she gathered her feet under her, preparatory to getting out. The ground was tinted red, like clay, and she could smell the richness of the soil.

As dust settled in the courtyard, a big burly man with an extravagant mustache, a bow to his walk, and vast sun lines crinkling his eyes strode up. "I'm the overseer," he said. "You will be taken to your quarters where you will settle in and freshen up for dinner. You'll receive your work assignments after you've eaten. Learn them. Tomorrow morning, you'll be taken to your assignments. You'll speak only when spoken to by Master Kalander or myself, Master Jack. This is your home now. You won't be leaving it unless you're dead." He dropped the wagon tail on that last for emphasis.

He handed Sharlin out first just before she nearly tumbled out, the support of the tail gone and the press in the overcrowded wagon leaning on her. Her arm gave a twinge of pain, which she suppressed. Her pallan tribe quickly surrounded her. The corner of her mouth quirked in a smile under her mask. She didn't

know if their attention was solicitous or if they were
trying to hide her clumsiness from the other pallans
who were sure to guess she wasn't what she claimed to
be.

Kalander's private buggy stood in front of a magnificent manor house. She saw its doors open, the master
step out and be handed to a seat in the buggy. The
buggy was then driven to them.

Kalander leaned out. "Which one of you is the
manager?"

"I am," Shar answered. The pallans parted before
her as if he'd driven a wedge into them.

"You will be maintained in the pallan quarters, but
you will report to me in the morning as soon as you've
been fed. Is that clear?"

"Yes, master." She gave a nod.

"Good." He looked to his overseer. "See they're
fed and watered."

Jack's mustache did a little dance before the man
said, "Yes, sir."

Kalander looked over them. His dark eyes sparked
with a hungry glint, and she felt suddenly afraid. "Which
one of you warned me at the auction?"

The pallans about her stirred uneasily. Then, with a
grace unstinted by fear, a red-and-gray-hooded pallan
stepped forward. Kalander's hand flashed up, filled
with a dart gun. He shot, and the pallan fell gasping at
Sharlin's feet. His heels drummed the clay in agony
and then he went stiff. Fear throbbed in her throat as
Kalander raised the gun to point at her. The darts
loaded now were fletched red, for poison death.

"This is how I reward disloyalty. Remember it well."
He lowered the stinger and stepped back into his
carriage. In a swirl of red dust the buggy was gone.
Her shoulder throbbed in memory.

The barracks was a long hall jammed with cots. The
middens were outside and, true to pallan fashion, fas-

tidiously clean and downwind. She was in luck there—
the latrines were probably in better shape than those
of the manor house, for the pallans were a clean and
precise people. The windows were barred, and the
doors gated. There would be little chance of getting out
of there without notice. Mahbray let her sleep until
dinner.

The dinner was served in pallan fashion. The little
meat given had been mixed into several grain and
vegetable dishes. The fruits were the last of the winter
fruits and fall-stored fruits. Sharlin ate around the
brown spots. Each table held pitchers of watered tea.
She couldn't get enough of the sweetened drink. The
clay in her throat had been forming a dam and she'd
never had tea so pleasingly refreshing. Her head cleared
and the dart wound's throbbing finally ebbed away.

Mahbray, eating meticulously behind her veil, reached
out and stopped Sharlin as she poured a third mug of
the tea.

"Don't."

"Don't what?"

"You mustn't drink any more."

Sharlin noticed Mahbray had scarcely touched hers.
"Mahbray, try the tea. You'll feel better for it. You
need to keep your strength up."

"If you need water, we'll get it from the horse
troughs. Listen to me, princess."

"The trough?" Sharlin stared at her in disbelief.
"What are you talking about?"

"The tea is laced with silth. It's done on purpose to
keep us here and working longer. Silth is a drug,
princess, and it takes very little to addict one. No
pallan ever leaves here because no pallan *can* . . .
unless death takes our brethren first."

Mahbray's voice trembled. Sharlin looked at her
mug. "A drug . . . like lyrith?" She grasped her drink.
She was still so thirsty . . .

"No. Far from lyrith. Our brethren hurried to warn us away from a trap that has taken many of them in. I spoke with one while you slept. In great quantities, it is very stimulating—the senses are sharpened and the body feels no pain. Even greater quantities bring prophetic dreams. It's used here in very small quantities— enough to addict us, and to keep the weariness from our bodies so that we will work harder. But in any quantity, silth wastes the mind and flesh. Every drop of it in our body feeds off us and gives nothing back until we've nothing left. I beg of you. Listen and believe me."

Sharlin uncurled her fingers from her mug. "I believe you. Why did you let me drink?"

"Because your wound pained you, and because I knew tonight wouldn't harm you. Because I hesitated to ask you to drink with the animals."

Sharlin put her arm about Mahbray's shoulders and gave her a light hug. "Never hesitate," she said, "to tell the truth." With great effort she pushed her mug away. Pallan constitution was different from human. Had Mahbray stopped her in time? She looked about the room. Every pallan sitting at the long tables came to her in a palette of vivid colors. She felt brand-new and enervated. It will pass, she told herself, and tried to let it go.

"Pallans, I'm told, are an acquired taste," Kalander said. He circled about Sharlin, household scrolls in one arm, his other hand free. He gestured elegantly with it. He swept it about the confines of her body, a slight caress that she could not be sure was intentional or accidental. She froze under his touch. "But I find, like silth, your people to be quietly seductive. You will come to understand me, and I you."

The manor house was dark, shaded and hidden. Banks of fans moved as if under their own volition, creating coolness within the house. Sharlin knew that, somewhere, pallan hands pulled the ropes that controlled those fans. She shifted away from Kalander, a subconsious movement that she hoped he had not noticed. He needed no cane now and she wondered if he affected it in public to obtain sympathy or if the cane was a weapon, subtly carried. The man was framed by a house opulent in its furnishings. The drapes and tapestries hung were rich in thread and yarn, depicting scenes of hunts and feasts, of dragongods and griffens, and of beautiful castles and manors. Kalander had a definite taste for the good life.

She found herself holding her breath lest he stroke her again.

Kalander stopped circling. He placed a scroll in her hand. "Here is a list of the pallan staff. Update it with my latest acquisitions. Master Jack will provide you with the names of those who were gifted to the dragonpriests or who have died in service. I want this done by this evening, at the latest."

She nodded.

"I want these other scrolls looked over. Read them and ask if you have any questions. The tithe for Geldart will be due in five days or so. See that you're prepared to have it ready. Under no circumstances will you allow the collectors to see the true accounts of the household. Is that clear?"

Sharlin did not smile, but a bittersweet feeling swept through her. No man was prepared to face the tax man squarely, if he could help it. "Yes, that is clear," she murmured in answer.

"Good. You may go."

Sharlin turned and headed quickly for the front door. She had almost gained it when Kalander's silken voice stopped her."

"Shar."

Her hand was on the latch. She pivoted, bending

her arm behind her back, the latch still in her grip. "Yes, master?"

"There are advantages to being my manager. Better food and drink. You are to stay away from the silth. I want you clearheaded and keen. Is that clear?"

She gave a bow.

Kalander's eyebrow went up. His sharp-boned face held a predatory look. "There are other, stronger, ties that will bind you to me." And then he turned his back on her, and she was dismissed.

Sharlin fled into the sunlight. She caught her breath in the courtyard. She shuttered her eyes but could not blank out the dark-eyed stare of the plantation owner. He held all the perversions that a man who owned the flesh of another held—and more. She had no doubt what Kalander wanted of her—and that a man would think of such a relationship with a pallan chilled her blood. Firstly, pallans were held in contempt and considered less than animals by men of his ilk. Most would use but not sully themselves sexually with their slaves. That Kalander would, made him even more perverse in her thoughts.

The sun brought her senses back. Sharlin grasped the scrolls to her chest and strode across the vast driveways toward the small outbuildings of the barracks. She would have to repel Kalander, but without the innate talent of the pallans, she did not know how. And as for revealing her true self—she doubted if that would sway Kalander, unless he killed her for knowing the dark side of his nature.

The longer she and Mahbray stayed here, the more desperate her danger would become.

Chapter 21

The road to Baalan's kingdom was paved with blood and bone. The crackle of charred and scavenger-stripped skeletons crunching beneath the horse's hooves unnerved Dar. The shards lay in a road so ripped and plowed by talons that he could scarcely keep the chariot on the track. Mwork said little, but his actions spoke. He nocked an arrow and kept it ready, his eyes watching the countryside alertly.

A skull was kicked aside by the left wheel horse with a dull *pock*. Dar watched it spin away into the mud. It was a goblin—as most of them had been this last stretch—and he wondered at that. So he asked.

Mwork grunted. "A small army of goblins laid siege to the watchtower. This is what's left of them. I'm told their commander got away."

Rilth lay on the horizon, but Dar didn't have his eyes on it. He was watching the jagged purple of a massive mountain range against which even the needle towers of Rilth looked small. The goblin's words penetrated, however.

"But why? Most of Baalan's army is goblin."

Mwork's lips tightened. "I'm told they're just naturally contentious."

Dar looked at him another moment or two, knew he would not get the full story, and concentrated on guiding the horses through the carnage. He wondered if anything green would ever grow here again.

"We're getting close enough to the tower," Dar said, "that we should be meeting the outpost soon. Any plan for getting past them?"

"Just the darkness. It'll be night soon."

"I can't drive in the night."

Mwork made a sound of scorn between his tusks. "You can't drive past Rilth, either. There's a ditch coming up on the right—Baalan blasted a hole deep enough to swallow two or three chariots. We'll leave it and the road when we get there."

The smell of death from the pit was overpowering. Dar could not get the horses close enough to unhitch them. They trembled as he stroked their necks and led them away from the tongue. Mwork put his shoulder to the cart and rolled it to the pit and cast the chariot over. It landed with such a loud crash that Dar froze a moment, certain someone must have heard the noise. The horses threw their heads up as if thinking to bolt, but he held them still. By the faint light of the two moons, he could see the whites of their eyes and the flare of the nostrils.

Mwork took his by the harness and mounted. Dar gathered a handful of mane and followed suit. The horse was lathered and slick. He could feel the beast's damp heat through his trousers.

"Follow me," Mwork said. He was a cloud of darkness on his horse's withers.

For a moment Dar wondered where he would be led. Then, he put heel to his mount's flank and followed.

They made slow time. The land bubbled warmly in spots, bleeding heat through the icy crust that was settled over it. "Mud pots," Mwork said. "Watch out for them. Warm enough, but one stumble and you've lost your horse."

Dar found himself nodding. The Shield and the Little Warrior glowed stronger and he knew Mwork could see him in silhouette. He pointed toward the orange glow on the next ridge. The goblin said, "One outpost we must pass, then we can take to the countryside. Away from the road, we'll find cover and forage. Baalan may be spiteful, but he knows better than to fire the entire land."

Dar pulled up the hood of his crimson cloak. Under his leather cap the silver helm hugged his head closely, but dragonpriests did not usually wear fighting gear. He touched his sword in case it might speak to him, but it stayed quiet.

"How do you intend to pass the outpost?"

"That depends," answered Mwork, "on who or what is manning it tonight."

Dar said grimly, "We'll pass them one way or the other. How far to the mountain?"

"On horseback, two hard days' riding."

"Are you with me?"

Mwork's horse stamped as the goblin said, "I wouldn't miss it. Besides, swordsman—you need someone at your back."

"That I do."

The outpost fire was small and neglected when they reached it. The soldiers manning the outpost were hunched over a gaming pit drawn in the soft dirt, throwing dice. Dar chafed his hands as Mwork stepped to the fore.

"Even quintains don't keep a hardhead warm on a night like this."

The watch looked up at Mwork when he spoke. The goblin captain spat to one side. "What's yer business?"

"It's Baalan's business and no one questions the great beast."

The soldiers stayed on their knees, dice clutched tightly in the greedy fist of one of them. "Faugh," said the captain who spat again, this time right between the

forefeet of Mwork's mount. The bay was illuminated
orange by the glow of the fire. "Take yer messages
and go."

"Just like that? No names? No password?"

The goblin captain thumbed at Dar. "I seen th' red
cloak. Ye got business too grand for th' likes of me to
know. Git on yer way before ye sour th' dice."

Mwork gave Dar a nod, put his boot to his tired
horse's flank, and rode past the watchfire. Dar followed after. The back of his neck prickled as if the
goblins watched him go. Would they notice his horse
had no saddle? Would they catch the length of sheathed
sword at his side?

And if they did, how many of them could he kill
before they pulled his horse down?

He palmed his sword hilt.

Hold, swordsman. I'll bite deep before the day is out.

He rode into the farther edge of night and soon the
grumbling of the goblins at the outpost faded from
hearing. The iron bar up his spine did not disappear
until he could hear them no more. The Mwork turned
his horse from the road, and Dar followed after.

By dawn the horses were staggering. Mwork found
a tiny knoll where green grass sprouted and hobbled
them with straps cut off the now overly long reins. Dar
snared a softfoot. They sat and ate in silence, overshadowed by the vast mountains. It was cold and even
the fire and hot meat did not warm them.

Mwork eyed the purple-and-blue-spiked peaks. Their
snowy tips were overcast by clouds laden with more
snow. "We'll cross the trail again, up there," he said.
"Can't help it."

"Why?"

"One of the main altars is inside that mountain."

Dar looked up. His memory of the Gates held no
such profanity. "What is this Night of Dragons supposed to be?"

Mwork cracked up a bone with his strong jaws and began sucking the marrow out. "It's a sacrificial night, I know that much. Rumor says old Baalan himself will be purified. That's why we attacked last fall. The canny old beast is showing his age. He uses as little magic as possible."

Dar said nothing. Could Baalan finally be confronted with the wasting sickness himself? There was no turning back from that. Had Turiana brought him all this way for nothing? To fight a dying foe?

Mwork tossed the bone into the fire. "We've not much time before the appointed day. It's said that when Baalan holds the Night of Dragons, that spring will never come to Rangard again. He will spread his shadow over the face of the world." He smacked his lips and looked at the two horses scraping snow from grass shoots. "Think he can do it?"

"I think what he'll spread is darkness in the soul until each and every one of us can no longer see the light." Dar threw his last bone into the fire as well. "Then what will the seasons matter?"

Mwork caught his glance. He nodded in agreement, lay back and went to sleep, his black and warty face shadowed by the mountains.

At high noon, Mwork found the trail into the mountains. It was rutted by the wheels of handcarts. He sniffed. "Dragonpriests bring their victims up here."

Dar picked up a handful of limp flowers. "We must not be too far behind." His horse nosed him and ate the flowers eagerly.

"Thought you'd not been this way before," said Mwork sharply.

"No," he said absently, remembering. "Only by dragonback." He found a stone and stood upon it to remount. "Let's go."

"In a hurry?"

Turiana waited close by with his son. Gods, yes, he was in a hurry. He snapped the reins and sent his horse plunging up the trail. Mwork followed. A tree branch with snow still clinging whipped after them.

It was a body that brought his horse to a skidding halt and nearly unseated Dar into a drift of gravel and ice. Mwork unhorsed and knelt to examine it. It was—had been—a pallan, its grace frozen stiff in death. Its clothes were badly torn and the mask and veil sunken upon its features.

"What is it?"

"A sacrifice that didn't make it to the mountaintop." He nudged the body with his toe. "Happens, sometimes." In the pallan's hand was a scrap of clothing. Mwork pulled it loose. It was a child's jacket. Dar froze at the sight of it.

Fort's.

His hand shook as he took it from the goblin. "What is it, softskin?" the being asked.

"This belongs—belonged—to my son." Had Turiana been found at the Gates and Fort taken from her to be brought back for sacrifice?

"Surely not. How?"

"I don't know how." He crumpled up the toddler jacket and stuffed it inside his chain mail. He ripped the crimson cloak from his shoulders and threw it to Dar. "Cover the body."

"The scavengers will have it soon enough."

"Do as I say!" His horse balked at being reined past the body. Dar clenched his fist and punched it in the neck. The mount threw up its head and mouthed the harness bit, and then minded. Dar set it at the steepening track, not caring if Mwork caught up or not. His son had to be riding that cart of victims.

The sun had begun its downward climb in earnest when the track widened, where melting snow and sleet washed it into a muddy run. Dar didn't see the victim, but Mwork did—the goblin's skin and clothing muddied as dark as the shadow he lay in. Once again, Mwork dismounted. Dar made as if to go ahead, but he reined in as the goblin said, "This one's alive."

But not for long. He was stove in and black blood leaked from the corner of his broken mouth. Dar listened to the dying creature dispassionately. The handcart had stuck in the muddy ruts. He had been volunteered to help shoulder it out. He'd done his bit, but then the freed cart had fallen back on him, rolling right over the top of him.

The dragonpriests had not even had the mercy to put the sword to him, leaving him to die alone.

"Is that all?" Mwork asked his fellow goblin.

The thing shuddered in this arms.

"How many victims left?" snapped Dar.

"Let him die," Mwork said.

"Not until I know how many victims are left."

The goblin put up a hand.

"Five," said Mwork flatly. He had his sword out, ready for a mercy stroke.

"Is there a child among them? A human boy, light brown hair, just walking and talking?"

The goblin's head dropped in a stilted nod. Dar felt as though a spear had pierced him through. He looked at Mwork. "Do it," he said, and turned his horse about so as not to watch it.

The cry was swift and short. Mwork came to his side, cleaning his sword.

"They use many children."

"He's mine! I know he is."

"We have to go cautiously here on out. We're not too far behind. Many of the dragonpriests are fighters, and the hardhead I left here is proof they have troops with them as well."

Dar stared down at him. "You're not sworn to

me," he said, "nor I to you. Stay here if you want. I'm going up there to fight."

Mwork's face split in a grin. "It's a little boring down here," he said. "I'll come with you anyway."

"Small comfort," the swordsman remarked. "But I'll take what I can get."

"Then do so quietly," Mwork told him. "The snow here is wet and heavy. I have seen avalanches wipe out entire villages on days like this."

Dar wet his lips. "Perhaps we can use that to our advantage." He waited for Mwork and continued upward.

Heavy smoke and the stench of burning flesh reached them long before they came to the ledge where the mountain opened to the world. They dismounted and staked the horses and finished on foot, creeping cautiously forward on an icy trail dwarfed by immense blue ice drifts. The stench of the burning left them sickened. Mwork rounded a drift and then ducked back.

"That's a dragoncarcass burning. There's been one hell of a fight up there."

Dar felt his breath stop in his chest.

Chapter 22

Casci, the glazier, gave in to the silth first. He made a scene at the dinner benches. Mahbray tried to keep the pitcher of drug-laced tea from him, but he fought her for it, eyes wild behind his veil.

"It helps me sleep," he said frantically. "This is all I have," And he wrenched the pitcher back from her. The other pallans stopped eating and watched, but did nothing.

Sharlin drew Mahbray away gently. "Let him have it," she said. "If he's already in their clutches, there's nothing you can do."

The little pallan shrugged her away. "You haven't seen them, have you?"

"Seen who?"

Mahbray considered her. She filled her pockets with biscuits, then she shoved her and Sharlin's food plates away. "Come with me," she said. They left the hall and struck out across the courtyard.

They had walked past the main buildings and pasture, woolie lambing sheds and a shearing and carding shed, past the hothouse and herb gardens, and toward the windbreaks where the feathery limbs of tall timber moved lazily between the plantation and the river Vandala. There were more sheds at the river's edge. The cold sheds, Sharlin thought. She'd not been down here—the cooks took care of that. As they neared the building, though, she could hear the cries of prisoners.

Reedy and weak, they could barely be heard above the movement of the river. The Vandala was both deep and wide here where a shore of rocks cut into its path, creating foam and fury. She might not have heard the voices if Mahbray had not motioned for her to listen.

The shed was barred with greenstick. She approached the door hesitantly behind Mahbray, who was already at the door, breaking open biscuits and pushing them through. The pallans huddled inside were sticks inside their clothing. Their veils hung on deathmasks. They took the biscuits listlessly, crying. "Tea. Give us tea."

"No," Mahbray said firmly. "I'll get you water." She picked up a filthy, eroded bucket by the door and took it down to the river. There she took sand and scrubbed and scrubbed.

Sharlin watched them pick listlessly at their food. Rations from earlier that day grew stale and rank in pans they had kicked to the corner. Flies buzzed around it, but surely the food had been edible earlier in the day. Mahbray came back with a bucket of water.

"What is it? Why won't they eat?"

Mahbray looked at her. "Why? Watch this." She held the bucket up. "The silth is already mixed in. Drink sweet and deep, my brethren."

The listlessness turned to lust. They flung themselves at the bucket, scooping up the water and drinking with their gloved hands. They fought for places close enough to the bucket to drink. They did not stop until the bucket was drained dry.

"It's the silth they want," Mahbray said wearily. "And only the silth."

"But you didn't—"

"Of course not! But it's sometimes the only way to get them to drink." She watched as the pallans flailed the air for more, only to cry in frustration when their hands met the bottom of a dry bucket. "Master Jack has put them in here until they can put aside the silth—or die. They've chained us with the silth. Those addicted must have it or die . . . and having it, die anyway. But he's not ready to let them go. They must be fit enough to work. Most of us can take silth for years before it reduces us to that. We'll work hard, ignoring pain, and being obedient. Silth is a better whip than the one the overseers carry. That one in the corner warned me of the doping. This is her punishment." Mahbray looked at Sharlin, her voice stricken. "Get us out of here before it destroys us, too."

Sharlin tried to look away, but the sight of the pallan huddled in the corner drew her. She could not turn away. The being had not taken water, nor food, but sat, rocking on her heels, singing to herself.

Sharlin motioned for Mahbray to fill the bucket again. "We bring you water, " she said, bringing herself as close to the corner as the bars would let her.

The pallan looked up. Her colors were bold, red and gold, as she herself must have been once. "Only water?"

"Yes."

"But the others—"

"It was the only way to get them to drink."

The pallan gathered herself and stood with ragged dignity. "Then I will drink." She waited for Mahbray and cupped the river water with hands that shook.

"How did this happen to you?"

The pallan did not answer until having drunk her fill. Then she said, "It was my fault. I found my dream better than my life."

"The silth dreams?"

The dusty masked face nodded.

"Dreams of what?"

The pallan regarded her. Mahbray said, "Trust her. She is the lost and found and lost again princess. Do you remember her?"

There was a long pause, then, "Perhaps," Another pause, "I dream of home and golden dragons."

Her simple words brought hope out of despair. "Golden dragons? What do you mean?"

Mahbray held her back. "Silth gives us fantasies," she said.

"No. It's more than that, it has to be." She grabbed at the pallan. "Tell me why you dream about golden dragons."

The imprisoned pallan reared back, just out of her reach. "Don't take my dreams! They're all I have!"

"I didn't come to take them." Sharlin withdrew her hand and tried to speak in a gentle tone. "Who are you?"

"My brethren call me Anya." The pallan hugged herself and her slim body was racked with soundless gasps. "Help me, please."

"I'll do my best," Sharlin promised. "Don't give up." Mahbray linked her arm about her and drew her away and walked her back to the barracks.

"I want the east wing stripped and readied for new furnishings," Kalander ordered her during the evening report.

Sharlin had been inking her pen and stopped in astonishment. Then she bent her face to the household accounts she'd been working on while the master ate his dinner. The desk in the corner was small and cramped, but it saved her from sharing the same table. She was hungry tonight—always hungry, any more, and the pitchers of tea and sweetstick and silth had been beckoning. Silth kept you from feeling the hunger. She etched in the numbers and laid the pen to one side. She and Mahbray had plans to visit the imprisoned Anya after dinner, and those plans now sank in disappointment.

"Yes, master," she answered as Kalander sat with fork poised to his mouth, waiting for her attention. "In what manner of furnishings shall the wing be done?"

"I'm taking a bride. She and I will be handfasted in Geldart and she will have her household goods ferried downriver. She will give you instruction on the furnishings and color she desires."

"Very well."

Did her flat voice fail to hide the surprise she felt? It must, for Kalander twisted in his chair.

"It is odd, is it not, for me to think of marriage? But all men come to this passage sooner or later, I'm told. She comes of a good family, highly recommended to me, and I will be gaining influence in the upper river valleys. But most of all, she comes to me with child, and because that child is not of my blood, we will be free to give it to the dragonpriests, gaining me even more sway." He tilted his head back, and a silver wing of hair fell loosely.

Sharlin said nothing, could not speak even if she had been bidden to do so, so callously he spoke of sacrificing the baby.

Kalander took a healthy forkful of cackle, cooked in the spicy sauces he preferred, "And, I'm told, she is not indisposed to raising an heir as well as providing flesh for the dragons. Proven fertility, coupled with a desire to please the gods. An altogether profitable bargain, don't you think?"

She choked out, "As master wishes." Her trembling hand caught the ink pot and sent it tumbling. She jumped up and blotted the ink before it did any damage—she'd used most of it anyway.

The sardonic wing of his eyebrow raised. "Upset, my Shar?" He put his napkin down and stood. "You mustn't be."

She mopped up quickly, but he closed the distance between them swiftly and now stood next to her. "Ah. Your hand shakes even though you do not speak." He grabbed her left hand and would not let go. Sharlin gave up blotting the ink spill and faced the man. His breath quickened.

He stroked her lightly. Kalander smiled and said, "I was right. I knew you felt it as I did. What is a human to you, who are surpassingly graceful in voice and movement? What is a wife to you, who could have anything she desires of me?" He drew closer until his breath made her veil quiver. "What is a rival to you, who could share my bed any time, if you but asked."

She tried to control her revulsion, but her arm froze in his caress. He felt it and stopped, anger flushing his face.

Master Jack entered the front door, out of sight but not out of hearing. The door latch jangled as it fell back into place, and his boots drummed on the wooden floors. "Master Kalander," he called. "I have the new ram in the lambing shed for your inspection.

Kalander dropped her hand. He looked deeply into her face as if he must pierce both her veil and her mask. "Remember that I own you," he said. "What is not freely given, *I can take*." He raised his voice. "Coming, Jack," and left her quaking with helpless fury.

"It's been burning for days," said Mwork. He hugged the crest next to Dar, their bodies making a hollow in a drift and warming the snow. "It's a big one."

Dar tried not to heed the smell, but it filled his mouth and lungs anyway. He could hear the garble of goblin voices above a biting wind that seemed to have found a gap between his skin and his clothing. "What are they saying?"

Mwork's bat ears went up alertly, cupping the wind.

He listened a moment and then looked to Dar. "The priests are inside, readying for a ceremony. The altar was profaned, they said, when the dragon tried to breach the mountain. It was slain by Baalan's watchdogs, Pevan and Atra. Must have been some fight. Anyway, Baalan's real pissed right now because he'd planned on using the boy for the Night . . . but the priests took him to consecrate the altar. They're throwing in a few others for good measure. Pallans, most like." Mwork paused to scratch himself. "Human flesh is dearer to come by. Baalan doesn't like to use humans unless they're freely given. For some reason he fears you softskins."

Dar took his sword from his sheath. "He should. Let's give him more reason to—" But before he could finish, the wind brought to them the piercing voice of a frightened child.

"Mommy! Daddy! Nooooo!"

Dar hurdled the top of the ridge, inflamed by the ring of terror in the child's voice. He cared little if Mwork followed him or not.

The sword cut cleanly in his hand. The goblin soldiers walking the parameter of the burning hulk for warmth never saw him coming. The light and ashes from the fire gave an eerie glow to the melting ice fields. Black blood splashed upon the ground, hissing in the snow. He had to kick a body off the end of his blade, where a rib snagged the tip. Then he whirled and dispatched the next guard.

It seemed that Mwork was with him, for his sword did the work of two. It sang into that biting wind and laughed at the feeble blows the goblin army met it with. He caught wounds of his own, but never felt them. He let the sword drink of blood and eat of flesh wherever he could find it. He stumbled over the wingtip of the fallen dragon, its point seared black. It brought

Fort and Turiana back into his mind as he gained the mouth way into the hollow mountain. He leaned against the immense stone that served as doorway and had been rolled aside.

Mwork bumped into him. The goblin gasped for breath. He wore a bloody footprint on the front of his shirt. "Gods," he got out. "Remind me never to fight you again."

"Are you all right?"

"Most of this blood belongs to the others." Mwork eyed Dar's thigh. "Would that you could say the same."

He felt nothing. The child let out another cry. Mwork caught his arm before he plunged into the cavern. "Most of the troops are inside."

"Stay with me, then!"

"They have to come out sooner or later!"

"Too late for me!" Dar let out a hoarse cry in answer to the child's and charged into the mountain.

The scent of incense and a golden glow that came not from torch or lantern washed over him as he crossed into the mountain. He had forgotten that the mountain made its own light, as it made its own fragrance, awash in sorcery. But the fairness of the sorcery had fouled. He gagged on its aroma and the light was dim. It served his purpose anyway, for he caught the first two guards by surprise. He cut one, pivoted, swung out, and gutted the second. Their death cries alerted the other twenty or so.

Dar took a deep breath, made it into a prayer, and began to slash his way into the interior of the hollow mountain. Two immense statues awaited him, sinuous of limb and standing upright, palms outward toward each other, their manes of marble falling to their shoulders. Their faces held the fierce look of dragons in their aspect. Veins of gold shot through the carved stone and glittered in the light. Dar knew now what he

had not known before: these were pallans who guarded
the Gates and the red, glowing life of magic beyond.

He was cut. He went to one knee. Mwork took care
of the assailant and hauled him to his feet. "Stay up,"
he said. "Or we'll never get out of here!" Above his
shout and the cry of the goblins was the high, terrible
terror of the boy being sacrificed.

Dar wrapped his hand more tightly about the sword
hilt. He'd found his sword buried in the dirt and stone
at the entrance. It sang to him now, a song of bloodletting, and he found new strength in it.

They fought back-to-back, painstaking step-by-step,
as the goblins tried to swarm them. Without shields,
their flanks were bared more often than not, but their
quickness made up for it. Mwork cut down a foe,
picked up his shield, and used it to bash another
solider over the head.

Dar felt his breath come in quick gasps. His arm felt
like lead. It was wet and sticky. He saw his shirt
parted there, and a crimson mouth. His chain mail
caught and turned aside more than one blow, but did
not leave him unharmed. The bruises spread like an
ocean tide and his ribs ached until he could scarcely
breathe.

He blinked sweat out of his eyes. Looked up and
saw the pallan statues looming overhead, their hands
outstretched as if in benediction. How much farther in
could the altar and his son be?

His sword dripped with blood both black and red.
His boots slipped in the lifestream he'd loosed. At his
back, he could feel Mwork lose the rhythm of his
strokes. *Injured*, he thought.

Then, suddenly, they broke through the wall of
flesh. Dar slipped and went to his knee. Three
dragonpriests, cloaked in the brilliant vermilion of their
order, swung about. Two held incense burners. One
held a wicked, curve-bladed dagger. It flashed upward

from the child's body. He was too late. A cry of anguish ripped through him. Their chanting halted. They half turned to him in annoyed curiosity.

Dar saw the stone altar to their back, with a writhing body upon it, and the rivulets of blood running out of it. His sight lost all color. "No!" he yelled, sound bursting out of his tormented chest. He took the sword in both hands and swung it, cleaving in two the only thing large enough to fall across the cavern floor and stop them.

The pallan statue rocked up on its base as the sword bit deep. Mwork let out a startled curse. Dar concentrated on getting the blade through the marble as its passage grew slower and slower. and then—clear. Impossibly the sword came up in his hand and the statue began to topple.

The dragonpriests stood with pale faces, their mouths open. They stared at the immense statue falling toward them. It hit with a crash and the altar disappeared under its weight. Two of the dragonpriests fled. The one with the dagger vanished along with the altar.

Dar stood, breathing heavily, sword point grounded as if it had died with the effort. He took a deep breath and never finished it as an arrow point drove deep into his back. With a spasm, he fell at the foot of the remaining statue. He blinked and saw Mwork standing over his body, and then the hollow mountain went dark.

Mwork washed his face with snow. The chill and wetness of it brought him out of dark dreams. He turned his face away to avoid it.

"Wake up, man," the goblin said. "We've got the arrow out of you. It's time to move."

His eyes blinked in spite of themselves. Dar looked up into a blurry monstrosity: Mwork's face hanging upside down and frowned in worry. "Go 'way," he said weakly to the apparition.

"Can't. You've wrecked the place and Baalan's likely to be here any second. Come on. Get to your feet. It's not far. I've the horses outside."

Dar felt himself heaved up. One leg was water—it wouldn't hold him no matter how loudly Mwork yelled at it. He had a pain in his back that felt as though a dagger still rode the wound. He stood, the uncooperative leg dangling. He looked up at the altar.

"My son," he got out. "Let me see my son."

"Softskin, we haven't time!"

"My son," repeated Dar. He squinted at Mwork. There were moving shapes behind him. "Who are these?"

"Pallans, They followed us up the mountain. Or rather, they were following you."

Dar dismissed them. With single purpose of mind, he took a shuffling step toward the demolished statue, with the canted altar under it. The unsteadiness of his passage reminded him of his son's first steps, Sharlin trailing him every bit of the way.

My son, our son, he thought. He thrust the pain away until he reached the altar. The hem of the dragonpriest's cloak covered the tiny figure upon it. Dar reached out and plucked it gently away. The boy had died a terrible death. His agony froze in his toddler's features. Eyes, wide and staring. Little round mouth opened into an O of a scream.

And, as terrible as it was, it was not his son.

A sob escaped Dar. Mwork caught him by the shoulders. "Now walk with me," the goblin said, "and I'll tell you what the pallans told me."

Dar hung upon the fighter's strength. The pallans stood by the gaping mouth of the cavern. It was impossible what he read in their faces. He knew what the mountain was to them.

"I am sorry," he said laboriously. The statue—there was no other way—"

"You needn't apologize to us. Our mountain was not meant for sacrifices. One day it will be ours again. Unfortunately, now we must hurry."

Dar did not recognize the pallan or its colors. His wounds had begun to throb miserably. His throat dried and his lips felt chapped. Fever, he thought. "Who are you? Why did you follow me?"

"My name is Silreen. I'm a renegade. We took your son. We knew of Turiana's visit. We knew what she, in all probability, wanted from you: passage to the Gates. We had to know where the mountain was—you see, it has been lost from our memory."

"Lost from pallan memory?" Dar gave a croaking laugh. Such a thing was unheard of.

"True. Burned out of our mind so that none of us might ever try to retrieve the powers we left here."

Mwork boosted Dar upon a horse. It was the chariot bay, but now it wore a goblin calvary saddle. The stirrups were too short. Dar clung to the cantle while Mwork adjusted them. "Where's my son if you have him?"

The pallan looked away. "He was taken from us by dragonpriests. But we knew that you would still pursue the mountain, and so we continued to follow. One of ours was caught—you found him dead on the lower trail."

Mwork was guiding his boots into the stirrup irons. "That's all well and good," said Dar bitterly. "But where's Fort now?"

The pallans stirred uneasily. "We," said the leader sadly, "don't know."

Mwork put the reins into his hand. "We've got to get out of here before the dragons come to reclaim the mountain. Those two priests lived to tell the tale. If we're lucky, there'll be snowfall tonight to hide our trail."

Dar looked at the goblin. There was only one way to keep his son safe from Baalan and all the Takings the dragon might ever make. His body began to shake in reaction to his wounds, so he made his oath through clenched teeth. "Take me and get me well," he said. "And I promise you Baalan will not live through his Night of Dragons."

Chapter 23

Sharlin staggered into dinner, every bone aching. Every spare minute when not working, she and Mahbray had been trying to coax Anya to live and to share her dreams. When working, she had been forced to go top and bottom of the entire manor, taking inventory in preparation for Kalander's upcoming wedding as well as for the dragonpriests' taxing. Then, with the master pacing at her elbow, she falsified a second record to actually be given to the priests. She had no experience with such falsification. Kalander had to lead her through it step-by-step. In so doing, he found a hundred obscene ways to touch her. When finally the household lists were finished, he demanded to see the roll of pallans. That list too had to be falsified.

"Else," Kalander had said, "the priests would strip my holdings of my best workers, and all in the name of blessed Baalan." His eyebrow went up as he found upon it the names for the pallans who still survived in the cold shed prison by the river.

"You told me to make a list of all pallans," Sharlin had said in response to his expression.

The master had nodded then. "This will serve." Then, again, he hovered over her until the second list was prepared.

She fairly bolted from the house when the dinner bell rang. Her weariness caught up with her as she picked up her tray of food and searched for her bench and table with Mahbray. The household inventory had led her up and down stairs and into cellars and pantries and under beds and into closets until she thought every muscle she had ached. She eyed the pitcher of silth with its sweet dreams.

She reached for the tea. Mahbray paused, fork halfway behind her veil for eating.

"What are you doing?"

"I'm exhausted," Sharlin said. "And I can't sleep at night. Just this once, Mahbray. Just this once."

The pallan said nothing more as Sharlin poured a mugful and drank deeply. Then she poured a second mug and sipped at it as she ate. The bread was fresh, and the grain dish spiced and good, though she wished more gunter strips had been roasted and scattered throughout it. Mahbray speared a few pieces off her plate and gave them to her. Pallans were nearly vegetarian and so Sharlin took them gratefully. In turn, she forked over all the fried green vegetables that squeaked between her teeth when she ate them.

She ate and looked for more, but their rations were kept low. The food was salted and spicy. She longed to drain her mug and take thirds of the tea, and knew she couldn't. Even so, the silth pounded into her blood and made her dizzy, Mahbray walked her to the barracks where she fell asleep without even knowing she had been laid on her bed.

The overseer woke her from a dream of broken wings and dragons falling from the sky. "The master wants you."

It wasn't even light in the barracks. Sharlin rubbed her eyes and shook her head, trying to clear the cobwebs of sleep. She groaned and sat up. The big man stood impassively, lantern dwarfed in his fists.

"Let me make my ablutions."

Jack looked at at her gravely. His mustache twitched.

"Hurry," he said, and let her go to the latrines and then to the washbasins without following her.

He waited inside the pallan barracks. There, she could see the gray edge of the Big Sister just over the windbreaks. "Why so late?"

"The master is master," the overseer said philosophically. Behind him she could see Mahbray raise up on her elbow. She signaled Sharlin, who could only shake her head in puzzlement.

"I've done with my duties for the evening," she said to stall.

"Fight, if you want. He won't care," the burly man said. And he smiled widely. Sharlin's blood went cold.

It was Casci who decided the impasse. He reared up on his bunk, a pitcher in his hands. With a *scree* like a wild hawk, he smashed the empty vessel down on the overseer's head. Jack crumpled to the floor. "Run," the silth-crazed pallan said. "Get out of here while you can."

Mahbray grabbed at Sharlin. "Anya," she said. Sharlin nodded. They would not leave without the brave pallan who huddled at the river's edge and who might know the way to Sharlin's golden dragon. They grabbed up their pitiful belongings and stuffed them in a thin blanket and ran.

Dew was cold and damp on the high grass. The Little Sister steadily followed the rise of the Big Sister over the windbreaks. Then, all they could see was the shadowy underdarkness as they ducked below the treetops. The cage stank. Since the last evening, one of the pallans had died. Flies buzzed hungrily about the corpse even though the air was dark and cold. By morning it would be unbearable.

Anya woke and came to the bars. "What are you doing?"

"We must leave. You've got to come with us."

"Free," the little pallan said, wonderingly. "Really free?"

"Yes! Get the others awake."

She shook her head. "They can't make it," she said. She gave a breathy laugh. "I'm not sure I can."

Sharlin paused, her fingers fumbling at the heavy knot on the cage door. "But you'll try?"

"Yes. Yes, I'll try!"

Mahbray tensed at Sharlin's side. "I hear something."

Sharlin could also. A heavy something thrashing and cursing through the brush. She bent over the knot. She could barely see the twisted strands. Her gloved fingers tore at it, and then a loop came free.

Mahbray screamed.

Sharlin rocked under the brunt of the blow, but it tore Mahbray away from her. For an instant, she stood all alone and she kept at the knot until it parted. Mahbray didn't stop screaming. She and a huge black form thrashed about on the ground. Sharlin threw open the cage and then turned, helpless, unable to see who was pallan and who was overseer. Mahbray's voice shrilled on and on.

The prisoners stumbled out. In the night they stood hesitant, blocking Anya from the open door.

Sharlin pulled them out and threw them to one side. "Run!" she shouted. "Just run!"

When Anya came into her grasp, she said, low and harshly, "Follow your dreams. If ever you should meet a golden dragon, tell her you knew Sharlin!" And then she shoved the little pallan away into the night.

Mahbray's screams cut off abruptly. Jack got to his feet with a grunt. He reached out and grabbed up Sharlin before she could bolt. He stank of blood and something else she could not quite identify. He held her hood in his fisted hand and then smashed the heel of his other hand into her cheekbone. Sharlin went to her knees with a gasp. Pain blurred her sight and burned her face.

"This is going to make Kalander very unhappy," he said, and hefted her over his shoulder like a sack of meal.

She awoke to the feeling of a hand caressing her throat. Kalander kept his hand there when her eyes came open and tilted her back gently. "I could have what I want," he said, "with just a tiny snap of your lithesome neck."

She stood in Jack's arms. The overseer's warmth at her back was overpowering. She felt him breathing like a bellows. Kalander seemed not to mind the witness. She swallowed tightly. He smiled as he felt the movement under his hand.

"Where is your bold tongue now!"

"Here," she whispered. Her voice grew hoarse as his hold tightened. "Under your hand."

"Jack, my boy," the man said, with a sardonic quirk of his ink-black brow. "Have you ever had a pallan?"

"No, sir," the other man answered. Sharlin could smell his interest, like musk. He tensed his arms about hers.

"They tease us, you know," Kalander said. "They hide their forms so that we cannot look upon them. Are they fair or gross? We don't know. But their bodies sing to us. They're cursed. The dragongods have proclaimed them the accursed on the face of Rangard. We are meant to be their masters. All that they have is meant to be ours." He loosened his grip on Sharlin's throat and slid in caressingly down her neck to where his hand rested loosely on the neck of her shirt.

Sharlin's heart began to pound. She knew what he was going to do next, and then next, and then next. And when she lay exposed to them, would they even notice she was a woman—or care? They were going to kill her anyway.

"Please," she said. "Please." Under her rib cage, next to her thumping heart, Dar's pouch lay like a fist.

"I paid as much for you as a horse," said Kalander. "Shouldn't I be given the chance to mount you?"

Her knees felt weak. She had nothing, nothing with which to defend herself. She looked wildly about the room. There was nothing she could grab if even she could get away from Jack. But the master stepped forward, and she was sandwiched roughly between them. Front and back, she could feel their hard arousals even through her clothes. "Please," she said again, her voice barely above a whisper.

Kalander's hand moved, whip-fast, and ripped her veil away. He sucked in his breath. "Gods, what eyes. So blue! So this is what has been hidden away from me." Greedily his hand roamed the shirt covering her breasts. "What are you, pallan? Do you suckle your young like we do? Will you enjoy the two of us? Do you fuck like we do?" He put his hand at her throat again and fabric began to rend.

A booming voice split the air. "Master Kalander, I think not."

The two men moved so quickly Sharlin hit the floor at their feet. She clawed at the planks in an effort to crawl away. Crimson cloak filled the front door of the manor house, a crimson cloak and voice like a thunderbolt.

Kalander went to his knees. "Telemark! You are early, exalted one."

"And you, I see, are embroiled in sin again. Jack, get out of here. This is between men."

The overseer stumbled from the house and his passage let in fresh air and retainers. They crowded the hall of the manor. Sharlin groped for her veil, found it,

and tried to pull it over her mask so that even her eyes
and mouth would not be exposed.

The dragonpriest was gangly, his height towering
over her. His eyes blazed with an anger that was
religious. His hair, when he dropped his vermilion
hood, was straw blond. He looked down at her. "Tell
her who I am, Kalander."

"Shar, this is the High Priest of Baalan," said the
master, in a voice still shaken, stripped now of all its
lust, quaking in its guilt. He got to his feet.

"And now tell her why I've come."

"He's come," Kalander said, and swallowed heavily, "to take his tithes for the Temple at Geldart."

He looked at her. Veil and mask or not, his eyes
blazed down, and she shrank before them. He was
more than a high priest. She felt the sorcery coursing
in him and tried hard, very hard to be small and
insignificant before him.

"What does this pallan do for you besides amuse
you?"

"She is my household manager."

"You do his accounting and prepare his scrolls for
him?" The high priest turned first his blazing attention
on one and then the other.

She hardly dared speak. "Yes."

"What will you do for me if I make sure Kalander
never bothers you again?"

"I—" Words failed her. Kalander shifted his weight
in agitation, guilt fleeing and anger returning.

"Would you give me the correct household accounts
instead of the falsified ones he had you prepare?"

Kalander's breath hissed in. "I never—"

"Quiet!" The dragonpriest looked down at her.
"Well, would you?"

Mahbray had died in the night, and Anya was gone.
There was no one here to help her. She was alone and
one day, Kalander and Jack would try again. His

death was a burden she could bear. She nodded. "Yes, holy one,"

"All right. Retrieve the scrolls."

Kalander made a move as if to stop her when she scrambled to her feet and fled upstairs to the bedroom where he kept his accounts, but she was past before even the high priest could fling out an arm to stop him. With hands that would not stop shaking, she searched the desk until she found what the dragonpriest required. She brought them downstairs and interrupted the two talking. Or rather, Telemark was talking and Kalander was listening.

". . . handfasting calls for a blessing of the highest rank priest available. With the Night of Dragons so close to commencement, I myself will be in attendance at Geldart. You could hardly ask for a beginning so auspicious. Contain yourself, Kalander, and think on what I've told you." His attention flickered to her. "Ah. Give them to me."

She laid the scrolls in the dragonpriest's hand. He snapped fingers about them. "Good." He looked over Sharlin's head at the oddly quieted Kalander who seemed resigned to his fate. "I'll take the first of the tithes now." He slipped an arm about Sharlin's waist and shifted her over to his retainers, who gathered her up.

"What—" A heavy hand stifled her surprise. Telemark's hand moved in a becharming and she could not speak.

Kalander's smirking face swam through her view. "Just desserts, my dear. We are both betrayed. You will be one of the privileged to die for Baalan."

Sharlin could not get her scream past her teeth as the retainers carried her outside.

A black dragon coiled in the drive, flanked by two griffens. The retainers stood her long enough to shackle her wrists and ankles. The dragon snaked his head about to watch with smoldering red eyes. Telemark came striding out, the household scrolls tucked neatly into his sash. He signaled for the retainers to loosen the ankle irons. "She will ride in the saddle in front of me," he said.

"Yes, mighty one," the retainers answered. They stank of griffen. Her eyes brimmed at the thought of the beasts perverted to the use of the dragonpriests. She was swung through the air and tied within the riding leathers. Telemark settled in behind her. The dragon got to his feet and stretched his wings.

Telemark turned her face to meet his. With a smile he ripped away both veil and mask. His smile grew wider. "For all his perversions, " the high priest said, "this is one he only imagined. Why a woman of your beauty would hide behind a pallan's mask, I can only guess. But my lord Baalan will know—oh, yes, there is not a secret hiding in your lovely body that he will not know before he drinks your blood."

Chapter 24

Telemark kicked off Pevan and stroked the black dragon. "You've done well," he said. He stretched weary muscles as priests in the courtyard came running. "Take her down to a single cell. Keep her clean, give her good food and water. Remember, she is Baalan's," he ordered and watched the woman dressed as a pallan marched away.

He stripped off his riding gloves and slapped them against his falroth breeches. Dust in the courtyard rose as Pevan took off again, his dark form shielding sun and cloud from view for a moment. The trip had been a long one, three days in transit, to allow the griffens to keep up with the dragon. In all that time, he'd had not one word from the woman but a glare from her clear blue eyes.

Baalan would be pleased with her, very pleased, not just because he enjoyed the blooding of human flesh but because this woman reeked of Turiana—carried the resonance of the golden dragon as nothing else he'd ever encountered. Telemark put aside his fatigue from the long flight. An acolyte bowed, took his cloak, and kept stride with him as he entered the fortress.

"Bring me lyrith and tea," the high priest ordered. "And then leave me to my meditations."

"Will you be speaking with our lord?"

Telemark looked at the inquisitive acolyte. "I am always speaking with our lord," he said shortly.

The minor priest went to his knees and then his face right there in the stairwell, knowing too well from Telemark's tone that he had angered. "Forgive me, Telemark. I am not worthy for this service."

The high priest paused over the acolyte's body. He looked out one of the narrow slit windows of the tower. The fortress had just been finished. It was primarily a storage center for the food and excess sacrifices to be taken into the Temple at Geldart. From the view he selected, the mountain range with the temple carved into it like a polished jewel could just be seen. The view overruled Telemark's anger. He placed a booted foot on the small of the man's back where, if he so wished, he could crack the spine.

But he did not. Having reminded the acolyte of his vulnerability, Telemark took his foot away and said mildly, "We are all unworthy. We all must constantly strive to be worthy. You had a reason behind your question."

"We've had word of the desecration at the Gates. I have had sightings here, high one."

"Sightings?"

"Errant dragons."

"Oh?" Telemark mulled that one. "Looking us over, eh?" He and Baalan were always looking for the few strays outside his influence. There was a natural attrition within the dragon order. Even the faithful occasionally died of the wasting sickness so that new blood could be brought in. It was Baalan's way of keeping the naturally contentious dragons in line. "Thank you for giving me this information. I will tell his greatness. Now see to my comfort," he finished and watched the acolyte scramble away.

The coming Night would draw every major dragon within flight of Geldart, Baalan being the greatest and foremost. Telemark would have ample time to look them all over, to mark their true nature for what it was. Old Baalan might view this coming ritual as his rejuvenation, but there would come a day when there was not enough blood in all of Rangard to cleanse him. When that day happened, Telemark intended to be very close. There were others with similar thoughts. He had seen them burning in the eyes of a man called Third, who had been left behind at Rilth. And then there was the geas Baalan had given him: to find and destroy the golden dragon. How close would this woman lead him? Telemark entered his chambers with deep and troubled thoughts.

Sharlin stood and chafed her wrists as soon as the shackles were taken off. She watched them shut the heavy planked door. As soon as they'd gone, she was at the window, kicking up to reach it and holding to the bars with hands gone pins and needles and letting the fresh air wash her face. When she could hold on no longer and see no more, she dropped to the straw. It was clean, at least, and they'd left her laving basins as well as a chamber pot. The cell held a cot, a chair, and table. The table bore a tray of food. She thought of ignoring its savory smells, but she knew that if Telemark wanted her drugged, it would probably be in the water. Food she could ignore but her body craved water already. Flight always left her dry-mouthed.

She sat down at the table and buried her face in her hands. The tears that had come so easily weeks ago now seemed dry and stale. With a sigh, she dropped her hands. Above the laving basin was a peg. A soft woolen blue gown hung from it. Not the height of fashion, but warm and clean. The invitation was obvious and she was a fool to resist. Turning an empty bowl over her plate to keep her food warm, she got up from the chair and went to the laving basin. It was full of scented, steaming water, and two pitchers beside it held more. She did not think she would ever feel clean again, but it was worth a try.

A simple bowl could not perform miracles. Her dinner was cold by the time she kicked her worn and dusty pallan clothing into the corner and sat down to eat. Her hair lay damp along her neck and her face felt strangely naked to the wintry breeze now licking in from the window. She belted Dar's pouch to the cobalt blue sash at her waist as if it were a bag of precious coin. Then Sharlin turned her table and chair so that she could meet the breeze head on. With its unfriendly cold it also carried the last slanting rays of the afternoon. She ate to an uncanny quiet in the cell—she might be the only prisoner in the wing for all she knew—punctured only by the occasional challenging trumpet of a dragon.

A goblin guard came and took her dishes and her basins, bringing a pitcher of water for the night. He said nothing to her, but flashed his tusks.

"May I have a candle?" she asked.

She got his back for an answer. Reminded that she was still a captive, she walked the cell until the last fading light from her window had fled and it was too dark to walk without stumbling. Then she sought her cot and lay down upon it.

Guards might be bribed, but she had nothing to bribe them with. Dar had never adorned her with rings or jewels. She remembered comparing him once to flint, rather than gems himself. And if he was flint, what was she? The spark ignited? The spark that still held dragonlight within it?

Sharlin folded her hands over her stomach as if to keep that wintry wind from blowing out the spark. If she had no weapons without, then she would have to reach for that within. Closing her eyes, she fell into a sleep and dreamed again of broken wings and falling dragons.

Telemark jolted out of his meditations. Like a blade falling across his spell and severing it, a silver bolt had disrupted the dark purple bridge of his communication with Baalan. He searched for the intruder and could not find it—but again, he heard the echo of Turiana and knew instinctively who the enemy had to be. He had nearly finished with Baalan and decided not to resume his message for the cost had exhausted him as it was. As for the dragonlord, Telemark doubted he would even have noticed the intrusion. He would chide Telemark for being peremptory and that would be that.

He pulled an empty scroll down and began to ink his instructions on it for the staff. Baalan would be leaving his stronghold at Rilth and crossing the straits in six days. The Temple at Geldart was to be readied for him. In the morning he would send the contingent of dragons at hand to check the preparations inside the mountain as well as acolytes to go over the temple itself. As for the woman, Baalan had been well pleased. She was to be kept in good condition for questioning.

The last thing Telemark did was write down instruction for the latest wagon load of offerings. He would be pleased to get the children out of the way. The one boy, a pleasant-featured sturdy lad, had no hesitation in standing up for his rights. He had even faced down Pevan, who had stolen him from a group of pallans who were, no doubt, hiding him for a wealthy family trying to avoid a Taking. The dragon had been more amused than annoyed by the child, but had Taken him anyway.

Telemark dusted the scroll and blew it dry, then rolled it up and left it for his secretary. He would sleep well this night in spite of intruders.

Dragonwings woke her in the morning. She kicked and shinnied her way to the rim of the window and watched them leave, flashing their brilliant scales and bating their wings against the sunrise. She wondered what their mission could be. Two black dragons stood on the far ramparts, then one of them took leave as well, winging a different direction taking it immediately from her view.

The stone tore at her fingers. Unable to hold herself up any longer, she dropped back down to the floor. Sharlin pondered how the knowledge might help her. Could the goblins be superstitious? Did they, perhaps, fear she might have sorcerous powers of her own? Would they be skittish with most of the fortress defenders gone? She put her fingers to her throat, lightly touching the mark of her house. No help there without enough bloodshed to seriously weaken herself. And even then, she had no idea what help the demonic Dhamon might bring with him. Gale-force winds to destroy the keep? She ran as great a risk as anyone getting buried in the rubble.

She stopped pacing and sat upon the cot. *Oh, Turiana,* she thought. *If only you could hear me.* She thought again of the spark within her. What would fan that spark into a fire, dragonfire, so that no one could keep her captive?

The goblin guard that brought her breakfast was different from the one the night before. An ugly sword wound had severed one bat-like ear from its head. It brought in a tray of breakfast and day foods. It scowled at her as she dared a step closer.

"Shtay away," it said, its immense tusks slurring its speech.

Sharlin moved her hands in what could only be charming. The beast froze in its steps.

"Th' mashter ssays you be kept ssafe. But accidents shappen. Do no witschery on me!"

The belligerent warning left her little doubt that the goblins wouldn't be frightened of her. She stepped back into the corner until it finished its chores and left, after gnashing its tusks fearsomely at her. It was, undisputably, the winner of the who's frightening who contest. Sharlin sat down ruefully and ate her portion of breakfast. The painful bruise upon her cheekbone had nearly healed, but chewing a dried greenfruit carried a reminder with it. She pressed her fingers to her face. Dar would kill the man who marked her.

Time weighed heavily on her hands. By the time the window light warmed her cell, she was restless. The sound of boots pounding through her corridor brought her to her feet and at the barred window at the door. Goblins, heavily armed and armored, running past. She heard a dragon's loud trumpet, and then a bellow, followed by more trumpeting and screeching. The scent of smoke filtered into her cell.

Sharlin pounded on the door as the smoke grew thicker. "Let me out! Fire! Fire! Let me out!"

She dragged her table to the tower window and pulled herself up to the window ledge again. Dragons circled, battling, clawing, and screeching. The lower walls below were aflame, smoke billowing upward. Baalan's followers warred fiercely with one another, heedless of the damage they inflicted upon the fortress.

Sharlin coughed. Already her throat felt tight and raw. There must be a fire within the wing. If she could just get out—she would have a chance of escaping in the panic. She watched the immense bronze bull and black one bait each other, jaws snapping and wings sculling frantically to keep themselves aloft.

The black began to throw sorcery. A thunderbolt split the sky with a roar. The very tower shook under the reverberation and she could see the bronze tumble through the air. It regained itself and struck back, not magically, but with brute force and cunning. Another thunderbolt struck, its explosion throwing Sharlin from her perch. She landed heavily upon the strawed floor and lay a moment, gasping for air.

The tower quivered. She heard the scrape of talons

outside her window. One of the battling dragons coiled itself there!

Sharlin staggered to her feet. She could hear its panted breath and smell the heat of its serpentine body. The talons scraped again—and her window was torn wide open!

Half the wall crumbled under the dragon's clutch. Sharlin pressed herself to the door of her cell. The beast whuffled and shoved its muzzle inward.

Silvery scales dazzled her eyes. She threw up a hand and then realized that this was not one of the beasts warring ferociously over the courtyard. She looked into its eyes. Benign interest met hers. It shoved a forepaw through, raking aside the stone and mortar as if it were sand and pebbles.

It extended the paw to her.

"Gods help me," Sharlin said. She took a step forward. The metallic toes pricked and gathered her, dragging her across the cell toward the dragon's mouth.

Then it tightened its grasp about her suddenly and with a powerful leap, launched itself from the crumbling tower, her body in its talons.

Chapter 25

"Is it safe?"

"Nothing, " the pallan said lowly, "is ever truly safe in Geldart. But the innkeeper has helped before and we've observed a lot of renegade activity coming in and out. And, dragonpriests avoid the place like the plague."

"It has possibilities, then," grunted Mwork. He shouldered Dar. "You're a convincing drunk."

"I try," the swordsman replied weakly. "I think I'm bleeding again."

"We'd better get you off your feet, then. It's the Broken Back for us." Mwork looked to the pallans who'd led them from the Gates across Baalan's wretched peninsula, and then across the straits to Geldart. "Are we farewelled, then?"

"No, sir goblin." Silreen looked about the fog-shrouded wharf. "We'll be meeting with you by and by. But the innkeeper already has a heavy burden to bear. We don't want to add to it if Baalan's spies are watching the place."

Mwork nodded in agreement. He watched them fade away on the wharf, almost like puffs of smoke. For a soldier used to their legendary meekness, the sight of armed and decisive pallans was almost a revelation. "All right then," he said to Dar. "I'll take most of your weight. Stay with me."

The swordsman could not answer. Mwork was as

good as his word and upheld most of Dar's weight as they crossed the foggy wharfs and made their way into the back streets of Geldart, where a city feasted and awaited the Night of Dragons. They found the Broken Back easily and staggered in. Mwork found the innkeeper at his bar and slapped a gold half crown down in front of him.

"My friend and I are here for the festivities."

The innkeeper was a dour looking man, with pinched lips, half an eyebrow missing, and bloodshot gray eyes. "Looks like you've not been missing any."

"I won't be sleeping in the streets!" roared Mwork. "Have you a room or not?"

The innkeeper did not flinch at the goblin's anger. For that, alone, he won respect from Mwork. The man, however, looked the two of them over. "I don't," he said slowly, "see too many goblin and human partners."

Mwork lifted his lips off his teeth. "We're free swords," he said. "Do you like the money or not?"

The innkeeper palmed the half crown neatly. "It's likable enough. It'll buy you four days. Where do you intend spending the other three?"

"There's more where that came from," Mwork lied. "Bed, meals, and drink?"

"Bed and meals. If you want drink, you pay as you go."

"Fair enough."

The innkeeper gave him a latchkey. Without batting a gray eye, he leaned over the counter and said quietly, "And your friend needs patching up. How came he by those wounds?"

Mwork cursed silently, for the wounds had indeed broken open if the innkeeper could see new bloodstains. He thought of what the pallans had told him. He leaned forward and lowered his coarse voice. "We took exception to a dragonpriest."

The innkeeper nodded slowly. "I'll send someone up to help you, later." He straightened and said loudly, "And no brawling in the premises."

Mwork growled at that and headed for the back stairs. He found his room, marked by the hexcharm on both the door and the latchkey. Grinding his teeth at the superstitions of humans, he knocked twice and entered.

Dar was limp in his arms when he laid him down on bed. Mwork took his face in hand and turned it carefully from side to side. All softskins looked pale to him, but the swordsman's was definitely sickly. The goblin secured the door and returned to his charge. He worked the mail coat off and could smell the metallic yet sweet scent of red blood. Good goblin blood smelled like the forge itself, poured out black and smoked when spilled. Softskin blood was like that of a gunter or woolie. The goblin smiled grimly. *Good eating,* he thought and opened the shirt. The bandages had crusted and fresh blood spilled through. Also, the thigh wound had slickened Dar's breeches wetly. Not good.

There was a soft knock at the door. Mwork opened it, glaring, and readjusted his sight to a gnarled dwarf woman who stood with a basket in her hands.

"Lykon sent me. I be Frieda." She shoved her way in past his kneecap, pulled up a stool, and hoisted her firm bottom onto it. "Nasty-looking. Who cut him?"

"None of your business." Mwork slammed the door shut and joined her.

Her busy hands paused in their rummaging of the basket of medicinal supplies. "Maybe Lykon wus wrong."

"Maybe," the goblin said.

Her fingers wove a pattern in the air. Mwork worked his jaws but nothing came out. He choked until his eyes bulged.

"That's a truthspell," Frieda said triumphantly, "Tell me no lies and you kin talk."

"Then I won't talk," Mwork got out. She made a fist and tears rolled from his eyes. "All right." She loosened her fist. He gulped for air. "Pallans sent us."

"They did?" Her round brown eyes rolled in consideration. Bow to the dragons?"

He spat on the floor.

She smiled widely. "All right then. Good enough. Run downstairs and get me some boiling water. Hot enough to scald the hair off a woolie, understand?"

He nodded. If he'd had any reservations about leaving Dar alone with her, the cooing she made as she touched his fevered brow soothed them. A goblin had to trust to luck, sometimes.

Lykon was waiting for him with two pitchers, one of beer and the other steaming with hot water.

"How can I express my thanks," asked Mwork dryly.

The dour man smiled. "Don't mention it."

Frieda was waiting impatiently at the door. She yanked the beer from his hand, took a hearty chug of the pitcher, gave it back, and took the hot water. With a mustache of foam still upon her lip, she poured the water into a basin and sprinkled dried buds upon it.

"Lyrith," she said. "It has a virtue."

A pleasant aroma filled the tiny room. Dar stirred upon the cot. "Sharlin?" he murmured.

Frieda smoothed his hair back from his forehead. "Who's that?"

"His wife," he said.

"Ah." She patted Dar's hand. "Husht, now." She dipped a clean rag into the water and began to bathe the scum-edged cuts. She rolled a dwarfish eye at Mwork. "He'll be a-right, hardhead. Sit down and pass me sum suds before it gets warm."

Dar opened his eyes. He caught sight of the dwarf

woman first, and then, squinting, saw Mwork. "Where
are we?"

"Th' Broken Back. Among friends, maybe. We've
not much choice."

"How long," Dar said, grasping the woman's wrist,
"until the Night?"

She was left no doubt as to what he meant. "A
week, sir,"

Dar let go of her and went limp on the cot. "I must
be up and wielding a sword by then."

Frieda twisted on her stool and looked wide-eyed at
Mwork. He nodded. "You heard him, stumpy. You'd
better start healing."

"Tch" was all she answered, and threw more lyrith
into the bowl.

The wind howled through the dragon's talons. Sharlin
wrapped herself about the thumbclaw even though the
beast kept his paw curled tightly. She stung in several
places. The cold pierced her like a sewing needle. She
would have screamed, but no one would have heard
her.

The dragon was young. He did not have the strength
and bulk of the great bronze who'd been fighting the
black. Her legs hung through his fist and her hair
streamed in the wind. He dipped and sailed over the
crags and valleys, catching thermals that would not
have tolerated a greater beast. Her weight, she knew,
dragged him down. As one bird will steal a crumb
from another, and then fly the length of the meadow
to eat in peace, so she'd been stolen and carried off.
He'd have a frozen meal if he flew much higher, she
thought wryly as her teeth began to chatter uncontrol-
lably.

They flew into the night and then into the morning
of the next day. He ate on the fly, snatching up
whurrlies in midflight, gulping them down, raining ex-

cess feathers upon Sharlin. His flight became ragged. She could hear his chest heaving in sobbing breaths. He would kill himself and her with him. She could feel his flagging strength and when he came to an awkward one-legged landing, she didn't know if it was because they had reached some mysterious, undefined destination or he was simply hungry or too tired to fly further. She crawled out of his paw and tried to stand. Her legs felt like frozen sticks. Her boots were stiff with the cold.

He curled his wings up and huddled, panting and miserable, upon the rocky ledge. He'd chosen one out of the wind, with a cupped kind of natural hollow to it. The sandstone was striated red and amber behind him, setting him off like a silver nugget. He turned gem blue eyes on her.

She stood transfixed in his sight for a moment, then shook herself. "Eat me and get it over with," she said. "At least I won't be cold anymore."

He did not seem to notice her any longer. He reared up, bolstered himself on one unfurled wingtip, and searched the skies. She looked, too. There seemed to be nothing major alive in this section of wilderness. She looked across the sweep of a valley cut out of the stone. A deep blue jewel of a lake reigned to the southernmost end. It was a long fall down.

She started to scurry toward the tag end of a trail leading toward the valley. If the beast heard her, he no longer cared, either. Sharlin stopped, puzzled. She clapped her hands. The noise thunderclapped. He did not react.

Sharlin approached him. She tugged roughly on his sail. He snapped peevishly at her, but no sound issued from his throat, though she must have startled him.

He resettled himself after giving her a hurt look and continued to scan the skies.

And, like the bronze, he was undoubtedly magicless.

From where had he come to rescue her? Did he do it knowingly? Why hadn't he passed the Gates where all dragons earned their sorcery?

"Who are you and where did you come from?" Sharlin said, as he put a wing protectively about her and gathered her in from the raw wind.

There was a sound of dragonwings and the ledge trembled as another beast landed. The silver creature released her as Turiana settled and said, "This one is mine. He comes from the eggs Aarondar helped me lay . . . and he is deaf and dumb and without magic unless I can somehow get him past the Gates. Even then, I do not know if he will be given hearing and a voice. So tell me, fair daughter. Did he do well rescuing you?"

It was warmer by the lake. Turiana warmed the rock they sat on with the furnace of her own body. They watched as the silver dragon tracked and pulled down a whitebuck and devoured it greedily, then joined them. The silver seemed to appreciate it as much as Sharlin as he settled upon the rock. She looked at the beautiful creature. "Can't he stay warm?"

"Not the way I do. It's sorcery that does this, just as it's sorcery that helps us to fly tirelessly or ignite the gases from our breath into dragonfire. He cannot hum to charm the softfoot and gunter. He cannot soar high enough to attract a mate when his time comes. All the life he has is before you."

"But he's young. He can't be more than—what four or five years old?"

"About that. He went through his strider period quickly. He was always quick and agile."

The silver watched her face and then Turiana's as if he guessed they spoke about him. There was a quickness about his face and eyes. She stretched a hand out and he took it gently between his fangs.

"Turiana, I don't know very much about dragons, but I do know that he can't have hatched only a few years ago."

"I bespelled them. I put on the eggs a charm to hold them as long as I could. He's one of the last. I still have a gold and that oddly mottled one left."

"That's all?"

"There was a bronze helping Silver, was there not?"

"Yes. He was a magnificent beast."

"That is Turan. He and Silver are the only ones left alive." Turiana watched as Sharlin carefully withdrew her hand. The gold put her muzzle close to her and looked her over. "You have suffered," she said.

"Only a little." Sharlin put her chin up. She would not take pity from anyone, not even the dragonqueen. She put her hand on her sash to reassure herself that Dar's pouch was still lashed there.

"Where is Aarondar?"

"I don't know. He was on the way to the Gates. He thought—he thought you had stolen Fort in order to bring him there and force him to help you."

The dragon tilted her head. "A thought," she said. "One more worthy of Baalan than myself. No, I decided to let destiny take its own toll of you and yours. Where, then, is your child?"

"I don't know."

"Did the dragonpriests take him?"

Sharlin shook her head. "No. Pallans stole him, although why, I don't know. I tried to follow—there was that inside of me which seemed connected to him, and tugged me after. But the pallans used it to deceive me. They led me astray."

"Pallans did this? Who and which nation?"

"I don't know. But I agree with you . . . whoever would have thought the pallans would move so openly? I hid among another tribe and that, too, was disaster. How did you find me?"

Turiana paused. She rumbled deep in her throat, as if mulling over a distasteful memory. "I have spent many years as guardian to a clan of pallans and one unfortunate day, left my post. My wards had grown feeble. The valley was raided. Only Silver here was left, and he could not defend them. Many were Taken. I have been searching for them since, when I could do so without attracting notice. I found one of them several days ago along the Vandala River, another like unto you, a fair daughter called Anya. She lived long enough to send me after you."

Sharlin's feelings were bittersweet. "I'm sorry," she whispered.

"I think you should tell me your whole story from the beginning. There is much I don't know and we have time for the weaving of a tale."

And so Sharlin told her story, with Turiana making sympathetic coos at appropriate places and dragonish anger at others. She finished by folding her hands in her lap, saying, "And where either Dar or Fort is today, or even if they're alive, I don't know. But I think they live. I hope I'd feel it if they didn't."

The silver dragon put its head up and made a rattling with its spines, and then entwined his neck about with his mother's. Turiana looked thoughtful. "He says that there was a boy child in the wagons this morning who loved the dragons flying overhead."

"He says? How does he say anything? What is he talking about? What wagons?"

"He can send me a few thoughts now and then. I have a picture of wagons leaving the fortress near the temple at Geldart. He and Turan were watching this morning before trying to free you." The golden dragon closed her eyes. "I'm sorry, princess. Fort is indeed the boy who loved the dragons flying overhead."

Her voice strained as she tightened her hands and

tried to keep calm. "What wagons, Turiana? Where were they going?"

"They were taking victims to the temple."

Sharlin felt as though her face would crack trying to release tears, but she still could not let them flow. "If you had not rescued me," she said slowly. "I would have been with Fort. I would have found him! Take me back."

"Even if all you could do is share his doom?"

"Even then."

Turiana shook her head. The silver appeared agitated and bated his wings. He trumpeted soundlessly. Sharlin could feel his frustration keenly.

"The boy is safe until Night falls six days hence. If you wish to expend your life, fair daughter, do it here, where it can be of some help."

"What do you mean?" Sharlin sat down slowly. "Why did you want Fort? Is Dar right . . . that you intended to sacrifice him yourself."

"Yes."

There was regret and even shame in the great dragon's voice.

Sharlin's heart felt as though it turned in her chest. She hid her face from the dragon's for a moment, uncertain of which emotions it showed. Not until she was sure of what her face and voice revealed would she look up. "How could you have asked that of me?"

Turiana stretched out a claw. She drew idly upon the grass bank of the lake. "I felt," the creature answered, "that it was the only way for Silver to gain his powers. I felt it was necessary not only for him—but for all of Rangard. Turan is strong enough to fight, magical or not. With Silver by his side, I could perhaps leave a legacy of hope . . . a dawn to follow the Night of Dragons. There is still a chance, Sharlin. We could rescue your son if we were strong enough."

Sharlin met the dragon's eye. She could see the fatigue within Turiana, like some ponderous burden she must carry. Then, she understood the dragon's desperation. "You have the wasting sickness."

"Yes. I have had it for some time. My strength is limited, my spells feeble. While Baalan is renewed again, I can only dwindle."

"What choice do we have?"

"If you would willingly exchange yourself for your son. Not in Telemark's grasp, but within mine."

Sharlin swallowed tightly. She did not understand all that Turiana spoke of, but she knew that to save Fort, she would have to give her very life. She reached out and grasped the talon that etched symbols into the ground. "All that I can give is yours, if you promise to try to rescue Fort later."

"Done, " said Turiana proudly and sadly. "And well done, fair daughter."

Chapter 26

They took a day of rest, for Silver's fine-boned frame fairly quivered with exhaustion, and Sharlin ached in every joint. She and Turiana took walks about the rock-rimmed canyon and talked about old times, adventures and times they had shared with one another. Then, when night fell, the golden dragon built a nest for her of evergreen boughs and sweet wildflowers and hummed her to sleep. She fell under the charming with Silver lying down next to her, her hand delicately held in his jaws.

She awoke from a dream of Dar and lovemaking, her face still flushed with the memory, to a stillness broken only by songbirds. Neither dragon could be seen. She got up and walked to the lake where she shed her boots and woolen dress, and bathed in icy water. She scrubbed her hair as well as she could. It had grown back to shoulder length. She dried it ferociously, with her dress for a towel, and the golden strands crackled with an energy all their own. She put the damp dress on, shivering slightly with the cold of it, and leaned over the water to watch it still.

She critically looked at her reflection. The girlish features were gone, never to return. There were lines about her eyes and gentle, subtle ones at the corners of her mouth. There was wisdom instead of daring and sorrow instead of anticipation. But she thought it was a face Dar could recognize and still love.

"How does it feel," she asked her reflection, "to wake on the last day of your life and know it?"

Before it could answer her, she dashed her portrait away.

A shadow blacked out the sun overhead. Sharlin looked up and saw the dragons circling, spiraling downward. Turiana landed with an awkward gait and Sharlin saw the age and weakness in the creature. It saddened her already melancholy mood. Silver flowed into the canyon like liquid fire, his brilliant blue eyes alive with excitement.

Turiana approached Sharlin and nudged her, gently breathing out warm air. "You're dampish," the dragon said.

"O great observer," Sharlin teased. "I bathed."

The nostrils flared and Turiana whuffed several more times, each gust of hot air drying her a little more. "Am I reduced to this," the dragon asked, "a bag of hot air to assure you comfort?"

"You could let me shiver."

"And catch your death of cold?"

Their banter stopped abruptly. Sharlin said lowly, "That was not a good choice of words." She turned to Silver and pulled a blue-gray whisker. "And you look in fine mettle this morning, sir." Then, to Turiana, "Where have you been?"

"Taking word to the elder of Anya of her fate and praising her courage."

"I'm glad," Sharlin said. "She deserved to be remembered by her brethren."

"She will be." Turiana flicked a look at her dragonson. "Have you eaten yet?"

"The grass looked a little green yet for me."

"Silver has brought back cakes and tea for you."

The dragon shyly uncurled his paw, revealing bulging packs. Sharlin grabbed them up. There was clean clothing as well as food for several meals. The honey cakes peeled away stickily from a napkin and Sharlin ate one greedily. She rolled her eyes.

"I think I dreamed of these last night." She licked her lips. Silver looked at her with eager eyes. "Beggar," she said, and gave him one of the cakes, though it would hardly have been more than a crumb to him.

Turiana remarked, "He has always been fond of sweets. Break your fast, Sharlin, and then we must talk."

Sharlin walked to the clearing where a small fire was banked. She began to rekindle it, to warm the jug of tea. "Go ahead, I'm listening . . . it's not going to get any easier," she added gently.

The two dragons hunkered down, the flames of the fire reflecting in their eyes as she prepared her meal. Silver got another honey cake—the pallans had sent half a dozen and she was not about to eat herself sick. "Tell me," Sharlin said, sitting down and making a tent out of her dress about her knees. "What have you learned about the rites?"

"Blood rites," Turiana answered. "Awful and torturous. Not long after our departure, a child of the East approached Baalan. She told him of ways to institute his rule as well as banish the wasting sickness. Where she devised her plan, I know not. To the East is another land, and a crimson dragon reigns there. Her mind is closed to me and she does not allow trespass. Perhaps she also rules in blood. At any rate this human child, Wendeen, became Baalan's high priestess. The sacrifices became ritual as well as necessary. Pallans and goblins serve those dragons of minor power. Humankind is preferred by the dragons of greater power."

Sharlin pinched off a strip of smoked gunter and chewed it reflectively. She shook her head. "That can't be all. How can blood cleanse away the wasting sickness?"

"Since none survive, it has taken me years to discover even now . . . I am not certain. But the powers we receive from our passage beyond the Gates are powers that pallans have put aside. This, I think, is what happens. The offered victim is given those powers. Then, the victims are slain, their death cleanses the magic, and the powers snatched back by the dragonholder."

"But how cleansed? Is it the dying that does it?"

"I don't know. And it also appears to me that many victims are necessary to filter away the sickness. But work it does—look at Baalan and his minions. They have survived far longer than any dragon could with the disease."

Sharlin sat thoughtfully for so long that Silver could no longer resist the last honey cake resting on her palm. His long, ash-colored tongue licked it away. She looked fondly at him. "Greedy," she said. She wiped her hand on her dress. She met Turiana's eyes. "Baalan is in trouble if anyone should realize what he's infused them with. Or if any of the other dragons realizes what he's doing."

"I think the elaborate ritual muddies those waters. From what I can gather, the ceremonies involve a great many steps. Even the dragons participate . . . there are drugs and other phases."

Sharlin felt sickened. "You must," she said firmly, "get Fort out of there."

"I have promised. You have my word we'll try."

"All right then." She set aside her jug of tea. "Before we begin, I ask one thing of you."

Just one?"

Her words threatened to fail her. She swallowed the ache back. "Be patient with me, great one. This pouch is Dar's—"

"As well I know."

"See that he gets it, when you bring him word of me."

Turiana's eyes glittered brightly. "I'll see that someone brings him word," she said. "I cannot guarantee that I will live much longer than you. It is magic that maintains me."

"But my death will cleanse it!"

"Yes, but I don't intend to take up my power. Silver must have it." Turiana looked to her descendant. "He is my hope for the future."

"I see." Sharlin stood. Not to her surprise, her hands trembled. "Make it quick. I—I'm afraid of hurting."

"My talons are ever sharp," the dragon reassured her. "You will not suffer. Why don't you lie upon your bed? There is lyrith among the wildflowers. Their scent will calm you."

Numbly Sharlin did as she was bid. She folded her arms over her stomach and tried not to think of what she faced. She took several deep breaths and remembered what it had been like the last time she shared dragonmagic with Turiana.

The golden dragonqueen loomed over her. "I cannot sing you into this sleep," she said mournfully.

"I know. I'm as ready as I can be." She coughed. "Fare thee well, Turiana, always."

The dragon lowered her head and Sharlin looked into her eyes. The world seemed nothing beyond those golden lanterns. She was swallowed whole.

The tide that engulfed her meshed them and there was no difference between woman and dragon. The rush of magic and the memory of other passages embraced both of them, she was Turiana and Turiana was she. In her thoughts the dragon gasped with pleasure and power . . . or was it she who gasped? She knew the river of Time and the flow of the sky . . . she owned dragonwings and Turiana birthed a human child

. . . let go she whispered to Turiana. *You must let go of them and give them to me.*

She felt the gushing of blood into her jaws at the moment of the kill. She arched her back in lovemaking and satisfaction. She rode a griffen into a sorcerous storm, and assayed the Abyss of Time into another age. But always she was paced by another, an aura of gleaming gold. *Let go, Turiana.*

And then she was alone.

She had the power. She was infused, she was fire and air dancing above the earth and seas. She could do whatever she wanted. She could save herself this death. She could look down and see her limp body upon the bower, braced by a dragon of silver and a dragon of gold. Sharlin knew she could strike out and protect herself from this sacrifice. Sorcery boiled in her blood.

The urge to strike like a ravening dragon or a vicious rock adder coiled in her. She wrestled with the power that ran through her in lightning strikes, melding her with fire and air and forces beyond her realization. She felt like a torch, consumed and yet an odd peace came over her as she hovered over the flesh that had been herself as well.

How tired I look and yet . . . how peaceful.

The golden dragon reared up with stately grace. She shook her crown of spines and the sun caught the molten sheen of her scales. Her claws came up. She wept, if a dragon could do such a thing. Sharlin sorrowed for her friend. She reached for Turiana to comfort her as the dragon put out a razor talon.

There was a rush. They swirled together briefly. Then Turiana disengaged in fury and with a keening cry.

"No!" she shouted. "I cannot. I have seen too much. Sharlin, you're with child. I cannot take two lives."

And Sharlin looked with amazement within herself

and saw the kernel of life perceived, life yet beginning these past three months and wept herself. A daughter lay curled within her womb.

Dragonmagic sucked her back into her body, swiftly and without mercy. She panted with the fire that raged in her flesh. She could not contain the power and Turiana would not thrust it from her. Now neither dragon had power, and she was being consumed by it.

She opened bleary eyes. Her voice husked through a fever-ridden body. "Turiana . . . I'm dying. Strike now."

She had not imagined the dragon's weeping. A great pale yellow tear shimmered from her eye and fell upon Sharlin's face. It could not cool her heated flesh. "I cannot, fair daughter. I cannot take both your lives. We will have to see what fate awaits us."

Chapter 27

"You walk like you've got a poker up your ass," Mwork snickered.

Dar turned stiffly and painfully and considered his fighting partner. He blinked slowly. "You're lucky I'm walking at all."

"Tell me a tale I haven't heard before. Stumpy's been telling me for days: 'lyrith has a virtue in't'." He grinned wickedly, having done a fair imitation of the dwarf healer's voice.

Dar put a hand to his ribs. The arrow wound in his back still ached horribly and he thought he could feel a wetness trickle down from it, but the rest of his injuries were scarring over. The street noise around them grew louder and Mwork moved alongside Dar to buffer him from the heavy and drunken foot traffic.

"The merrymakers are out in force," the swordsman commented.

"And why shouldn't they be? The dragonpriests have knocked open the kegs and thrown bags of grain into the streets. And they tell me silth is for the begging. And the greatest celebration is this—the Takings are over for the year. You see the feverish relief of the living." Mwork smacked his tongue along his tusks. "Wouldn't you dance too?"

"I'll stick to walking upright. How far do we go?"

"Two blocks down and then right to the Singing Adder. The jobman should be inside."

Dar nodded wearily. He had been practicing walking for two days—gods knew he should have it right by now—and his sword hung from his hip like a multitude of weights. A dragonpriest was hiring free swords for crowd control at the temple two nights hence. Mwork had found out through a lively goblin lass who was doing a fair amount of business at a local brothel and brought home the news with a smirk. If they were hired, it would solve at least one major problem of getting inside the temple. Once inside, he didn't intend on leaving until he had Baalan carved into mincemeat.

"Where's Silreen?"

"He said he'd meet us later. He didn't want to create a scene."

Dar nodded a second time. Even in this confusion, armed pallans would stick out like a walking headless man. Mwork leaned on him slightly and pointed. "There it is—the Singing Adder."

It looked as though it deserved its reputation. In the streets that intersected at its corner, footraces were being run. Dar noted with a raised brow that the racers were nude and the course lined with women carrying switches. The losers tended to invite blows urging them to catch up with the front-runners. All of this was done with a great deal of drinking and cheering and staggering. By the time they reached the inn, the race had changed again and this time the fully clothed were running—handicapped by carrying a wench over their shoulder.

Mwork stalled in the doorway, watching such a race. Dar pulled on his vest. "We've business inside."

"But the business outside is so peculiar," the warty goblin said. He rubbed his hairless pate. "I wonder what the hardheads are doing."

"Drinking and complaining, no doubt. Now where's that dragonpriest doing the hiring?"

Mwork stood up on his toes and cast a look about the dingy inn. "There," he said, and pointed to an even darker corner.

Dar started gingerly across the inn's interior which was filled with raucous drinkers and an off key piper's band. Food deemed not worthy of eating flew through the air with regularity. He ducked and weaved, and then pulled up short.

He knew the man wearing the crimson cloak who was sitting in the corner with an expression of bored tolerance. His hair had grown back and a prosperous costume covered it . . . but he knew the air of wounded superiority. He nearly turned heel.

Mwork bumped him, then caught him by the shoulders to steady him.

"What is it?"

"I know him," said Dar.

"Would he know you?"

Dar thought on that. He'd not know the silver helm, for he'd kept it covered by that silly straw hat Sharlin had hated. Nor would he know his face . . . having gone without hairroot for so long, his face had finally begun to sprout a soft, wispy blond beard. Both Mwork and the healer Frieda teased him on the boyishness of his new appearance. Finally, he said, "I don't know. I don't think so, but—"

"Then press on. He won't see what he's not expecting."

"What are his chances of recognizing *you*?"

"Not much if I don't recognize him and I don't."

Dar ducked a soggy tuber thrown through the air, and said, "Stay close in case there's trouble," and began to to cross the room.

Telemark sat watching the Geldartans drink themselves into stupors. He derived a kind of pleasure from it, for it had not been all that long ago that he had been forced to drink himself into stupors in order to enjoy a squalid life. Now he had sorcery and power and that was his joy, and he could no more afford to be in a stupor than he would jump headfirst down a dragon's throat. There were others jockeying for his position and influence with Baalan. It was a heady game and worth more, by far, than what he'd given up.

It was the game that drove him to this backwater den. His plans for Baalan entailed a certain amount of risk—risk that would be greatly lessened if he had a guard of his own, endowed with a certain sense of loyalty. *You get what you pay for,* he reminded himself. Swordsmen with loyalty would be hard to come by in any city, let along the dingier side of Geldart. Mayor Nicommen probably had bought up all the good men long ago.

His gaze narrowed as he spotted the two making his way from across the tavern. Goblin and human were an odd couple, indeed. He searched his memory for word of such a duo, found none and watched them approach. There was little doubt they were coming toward him—and they were dead sober.

Telemark consulted his power and found little remarkable about the two. The only thing extraordinary was the blade the swordsman carried and that only because it was a quality blade, metal the common fighter couldn't afford. Undoubtedly he had picked it up as spoils from a previous engagement. The high priest did not notice that his sorcerous inquiry slid off the two, as if repelled.

He dropped his gaze to his cup and took a sip of mulled wine. The sweetstick and spices were the only things that made his cup palatable. The pair reached his table by the time he set his drink down.

"Word is you're hiring swords."

"For the Night, that is correct." He kept his voice

bland. "Only the two of you? Or do you have a troop you feel comfortable with?"

The goblin and swordsman regarded each other. Then the man said, "We could pull in four more."

Telemark sniffed. He could not detect silth on either of them, another plus. He drummed his fingers upon the table. "What's your price?"

The goblin said, in gravelly tones, "What's the job?"

"The high priest needs a guard. The revelers tend to get boisterous at the rites. He is new to his position and the politics inside the priesthood—well, let's just say they're chancy."

"They're more than chancy if he can't ensure their loyalty." The swordsman scratched his beard. He looked young, but his eyes held experience. "What's the pay?"

"Four gold crowns each for the Night. And, if matters are satisfactory, you can expect a regular salary of a gold crown a month, plus room and board and other benefits."

"What can we expect?"

"A little jostling. You'll be at the main altar, elbow to elbow with the high priest and great Baalan himself."

A light flared in the swordsman's eyes. "What more could the faithful ask," he said softly.

Telemark cleared his throat. "Indeed." He stood. Even standing, the swordsman was taller. A feeling of déjà vu swept over Telemark, but the cogs of his plan were beginning to turn and he pushed the feeling away. "Can you vouch for the other four?"

"We can." The goblin, rumbling in irritation.

"All right then. Here's a gold crown each. They're cursed," Telemark warned, setting them into their palms. The two looked uneasily at the money. "Meet with the high priest at the first rising of the Shield on the Night, and the curse will be lifted, and you'll be paid the other three crowns. Agreed?"

Mwork rubbed a gnarled finger across the coin. "It feels greasy," he said.

Telemark smiled thinly. "Try to disappear with that in your pocket, and the high priest will hunt you down wherever you go."

"Don't worry," the blond told him. "We'll be there."

"Good," Telemark said. "Very, very good." He wrapped his cloak about him. When Baalan gave his powers to the first sacrifice, the boy Telemark had chosen, he would be at his most vulnerable. If all went as Telemark planned, when he usurped the powers, the dragon would be at his mercy. And, if the old beast still had snap left in his bite, well then, there would be six hired swords between him and the dragon's maw. The thought of that was heady, indeed.

"She cannot last much longer," Turiana said. She watched the woman upon the bier, her face in alabaster paleness, her hands weaving in useless signs upon the air. Food and drink she'd taken sparingly, but it was the sorcery eating her—and the golden dragonqueen knew she'd risked all, and lost. Silver rubbed his muzzle along her neck, as if knowing what she'd told him.

Turan had come and gone. He brought news that Arel had been cut down trying to pass the Gates. She'd sent the big bronze on this way, though he'd refused to go. His flanks were covered with the scars of his fight with Pevan. "Go," she'd pleaded with her son. "Go and try the Gates again someday when fortune smiles. To stay with us is to invite disaster for us all. You, at least, must live."

And he had left her then, her and his strange mute brother of the gem blue eyes, himself an aberration among dragons.

There was no hope left, and little time. Turiana put her sail over Silver's shoulders and noted that he had grown. He no longer fit neatly under her wing. How could she have missed that? Indeed, he threw his head up huffily and glared at her as if to say that he was adult now and too big to be coddled. She looked at him fondly. Who was to say what powers he might have invited if he had ever passed beyond the Gates? Or even what he might have accomplished if she could have passed her own talents onto him? She could have tried, but she did not want to see the wasting sickness drag him down, and it would have . . . it raged in her now and she grew weaker by the second. Sharlin and her son had been her only hope.

Still, Turiana gazed at the woman. She had gained much since the resurrection. This bit of flesh that weighed so lightly on her back whenever they had flown—this fragile life had given her a second lifetime, and given her dragonets to raise and bond with as no dragon had ever done before. Who is to say that all this had been futile or wasted?

"Sharlin," she whispered lowly. "Stay with me. Stay with me so that we can find Fort and fight together."

Such things she had whispered to the woman all through the days and nights of her fever. Nothing had helped. She was beyond lyrith and whispers. She was where only the gods could touch her, and Turiana was not of the sort who believed in gods. Only the small ones did.

She wrapped her tail about her and hunkered close. Sharlin burned like a bonfire and it was she who kept them warm.

Sharlin longed for tea and silth. The memory of cool sweet and pain-relieving drink surged down her throat, but when she swallowed—it was gone. Gone as if it had never been. She tossed and turned in her night-mares, reached for surfeit, and found none. The sorcery had her in its grip and would not let go.

Then the pains began in her stomach. Her womb

clenched fitfully. She could feel the frail purchase the child had begin to loosen. Sharlin came half-awake, batting her eyes against the glare of the sunlight, and tried to speak. Her bones ached as if poison coursed through every fiber. Turiana could not hear her. Silver could hear nothing.

"Help . . ." she rasped.

The golden queen lay near her, her wide eyes open and surveying the valley. What her thoughts were, Sharlin could not tell . . . and she could not gain her attention. Sweat plastered her hair to her face. She shivered and chattered in fever. The argent dragon turned his eyes to her as if drinking her in. She raised an unsteady hand and he took it, as had been his custom, gently with fangs that could slice her in two.

The dragonmagic wanted to feed on her. The life within her was feeding as well, and she could not sustain either. The life of her child was flickering like a torch in a high wind. For the babe to live, she must defeat the sorcery. Her stomach clenched in another spasm.

Or pass it on.

Without thought she gathered every ounce of strength available to her and thrust the witch power at the silver dragon.

He took it. He swallowed it and gulped for more, sucking at her hand as if it were a teat. She could feel the flowing river move through her and down her arm, a molten flow of energy that sparked and lashed as it flowed. Excess energy filled the silver dragon's jaws, sparkling and twinkling until Sharlin had to turn her gaze away. And then, nothing.

He held her hand but a moment longer. Then, with a massive convulsion, he reared back on his tail and clawed the air, wings thrashing. She was thrown from her bower, rolling underneath Turiana's flank. The dragonqueen trumpeted in alarm. Sharlin shaded her eyes at the splendor of the dragonlord, for lordly he had become, wildfire dancing up his silver scales and pouring forth from his jaws like music.

With a cry of jubilation the beast sprang into the air. An aura of blue and silver surrounded him as if he contained all lightnings. Impossible, he held himself in the air above them, wings flung up, head thrown up in triumph. And when he sounded his cry of elation, the very air shook.

Turiana seconded his cry, for her son was mute no more. She cradled Sharlin close. "What have you done?"

Sharlin clung to the dragonqueen's side with all of her feeble strength. "I gave him . . . the magic."

"And live?"

"I think so." She laid her cheek against the warm, feathery, soft-scaled throat of her friend. "There's no sickness in that wonder."

Turiana watched her dragonlord avidly as he began to soar above them in a fierce, triumphant conquest of the skies. "No," she said in awe. "The powers are clean and pure."

"We've done it."

"Yes."

The two stood close and watched in silence as the creature once deaf and dumb and magicless conquered the wind. Sharlin curled her hand over her stomach, where her womb relaxed and the babe seemed secure again.

Baalan flexed under the scented oiling. Suddenly, like a wire springing taut and then snapping, his universe echoed with the repercussion of dragonpower. He rolled to his feet. He bayed in triumph. What need had he for Telemark *now*, for here was Turiana. The flare of sorcery was like an explosion, though it be halfway round the world from him.

He summoned Atra. The big black came slithering down the rocks to him, silver eyes ablaze.

"I have found her," he said. He gave the black the echo of her location. "Pick up Pevan on your way across. Destroy her utterly.

The black dragon snapped in agreement and left. Baalan looked at the servant he had smashed upon the rocks inadvertently. Nothing could spoil the Night of Dragons now. It did not matter that a valuable prisoner had been lost. He had found the only enemy who could disconcert him. His power would be purified and refined and returned to him, and the vigil of seventy-five long years finished.

Nothing could stop him now.

Chapter 28

"Tomorrow the Night falls."

Sharlin flexed her back as she stood. The fever had left her pale and thin and still a bit shaky . . . and her tiny pout of a stomach that much more noticeable. The pallans had sent over more food, which Turiana had had to fetch because Nazar, as the silver named himself, was still so full of himself he was difficult to contain. Magic effused from him, sparks and rimfire fountaining from his very skin as he danced over the ground. He crackled like St. Elmo's fire through the air when he flew. She smiled in spite of all they faced. Take your triumphs wherever you can, Dar used to tell her. She looked at Turiana. "I'll be ready," she said.

"You'll leave at nightfall. You'll be chasing the sun across the continent, but you dare not leave earlier. Nazar must bring you to the temple when the doors are thrown open for all dragons to enter, not a heart-beat sooner. Baalan will be vulnerable only when he passes his power to his victim. Then and only then can you strike."

Sharlin smothered a smile as she answered, "I know, Turiana."

"I can't be there with you."

"I know."

"Do you?"

"Yes." She kissed the beast gently. "I know." The

dragonqueen leaned against her shoulder with a contented hum. "Your illness is gone."

"Yes, along with my magic. But I will grow strong
before I grow old. Retrieve Fort, and then we shall
find Aarondar. And then . . . I shall begin a quest that
I will not see the end of."

"We'll bring down the reign of Baalan and the
dragonpriests."

"Yes." Turiana closed her eyes in contentment as
Sharlin carefully scratched her eye ridges.

Nazar skimmed the ground and alit near them. His
fine-pitched tenor voice called out, "I nearly have
it."

Sharlin laughed. "Your hide will burst."

"Not so. I'll grow into it." His eyes fairly shone.
"Take a ride with me."

"And be struck by levin bolts? I'd sooner eat a
treefrog raw."

Nazar put his head to one side. "But they're good,
Sharlin."

She stuck her tongue out. Turiana nudged her. "He
needs to feel your weight."

Sharlin was dressed in pallan garb again, her trousers finely wrought, with a quilted vest over a shirt of
deepest blue. She picked up a matching cloak. "All
right, then, but mind you—there's no harness for me
to hold to." She stepped to him. He dropped his
shoulder and bent low to the ground for her to reach
up to his withers and pull herself aboard. There was a
discharge of sparks as she touched him. It didn't hurt,
but disconcerted her, as the cold sparks showered over
her hands.

"Nazar!"

"Sorry," he said smugly and without conviction.

She clung to his mane of spines. A cloudburst of
silvery light enveloped her, and he dampened it just as
quickly. He got to his feet and poised for a quick run
across the meadow and powerful launch to follow.

There was a terrible pressure upon her eardrums. She could almost hear a drumming—

Turiana bellowed and reared. She flung a cry after them. "Fly!"

The sky ripped open.

The dragonwings thundered into her hearing as two dark shapes fell upon them from the sky. They hammered Turiana down with hisses and roars. Nazar gained the air and sculled in hesitation. He spat at the two blacks and lightning ripped the air. The black with ruby red eyes fell back squalling. The black with gray eyes struck, his jaws aiming at the golden's throat.

Turiana got up, raking furiously. "Fly!" she spat. "While you can!"

Sharlin recognized the desperation in her voice that Nazar, newly gifted with hearing, could not. She gripped the silver creature tightly. "Go, Nazar. She's fought the best. She'll hold them off until we're gone, then go to ground somewhere where they can't get at her. She's giving us precious time. Don't waste it."

The golden dragon launched herself into the air with a shrill keening of agony, for Pevan clung to her flank, jaws sunk deep into her side. Once in the air she shook him off. Crimson drops of ichor rained gently to the canyon floor.

Nazar shook himself, circled once, and windfire struck with every bolt he spat. Atra danced in pain, his red eyes blazing. Then, with a surge of his newfound strength, Nazar gained the heights. The wind billowed the sails of his wings.

Sharlin called back, as loudly as she could, desperately afraid Turiana would not hear her and knowing that she may never have the opportunity to say it again. "I love you, golden one. God speed you and fare you well!"

The canyon walls echoed with her voice, a clear sweet note amid the trumpets of dragon fury. Sharlin bent low over Nazar's back and never looked back.

* * *

Silreen and his three companions met Dar and Mwork at the livery. Dar stood impatiently on the platform, a garish sash about his waist decorating his much washed and patched clothes. "About time you're here." He signaled Mwork, and the goblin fastened like sashes about the slim pallan waists.

"A pallan with a sword is a great oddity. We had difficulty getting through the crowd." Silreen hesitated, then said, "Dar, there is something I should tell you—"

"Not now. We're going out on the next wagonload to the temple. Our boss has given us free transportation. Keep quiet and on your toes. You know what we face once we're inside."

"I know well," Silreen said, and his voice sounded unhappy. "We are ready then."

Mwork knotted the last sash in place. "Don't lose those. They were delivered to us this morning with instructions. Hired or not, we won't get into the temple without them."

"We understand."

Dar looked at Silreen and his three companions. They had never been named to him since the day they met in battle at the Gates, but he knew their ways well and it was as if they had been. "May you all be remembered," he said, knowing a little of pallan lore. Their masked faces turned to him in startlement, and then they bowed in thanks.

A driver pulled a flatbed wagon out of the livery, and it was filled before he'd driven it free and up to the platform. Mwork hauled ten celebrants out by their hair and collars and whatever else he could reach. They protested loudly until the dragonpriest striding up took a look at the sashes and said, "The high priest is waiting for these fellows. Make room."

Mwork dusted his hands. "I already have." He helped Dar be seated and the pallans jumped in nimbly.

Two or three of the celebrants were bold enough to jump back on, but the rest of the wagon load gave them a wide berth. Dar felt his newly healed wounds stretch, and winced as he settled himself. He kept his sword sheath across his lap and the hilt warmed between his palms. It did not speak, but he and it knew the hour of readiness was soon at hand. It would be a long and muddy ride to the Temple. The leaden sky had cleared of the cold and sleeting rain. Tomorrow, if they lived to see it, would be the first day of spring. It had been nearly four months since he had seen his son and his wife. He had spent most of the night before in stretching exercises to limber tender skin and ill-used muscles. The rest of the night he'd spent scratching out a map so that Mwork could find his way to the Shalad Mountains with Fort if he himself could not make the trip. The last hour he'd spent wrestling with the goblin to extract the promise that the goblin would take the child and leave him when ordered to do so. He'd won, but only, Mwork insisted, because he was trying not to break Dar's wounds open again.

Nazar pulled up at dawn. They found a high desert with cold clear water that spilled out of a shattered rock, and drank, and then he charmed the softfeet and desert gazelles to come to them, and they ate. Then they slept for a while in the white-hot sun until the heat woke them.

He looked at her with his eyes of sapphire. "I will avenge my mother," he said.

"We'll try the temple?"

"Yes, if you're willing."

The odds were no greater than before, but she hesitated. Then she nodded. "Do you know which way?"

"It is burned upon my heart," the silver creature answered her. He knelt so that she could mount.

*   *   *

Dusk fell, Mwork handed Dar off the wagon bed and they fought the jostling crowd, having been instructed to look for the red cloaks and enter where the dragon-priests congregated. The great doors of the immense temple were thrown open and even a dragon would not have to bow his neck to pass through. Dar was impressed in spite of himself by the gold-veined marble pillars and veneers, and the scented woods, and the hand-pounded gold sheeting that layered the cornices.

Mwork showed his tusks. "Built on blood and bone," he said. "Just like the road to Rilth."

Silreen made only a hissing through his veil. Dar shushed both of them as they approached the small door where dragonpriests firmly guarded the entrance.

Their faces weren't even noticed. The priests' gazes fell on the sashes and they parted so the six could enter.

Telemark left the pool as late as he could. The lap of warm water soothed him. He paused at the jug of water set upon a table carved of lapis and looked at the packet of silth beside it. He was not a user, but knew its calming property. Perhaps just this once, to hide his thoughts from Baalan. His hand trembled as he reached out for it, then violently brushed it away. The powder spilled along the polished stone floor of the mountain's interior. He poured himself a goblet of water and drank it down, quickly. Then he appraised the area again. This gilt cavern with its pool was only one of many within the mountain's hollows. Baalan had wrought well when he planned this temple. When this was all over, and Baalan's powers coupled with his own, he would make this the center of his rule. The cold and drafty fortress at Rilth would be left in Third's care, as good as a banishment.

Telemark dressed himself with caution. If Baalan even sensed the presence of the mail beneath his robes and crimson cloak, all could be lost. The great beast sometimes seemed to know every thought in his mind. And where had Baalan sent Pevan and Atra? The purple majesty arrived alone in the morning and would not tell him on what errand they'd been sent. It made for an uncertainty he did not like.

He put the thought aside. To think of defeat was to open the door to it. Neither Pevan nor Atra could challenge him *now*. When he had Baalan's power melded into his own, he would be unconquerable. Let them show their faces or slink away from the Night of Dragons he was going to loosen upon Rangard. It would make no matter to him.

He mounted the steps toward the inner sanctorum as a gong tolled. Upstairs, he passed the cells where the victims were being held. They had been bathed and dressed in white cloth so that the red blood of their wounds might be most visible. They pressed themselves to the barred doors and cried for mercy as he passed.

All except the last cell. It held but one occupant, the child, and the boy was playing in the corner, quite absorbed in some game. There were other children to be slaughtered tonight, but this one had always been quite exceptional.

Third had explicit instructions to bring this child as the first sacrifice for Baalan. Telemark had no intention of absorbing tainted magic. The child looked up as Telemark's shadow fell across the cell's meager light.

He got to his feet and ran to the door. "Are you the dragonman?"

"One of them," Telemark had to admire the child's fearlessness. He bent down so the boy could talk.

"Bring me one."

Was he hungry? The child was supposed to have been drugged along with the others. He should be able to smell the silth on his breath and see it in his too bright eyes. Telemark's gaze flicked to the tray. Some fool had put a wine jug out. "Bring you what? Are you thirsty?"

"Yes." The boy thoughtfully put his hand to his mouth and added, "I want a dragon."

"Oh, you'll get one before the night is out, don't you fear." Telemark straightened. "And I'll have some milk brought to you, too." He turned heel, but the boy said, "Do you know where Mommy is?"

Telemark's lids half shuttered his eyes. "No," he said, thinking of his own hated mother. "If she cares, she'll be with the dragons, too." He stayed another moment. "What is your name, boy?"

"Balforth, but Daddy calls me Fort."

"Indeed. Be a good boy, Fort, and tonight you'll see as many dragons as you could possibly wish." This time, Telemark gathered himself and left the corridor. The cries of the prisoners faded behind as the silth began to take hold.

The minor ceremonies were already in progress when he took the great stairs at the back of the dais. A functionary straightened his robes and he told him to drug milk and give it to the boy. Telemark took a deep breath and listened. It must seem as if he appeared from the bowels of the earth just as the first sacrifice rendered up his life with a great scream, and the fountaining of blood produced the high priest.

"There he is," said the acolyte. "Flank him and stay out of the way." The ranks of dragonpriests opened an aisle to let Dar, Mwork, Silreen, and the others pass.

A roar accompanied the first splatter of blood and the high priest's appearance. Mwork stumbled and muttered, "Holy shit, Dar—it's *him*!"

Dar looked through the press uneasily. Throngs danced on the temple floor, weaving in a drug-and-drink and excitement-filled ecstasy. There was no quick way in or out. "Keep moving," he said. They gained Telemark's side and he split them, three and three. There was a radiant look to his features and he never noticed that four of his guards were armed pallans.

He spread his arms out and silence fell. The multitude swayed in a prismatic blur of their festive clothing.

"Tonight," High Priest Telemark said, "is the end of winter."

A roar of approval.

"Tonight," he said, "is the eve of spring."

Another roar.

"Tonight," he said, "is the Night of Dragons."

Frenzied shouting drowned him out. He stood patiently a moment. Silence fell again.

"Tonight," he said, "we give our oblations to the dragongods who bless and enrich Rangard. We give ourselves, that our land might ever be enriched. We give our voice and thanks to those who have been Taken, so the gods might be appeased."

Music struck up, sounding from the balconies high upon the walls, and the shouts became rhythmic to the melody's sway. Inner doors opened, and the Taken began to step upon the serpentine stairs that would lead them to the altar. Another roar, sounded, but this one came from a bestial throat and announced the arrival of Baalan the great. His purple bulk shadowed the rear of the foretemple.

"Gods," said Mwork lowly, pitched for only Dar's hearing. "He's bigger than I remember."

Dar palmed his sword hilt.

Hold your strike the sword told him.

Dar took a deep breath and then his gaze took him to the staircase that had begun to fill with a line of people. His heart did two or three rapid thumps when he saw the boy who led them.

Fort would be first.

He closed his eyes in agony. He had counted on the frenzy and confusion of the rites to give him time to spirit the boy away relatively unnoticed. But with the exception of the man who'd bloodied the altar and whose body now lay in a pit underneath it, his son would be the center of attention. He tried not to look at the boy. How he'd grown since early winter! In a season's passing, he'd gone from toddler to lad.

He moved into Baalan's shadow to hide his face from his own son. "Get ready," he signaled to Mwork.

The goblin flashed that he understood.

After long moments Fort stood at the step leading to the altar. Baffled, he stared at Telemark. The high priest smiled and took his hand. Softly so that his voice would not carry to the masses, he said, "And lo, your dragon appears."

"He's big." Fort whispered back. His cheeks were too bright, and his eyes too wide. Unresistingly he stepped into Telemark's arms.

The high priest swept up the boy and laid him on the altar.

Dar tried to clear his throat. He wrapped his hand about the sword hilt.

Stay the weapon told him. His heart threatened to burst inside his rib cage.

Fort twisted his head so that he could look upon great Baalan. The dragon leaned down so that his great fangs flashed within the boy's reach. Never had a throat been so conveniently offered to a blade. Mwork's wild eyes met his a second and he knew the goblin thought the same.

Hold.

Dar's muscles trembled with eagerness. As in lovemaking, he had reached the point where muscle and nerve and fulfillment could be withheld no longer . . .

Telemark parted the boy's robe at his unblemished neck. Fort wrinkled his nose. "That tickles."

The singing and shouting began to still. The hypnotic swirl of the music quieted also.

"For Baalan, I offer thusly. For Baalan, I promise me and mine. For Baalan, I bow most humbly. For Baalan, I—"

Strike.

Dar froze. His sword in his hand, but he knew not which target to strike! Telemark with dagger over Fort's breast or the scaly throat exposed to his flank.

The dragon breathed deep and swayed. Young Fort on the altar block suddenly opened wide his eyes and yelled, "I can fly!"

He put a hand on the high priest's, and purple sparks flew. Telemark rocked back on his heels, jolted. Then, the dagger began to descend in his fist. The crowd screamed in ecstasy, anticipating the killing blow.

Mwork swung at Baalan's underthroat. Dar saw the beginning of the swing and knew his target. He swung out as well, and the dagger went flying from Telemark's hand with a clang as the blades met.

Baalan bellowed in pain and anger, rearing up. Mwork swung from the hilt of his impaled sword, unable to let go, lifted in the air. Dar pivoted and cleaved at the beast's paw as he lifted it to claw down his assailant. The dragonlord trumpeted, "To me! To me!"

It seemed the bowels of the mountain did not answer him.

Telemark hugged the child to him and squeezed his long fingers about the child's neck as Fort cried in exultation, "I can fly!" once more. As his throat closed under Telemark's hold, his body went limp upon the bloodied altar. Telemark's body shook with frenzy.

"Give them to me!" he screamed at the fainting boy. He squeezed tighter. "Give them up!"

Baalan thrashed about, his tail lashing. He knocked the altar out from under Fort's body. It shattered and exploded into the crowd. Wounded screamed in fear and began to run. A lamp shattered. Wall hangings went up in flame.

Dar danced to avoid Baalan's fury. He slipped and went down. The dragon stepped on him with a crippled paw. His muzzle snaked about to snap him in two. Silreen stepped in calmly. Even as the dragon struck, he arrowed his sword down Baalan's nostril. The other pallans disappeared as the dragon skewed his tail about, smashing everything within reach.

Mwork pulled his sword out with a goblin bellow. He slid down the bloodied throat and chopped it deep into Baalan's breast. But the beast never slowed a second. He opened wide his jaws.

The temple exploded. The massive domed ceiling burst and the night rushed in on silver dragonwings. Lightning bolts licked the floor and walls. The throng bolted from the sanctuary, trampling dead and wounded and living alike. Fire and falling beams could not stay them. They screamed in terror and fled their gods.

Telemark stood. He dropped the limp body of the child to the dais floor. Unseeing, he stumbled down the back stairs. Purple sparks marked his shambling passage.

Baalan looked after the betraying priest. "Telemark!" he shouted and the temple shook with the noise of his fury.

Strike now the sword told him, and Dar cleaved across the serpentine neck as hard as he could.

The pits from the rear of the temple, where it opened into the hollow mountain, filled with the dragonflesh as they answered the call of their leader.

Too late. His severed head bounced along the polished stone floor before them. With cries of hatred they reared up and dragonfire licked the ruins of the temple walls still standing.

The silver dragon sculling before them answered, and the mountain itself rumbled under his bolts.

Dar stood, exhausted, sword trailing from his hand. Mwork crawled to him. Together they managed to lift Fort's limp body. With a sob, Dar looked for the high priest, but he was gone.

"Dar! Run!"

He looked up. Sharlin rode the silver beast and she leaned from his back. The mountain shivered as an anvil does under a hammer. He shouldered his son's lifeless form and ran across the now deserted temple, Mwork at his heels.

They reached the opening where the great doors had once stood when the blast at their backs threw them to the ground. With a clamor that sounded like the end of the world, the mountain collapsed.

When the dust cleared, the silver dragon had landed near them. Sharlin slid off his back and came running.

Dar had fallen with Fort's body under him. He got to one knee and caught her, pulling her away from their son, saying, "Don't look."

There was joy on her face and her tears were those of gladness. She fought his grip. "What do you mean, don't look?"

Dar could barely get his words out. "He's dead, honey. Mwork—"

At his choked attempt, the goblin tore off Sharlin's cloak and moved to cover the body.

"No!" Sharlin pounded on him, "No and no and no!"

"Shar." He wrestled with her and his own eyes blinded him with tears. Too battered and weak to contain her, he let her go.

"Mommy? Don't hurt Daddy," a small, hoarse voice said.

He turned. The boy stood in the goblin's embrace, wrapped in a blue cloak against the chill of the night.

The silver dragon trumpeted in victory.

Chapter 29

Mwork and the boy slept as dragonwing carried them back to the only home Nazar had ever known. Magic fueled their flight as much as his sail did. Sharlin rocked back in Dar's arms, but they could not sleep. They talked much of the night away.

"Telemark," Sharlin repeated thoughtfully. "If he survived the destruction, he couldn't get far. The powers he absorbed from Baalan through Fort will probably kill him. As for the rest of the dragonpriests—"

"The ones that lived will never be the same. Their loyal flocks saw ample proof of their cowardice." Dar kissed the hollow of her cheekbones. "You saved my life."

"And you, mine. Or maybe I should say, you are my life." She snuggled the hand that cupped her stomach closer.

"Mmmm," Dar murmured. "A feisty daughter this time, eh?"

"So I'm told. Would you mind?"

"Never."

The sun tipped Rangard's horizon. He straightened and then groaned as old wounds and new reminded him he was not the man he used to be. Nazar made a sound that was halfway between a plea and a moan and quickened his wing strokes.

In the hollowed canyon, two dark bodies lay slashed and torn. Nazar wheeled about once, but the reek of death was plain and carrion crows ripped at the carcasses. With a singular cry, the silver dragon headed over the peaks to the cave where he had been hatched.

Her golden form lay across the entrance. Sharlin let out a harsh sob as she saw its scored and wounded hide. Nazar landed on the precarious ledge and shook himself as his passengers slid off. Sharlin went to Turiana first. With great effort she slid under the head so that she might cradle it with her body and close the eyelids over the dimmed eyes.

With so slight a movement the dragon awakened. Faint candlelights shone in the depths of her wondrous eyes.

"Fair daughter," she whispered. "You have come back to me. Are you well?"

"Very well," Sharlin said. She put a trembling hand to her mouth suddenly and looked to Dar.

"Mother," the silver dragon said. "I have destroyed the Temple at Geldart and most of the dragons who followed Baalan did so to their doom."

"And the Gates?"

"Guarded by only a few. We will wrest them back."

Turiana let out a shuddering sigh. "You have done well, my Silver. Tell Turan when you meet him next that my last thoughts were of you two. And, if you can find it in your dragonish nature—dance the dance of mating while you are still young, and enjoy the hope your children will give you." She fell silent and gave a few heaves as if spent.

She looked again at Sharlin. Dar and Fort now partnered her. The dragon appeared to smile. "To the three of you, I bequeath my last two eggs. They will hatch when and if they are ready. The gold, perhaps soon. There can only be one golden dragon in the world at a time. Promise you will care for them."

"I promise," Sharlin said, her voice thin and patchy.

Turiana turned an eye on Dar. "Promise," she said, her voice an echo of her old, imperious self.

"So vowed," Dar said.

Fort placed his hand upon the dragon's muzzle. "I like dragons," he said.

Turiana looked last upon her silver dragonlord. "Nazar?"

"Here, Mother."

"Move into the sunlight. I cannot see you."

Nazar let loose a little of his magic and his body shimmered with the sparks and aura of lightning.

"There. As was once said to me, and now I pass on to you, words that were never meant for dragonkind, but . . . I find mean much to me. I love you." With that, the breath rattled in her throat and the dragonqueen could say no more. The light faded from her golden eyes, and the life from her flesh.

Sharlin leaned over the still head and grieved again. Her tears mingled with the silver-blue ones of Nazar. When she was done, she raised her head to find Fort gone.

His raspy little voice pealed out from the depths of the cave.

"Mother! There're eggs in here—and the golden one *moves*!"

ABOUT THE AUTHOR

R. A. V. SALSITZ was born in Phoenix, Arizona, and raised mainly in southern California, with time out for stints in Alaska, Oregon, and Colorado. Having a birthplace named for such a mythical and mystical beast has always pushed her toward SF and fantasy.

Encouraged from an early age to write, she majored in journalism in high school and college. Although Rhondi has yet to drive a truck carrying nitro, work experience has been varied—from electronics to furniture to computer industries—until she settled down to work full-time at a word processor.

Married, the author matches wits daily with a spouse and four lively children of various ages, heights, and sexes. Hobbies and interests include traveling, tennis, horses, computers, and writing.